Dedication
As always, dedicated to Lee Lee.

Acknowledgments
Thank you to my critique partners

Dangerous Web

Dangerous Series Book 1

Reggi Allder

About the author

Reggi Allder writes suspense and contemporary novels. In both genres, as in real life, her characters must overcome difficulties. The males are strong. The women are determined to make changes in their lives to manage their future. They cope with life as each fight to discover a hidden strength and work toward a lifelong goal.

Reggi studied creative writing and screenwriting at the University of California at Los Angeles (UCLA). She enjoys hearing from readers.

Praise for Reggi Allder

Dangerous Web keeps the reader's attention from the first page & never drops. Characters the reader cares about & a complex plot makes for a satisfying read. -Verified reader.

Dangerous Web by Reggi Allder will hold you on the edge of your seat as you follow her real-to-life characters. She nicely blended the heroine and hero into a romance intertwined with suspense at a pace just slow enough to hold your attention then increased it to keep you going! If you love romantic suspense, then treat yourself and grab this novel, you won't be disappointed. - Nicole Reviews

Dangerous Web had people so real it was easy to care what happened next. -Carmen Reader

Books by Reggi Allder
Suspense: Dangerous Series
Dangerous Web
Dangerous Denial
Dangerous Money
Dangerous Moves
Shattered Rules
Small Town Romance Sierra Creek Series:
Her Country Heart
His Country Heart
Our Country Heart
My Country Heart
Her Country Heart Christmas Edition
Historical
With Glowing Hearts
Coming next
Dangerous Sisters
Growing Up in a Small Town

Oh, what a tangled web we weave when first we practice to deceive- Sir Walter Scott

Chapter 1

"Do you know what day it is?"

Emma Craig looked up from her desk at the Palmer Real Estate office in San Francisco and stared at her friend and business owner Karen Palmer. The middle aged and fashionably dressed woman deposited her designer bag and paper coffee cup on the desk next to Emma's.

"Well, do you?" Karen asked, presumably waiting for an answer to a question Emma considered rhetorical.

She'd never forget the second anniversary of the day her husband went to the store for a quart of milk and never returned. She recalled every minute, every hour, and struggled with the memory. She relived the terror of thinking any second the phone might ring with the news he'd been killed in a horrific accident on Highway 101.

Webb's voice, like a warm breeze, use to heat her on cold nights. His gentle touch had sent desire flowing within her, his smile promising forever. Of course, she damn well remembered what day it was.

"Emma, what are you going to do about it?"

"He's gone. No trace. The police couldn't find anything, not even his body. The officers think he abandoned his wife—me. It's becoming clear they're right and I can't go through anymore torment."

"So why are you still wearing your wedding ring? For pity's sake, take it off. Face the fact he disappeared without so much as a goodbye and forget the jerk."

Easy for Karen to give advice. She hadn't loved the man, promised her life to him. She griped. They'd vowed to be together for eternity. She might learn to hate him, but never forget him.

"Karen, I don't want to think about it. It's a Friday like any other, not an anniversary." She slammed the desk drawer closed harder than she'd meant to, slumped deeper into her desk chair, and held up her hand. "Please, Karen, stop. Don't say anymore. Okay?"

"One more thing and I won't mention it again." Karen dug into her purse and yanked out a smart phone. "Someone's interested in your Sierra Nevada cabin. Here's his Facebook profile."

Emma pushed the phone away.

"You spent your honeymoon in the place, Em. I understand, but it's time to let go and move on. A chance like this might not come along for years. The cabin's rural, exactly what the guy wants. Do you know how often someone has asked for a place in the Sierra's away from the lake, casinos, and grocery stores?" She paused. "Never. I quoted a high price and he didn't blink. Guess he's used to Bay Area real

2

estate. He's some Silicon Valley dude looking to get away from the hustle and bustle."

"Yeah, but…"

"Hey, it's been tough and I don't mean to be a bitch, but face it, you need the money. Emma, they aren't supposed to, but bill collectors have been calling here at work. I know your husband left you in debt. As if that wasn't bad enough, he disappeared like a coward."

"What can I say?" Emma shrugged.

"Say you didn't do anything wrong. He's a bum."

"He didn't know I was in a car accident after he left. How could he?"

"Maybe so, but you told me how high your medical bills are. Even with insurance, there are co-pays. You don't make enough to take care of those, do you?"

She shrugged again.

Karen held her hand to her ear. "Listen. The phones aren't ringing. The doors are open, but no one's here asking to see homes. We're a new company, just getting our ads going and starting to network. It takes time to build a business." She took a sip of coffee. "The cabin's in your name. You might as well get the benefit. Close out your debt."

"I…"

"If it sells under the Palmer Realty banner, it would be good for my company. The guy's Silicon Valley friends might use this office when they are ready to buy something. It could be the start we both need."

As usual, Karen was right. The cabin belonged to her, a present from Webb. Her husband had insisted the deed be put in her maiden name. At the time, she'd protested. Now, she almost thought he understood he was going to disappear and wanted to give her a consolation prize. Emma shook her head. *What a crazy idea.* "I'm not going to deal with any of this today."

Karen sat down at her desk and took another sip of coffee.

Emma waited. She'd known her friend too long to think the woman had finished pushing the idea of listing the cabin. A good business woman, relentless, striving, but sometimes it was hard to be her friend.

"Emmy, don't be mad. I told the tech guy he could look at your cabin next weekend. You have a week to get up there and give it a quick once over before he comes to check it out. Sweep the cobwebs, vacuum, and whatever. You know the drill. I mean it's dead here. You might as well. It's been two years. You know what they say, time waits for no man or woman, and money talks, you know what walks." Karen smiled.

"I guess."

The office phone sounded. Karen grabbed it on the first ring. "Palmer Realty, how may I help you?"

"Emma, it's for you. I think it's a bill collector."

***

Scent from the sugar pine filled the Sierra Nevada mountain air. Emma took a deep breath and wiped her forehead. Hot and tired, she squeezed the wheel of her old sedan to keep it out of the ruts in the single lane, dirt road. How much further? It seemed forever since she'd left the main highway. As the car hit the bumps in the road, she could hear the bottles of cleaning solution rolling around in the trunk and hoped they didn't pop open.

When her husband had searched out the remote place to buy, he'd told her he was looking for a love nest. Of course, she'd been wildly in love and had believed him. Today, she laughed bitterly at how naïve she'd been and tried to ignore the heartache dredged up by the memory of their honeymoon night spent in the cabin. Her body heated. *Damn.* She still wanted him. How could she detest Webb and desire him at the same time?

The car's front tire hit a pothole causing her to focus on the road. She brought the compact under control and slowed down.

The sky flamed orange as the sun lowered on the horizon. A cold wind came through the open driver's side window and she shivered.

As the country road made a sharp left turn, the cabin came into view in a grove of ponderosa pines. The house stood strong, but weathered and unwelcoming. The perennials she'd planted in the front yard lay lifeless, as dead as her relationship with her husband. Seeing them sent a shard of pain through her. *Don't think about what might have been.*

Why had it taken so long to understand Webb wasn't coming back? Until now, she'd held out hope. In the waning daylight, she stared at their vacation home and finally accepted the truth. The marriage was over.

She parked, turned off the engine, and let out a single sob. *Stop. No crying. You've done more than enough in the last two years.*

The wooden stairs squeaked as she climbed to the large front deck. With shaking fingers, she held the cold metal door key in her hand.

"Miss."

She jumped at the sound of the male voice and glanced at a forty something man dressed in jeans and a khaki shirt. He wiped his brow before putting a black and orange baseball cap on his brown shaggy hair.

"Yes."

"I can finish weeding the backyard garden, but I'll have to come again later and get the fallen tree behind the house. Got to get a bigger truck if you want the whole tree cut up and taken away." He rubbed the stubble on his chin. "Or I can leave the wood for your fireplace."

A chill ran down her back. It wasn't as if he said anything menacing, but she hadn't sent for a gardener. "There must be a mistake. I never called for a gardener."

"I've been coming here for two years."

"Impossible. I—two years?"

He sniffed and rubbed his nose.

"Look mister, I own this place. I never ordered or paid for anyone to do work in this garden."

"I wouldn't know. I only do what I'm told." He pulled a kerchief from his back pocket and rubbed his neck. "You got a branch in the backyard, almost broke a window. If it's not cut and pulled away from there today, you could end up with trouble. A storm is coming." He sniffed again.

"But I..."

"Lady, I was sent to do a job. You got a problem, call my boss. I'll move the branch from the window before the glass gets broke. You can take up the bill with the company. You'll be glad I was here when the rain and thunder come tonight."

"Okay—if it'll prevent the window from shattering, but..."

He walked toward to a nearby truck, apparently finished with the conversation.

Stunned, she stood on the deck trying to make some sense of who would pay for the yardwork.

She glanced at the pickup's door. "Sierra Gardeners." Later, she'd call and find out who was shelling out money for the job.

Carrying a dust pan and broom in one hand, her keys and purse in the other hand, she put everything down and pulled her phone from her jacket pocket.

No signal, she should have understood being so rural there wouldn't be a cell tower nearby.

As she headed for the front door, the sound of a chain saw broke through the quiet.

When she turned the key in the cabin's lock, the door squeaked open. The knotty pine walls had darkened, but the handmade sofa and chairs were still where she'd placed them. The turquoise and sage green upholstery, chosen so carefully, now appeared to mock her. "Our love nest," she whispered to no one.

The smell of smoke wafted toward her. She'd expected mildew or dust, but a burning oak log in the brick fire place—never. Had the gardener started a fire? Would he have the nerve to come into the house? She set her purse and keys on the entry table. Coffee?

She took another whiff of the indoor air and smelled freshly brewed coffee.

A chill jogged down her back. "Hello. Is anyone here?"

Silence.

In the kitchen, a French press coffeemaker sat alone on the Formica table. She touched it. *Hot.* It had to be the gardener. After all, he hadn't expected her. Being far from anyone, it might be his routine to make himself at home. She shook away her fear.

Nevertheless, to be sure she was alone, she'd check the rooms. First the extra bedroom, empty. She froze at the door of the master bedroom. Her wedding night played in her mind. *Honey, don't be shy.* Webb had coxed her. *You're beautiful. I love you, Emmy. Come to me.*

"No." She wouldn't relive the night, not now, not ever.

The pine floorboards squeaked as she entered the bedroom and flicked on the overhead light to illuminate the dark wood walls. The pale green and blue landscape, she and Webb had found in an antique store, still hung-over whitewashed pine bed. She pushed back the closet curtain. Men's shirts hung on the wooden rod in the cedar clad closet. A duffel bag sat on the floor.

A squatter's living here. Oh God. Wait, would a squatter hang up his shirts?

She ran from the room to the backyard. Waving her hands to get the gardener's attention, she yelled, "Are you living in the cabin?"

"What?" He brought his hand to his ear as a hard of hearing person might.

"Are you staying in the house?"

"What the hell are you talking about? I got my own place miles from here."

"Oh—I found—never mind. I'll let you get back to work."

He started the saw immediately, leaving her to wonder what to do next.

Her cheeks burned as she stumbled toward the cabin. *Call the police. Can't. No signal.* Unsure if she should enter her home again, the minutes ticked by. Afraid, she paced at the front door to the cabin. Maybe she could ask the gardener to come into the house with her. Too late, the truck was driving out of sight.

Should she leave too? *Shit.* Her keys and purse were on the entry hall table. She had to go back inside. With a deep breath, she turned the door handle and, as quietly as possible, entered.

The small log in the fireplace still burned, but someone had added a larger one and the lights in the room were on now.

"I didn't remember your eyes were so incredibly blue."

There it was the deep warm breeze of Webb's voice. *It can't be.*

She struggled to catch her breath and stop shaking, tears would soon follow. She blinked, moved closer, searching his features. Her husband, not a mirage. "Dear, God. I thought you were dead."

"Sorry to disappoint you, Emma."

"How dare you?" Before she could think, her hand collided with his face, making a hollow sound in the quiet room and leaving a red mark on his cheek. His eyes narrowed and he swayed. Had she hit him that hard? Well, he deserved it.

"You jerk. Hold dinner, Emmy. I'll go get a quart of milk and be back in a minute. That's the last thing you said to me when you left two years ago. Damn you! I thought you were in some horrible accident. Years of despair and all you talk about is the color of my eyes. Why don't you say you're sorry and ask for forgiveness?"

His eyes widened and his skin had a gray pallor. He favored his right side and held his arm against his body. After a shallow breath, he said, "You weren't supposed to be here."

"Well, I am. What do you have to say to me?"

"No words will change what happened." He coughed and grimaced. "I didn't expect to see you again."

"I bet you didn't." Suddenly cold, she trembled.

The log in the fireplace crackled and spewed the scent of oak into the room as the air heated.

"They said you never come to the cabin. Hadn't been here since I left." He stood tall and frowned.

"Who said I never come here?"

"It doesn't matter. They were wrong."

***

In a dingy motel room in the low rent district of town, Smith glared at the stocky man slumped in the stained beige sofa. "Leonard, how did Ethan Lancaster get away?" Smith paced in front of the man. "Couldn't you get a decent room?" he asked, not expecting an answer. "It's not for lack of money. I pay you well." He brushed the perfectly pressed slacks of his impeccably tailored charcoal gabardine suit and stood his full height, then sniffed. "The damn place stinks." He glanced at a club chair but decided not to risk sitting in it. Who knew what the hell lived in the upholstery?

"How did Ethan slip out of your grasp?"

Waiting for a reply, he stared past the pathetic man and caught his own image in the darkened motel window. The lines in his dry skin appeared deeper than they had this morning. He looked older than his fifty years. He grunted. *Shit, it's been a long day.* He'd planned an early dinner, a steak, baked potato, and a large glass of cabernet. For dessert, he'd expected to bed his young, amply breasted wife. Instead, he was forced to deal with this wretched man with the eyes of a trapped animal.

"I told you. The prisoner was hardly breathing and he was bleeding like a pig," Leonard finally said in his defense. "He didn't look like he could get to the bathroom let alone get out of the room."

Smith sniffed again and waited for the next insufficient excuse the underling would soon deliver.

"Look, Mr. Smith, I had to untie Ethan to roll him over and stop the bleeding. He wouldn't be any good to you dead. Couldn't tell you anything if he bled to death." He ran his trembling hand through his thinning blond hair and sat a little straighter. "A stiff wouldn't be any help to you, would it?" Leonard pleaded for agreement.

"He sure as hades is not any good to me now," Smith grunted.

"Lancaster clocked me with the God damned water pitcher I'd set near the bed. I'm lucky I didn't lose an eye."

For the first time, Smith spotted a small cut over the man's left brow. If he couldn't stop Ethan from getting away, Leonard shouldn't have a cut. He should be deceased, but here he was sitting in a cheap motel making justifications.

"Tell me what you learned while you had Lancaster?"

"He was shot—unconscious most of the time. I beat the shit out of him, but he didn't say nothing." The man's eyes widened as if he, for the first time, comprehended the trouble he faced. He fidgeted and seemed to search for something more to report. "His wound was festering and he came down with a fever. In his delirium, Lancaster said one name over and over."

"What name?"

"Emma, Emma Craig."

"Who the hell is that?"

The man shrugged. "Thought you might know."

"Another operative? His contact?" Smith had to find out. "Any idea where she is?"

The blank expression on the man's face said all Smith needed to know. Still, he asked, "Are you positive that's all you got? Anything could be important."

"If I had something, I'd give it to you." The nervous man leaned back into the sofa. "Nothing. Only the name and he wasn't even conscious when he said it. Emma Craig."

"Stay here tonight, tomorrow get out of town. Go north. I hear Canada's a good clean place. Or walk across the border into Mexico, if you like a warmer climate. Don't come back to the U.S. until you're told it's alright. Got it?"

"Yeah, yeah. I got it." For the first time Leonard's strained features relaxed and he stopped shaking.

Without a backward glance, Smith walked out of the motel room. He let the door slam behind him and took the first breath of clean air since he'd entered the motel.

In a nearly empty parking lot, a young man sat waiting in a grey nondescript sedan.

Smith went to it, sat in the back seat, and leaned forward to speak to the driver. "Tyler, take me to my car and come back and kill Leonard before he causes us anymore trouble."

"Done." Tyler smiled.

In his new luxury SUV, Smith shut the door and inhaled the aroma of fine leather. The car didn't have license plates yet, but the payments had already started. It was metallic gold the exact color his wife, Julie, wanted. Not the best choice if one wanted to be inconspicuous, but it'd be a cold day in hell when she didn't want people to gawk at her. It was one of the things that attracted him. Still, her behavior was beginning to wear thin. In his line of work, decorum and humility went along way to keep his real agenda undercover. A flashy car and a showy wife could be a liability. His muscle tightened thinking of her sighing while she moved under him. *Damn I want her.* Even so, he'd have to be certain she understood to keep a lower profile, if she wanted her affluent lifestyle to continue unabated.

He grabbed his smart phone. Calling his superior couldn't be avoided any longer. The boss had to know the assignment had failed. Ethan Lancaster was out in the world with information that could stop their expertly planned mission. The only hope was Ethan had bled to death somewhere before he could talk.

Smith clenched his jaw. He shouldn't be tainted with the failure of letting Ethan get away. After all, he hadn't hired Leonard. Yet when he dialed his boss, he'd be the one bringing bad tidings. As the bearer of the bad news, his employer would always recall this as his failure.

Shit.

He took a deep breath and dialed.

Chapter 2

Emma watched Webb track a cloud as he stared out of the cabin's great room window.

"A storm's coming, Emmy. You better get back to the city before it starts."

"I'm not leaving. This is *my* cabin. You go." Would she let him take off before he explained where he'd been the last two years? Not likely. She waited, but when he didn't speak, she added, "Nothing to say to me? Not going to tell me anything? Why you left? Why you stayed away?" Anger grew as she stared at his stoic expression.

He leaned against the hearth and closed his eyes as if in pain. He blinked and for a second, she thought he might not answer. "Emma, I don't have time for this. We're over. Get the hell away."

As if she'd been socked in the gut, she gulped for air. "You can't talk to me like that. Not after what you did. You're my husband."

He moaned and grabbed his side.

"What's wrong? What happened to you?"

"Accident," he said through gritted teeth.

"Let me see."

"I don't need your…"

"Webb, I want to look at it."

When he moved and she could see blood had oozed through his shirt. She gasped.

He grimaced.

"What kind of an accident leaves a gash in your side?"

"Never mind. Just get the first aid kit—duffle bag in the bedroom," he said almost spitting the words. "Hurry."

He moaned and slumped against her. She tried to hold him up, but his height and weight was too much for her. Together they tumbled to the floor. He rolled onto his back. His eyes closed.

"Webb!" *Dear God.*

"I need the kit." He choked, then coughed.

She stumbled to her feet and ran toward the master bedroom.

Still on his back, he hadn't moved when she returned. Without checking to see if he was conscious, she tore open his shirt and pressed gauze against the open wound. Holding it with one hand, she pressed several more layers of bandage on top of the first one. She ripped strips of medical tape with her teeth and placed them to hold the everything in place.

He rolled to a sitting position, took a shallow breath, and tried to stand up.

"Let me help."

"Emma, you're not wanted here. I don't need you." He sank down again.

"Yeah, I can see that."

"Leave me alone. Get out."

She recoiled from him, but something in his expression prevented her from leaving as he had two years earlier.

Without her, he managed to stand. Still, she could see in his condition he'd never make it to the bedroom without her, if that was where he was going.

She took his arm. With it over her shoulder, they slowly staggered toward the bedroom.

Who was this man? Yeah, Webster Craig, her husband, but what had changed him from the thoughtful, fun-loving guy with a wonderful sense of humor, to the dark, brooding person with her now?

In their old room, she helped him sit on the bed and lean back against the whitewashed headboard. She placed a pillow under his head and with a deep sigh, he relaxed.

The pain killer is in first aid kit." He coughed and blood marred the make shift bandage she'd used.

"Tylenol and Codeine one or two tabs every four hours as needed for pain," she read on the bottle. "No refills." The name on the label said, Ethan Lancaster; who the heck was he? She shook the bottle, more than half full. Was it okay to give him someone else's medication? What if he was allergic to it?

She put her hand on his forehead. *Fever.*

Carrying a glass of water from the bathroom and touched his shoulder. His eyes flew open and for a moment, she thought he might strike her. "Webb, it's me."

"Oh—I" He sagged back in the bed.

"You're burning up, take these to bring down your temperature." She handed him two tablets.

He swallowed hard. "Go. I can manage from here on."

Startled by his directness, she hesitated. "I—I deserve a few answers first. You can't deny me." She set the empty glass on the bedside table and folded her arm across her chest. "Webb."

The wind rustled the large pines outside the bedroom window and he glanced away from her. "Hey, you better leave before the storm hits."

Was a rainstorm coming in or was he using it as an excuse to get rid of her? With her gone, he could disappear again and she'd never hear an explanation, no understanding why he'd walked out of the marriage without so much as it's been fun. She wouldn't allow him to get off that easily.

A crack of thunder rumbled and lightening lit the darkening night. She shivered when the sky opened up, and hail stones pelted the cabin.

"Maybe we should both get out of here. Webb, I could drive you to an emergency room," she yelled above the noise of the thunder.

"Not safe to drive with the lightning. Looks like you got what you wanted. You're stuck in the cabin." He rolled toward the wall ending the conversation.

"Damn you," she said under her breath.

Webb was here, but something dreadful had happened to him. Still, he was alive. She should be grateful. Right?

***

Unable to sleep, Webb struggled to a sitting position. Pain throbbed in his gut, but it wasn't the worst problem. He'd never meant to see Emma again. In the bedroom sleeping in a club chair, she was near enough to help if he called for her. The good wife, she hadn't left his side.

"Hell," he whispered under his breath. All the plans he'd made two years ago were now ruined. For her safety, he'd designed a clean break in a manner that caused so much anger and hurt she wouldn't search for him. Instead of moving on with her life, as he thought she would, he'd only caused her to hate him. Great, he'd managed to take a happy young woman and turn her into the angry person sleeping in the chair near him. He closed his eyes against the thought of her loathing. He had comforted himself by believing she'd started a new life. It looked as if nothing he intended had come to fruition.

Here he was in bed like a weak fool, depending on the woman whose trust he'd betrayed. With a quick change of position, pain ran from his right shoulder to his abdomen. He hissed and held his arm close to his body until the throbbing subsided—somewhat.

Today, Emma had stood in the cabin, her dark hair glistening in the overhead light, as shock flashed in her blue eyes. She'd frozen in place, a confused expression on her sweet face. Right then, he wanted to take her in his arms, comfort her, and feel her soft body pressing against him. He took a slow breath. The pain in his side didn't compare to the ache caused when, two years ago, he'd left her.

The first time he'd seen her, she was standing on Union Street in San Francisco waiting for the traffic signal to change. Her dark hair had glistened that day too and her innocent smile had drawn him to follow her into a bookstore. He should have known she was a romantic when she went to an aisle marked English poets.

He could have admired her for a few seconds, as he'd done with so many other attractive women, and been on his way. For some reason, he'd needed more.

Why? Not being one to ponder questions without answers, he'd never asked that until tonight. Yet on that day, he'd engaged her in conversation. Standing next to her, he'd pulled a book from the shelf and said something inane.

Emma had laughed, a lilting sound. With eyes wide open, she'd said, "Are you trying to pick me up?"

"If you'll let me," he had replied.

He forced his thoughts from the past and grabbed the pain meds. The only thing he needed tonight was sleep. Tomorrow plans had to be made, foremost, get Emmy out of here and back to her current life.

A crack of thunder shook the windows and a second later lightning flashed. Years ago, Emma had been terrified of thunderstorms. Was she still afraid? He was hit with the desire to protect her, stupid since he was the person putting her in danger.

***

He didn't remember dozing off, but he must have because he woke in the cold dark room in pain. In the corner chair, Emmy purred in her sleep. His body heated as he recalled sharing a bed with her. *Stop.*

He scratched the stubble on his chin. In the morning, if he could make it to the bathroom, he'd shave. He stifled a groan and managed to slide to the edge of the mattress. He pushed his body to a sitting position and forced two pain killers into his dry mouth, hoping he could swallow them.

Outside the sky had turned to a timeless charcoal gray. It could be middle of the night or early morning, no way for him to tell. It didn't matter because he wasn't in any shape to go anywhere. Even so, his heart pounded knowing the schedule he worked under didn't allow extra time to rest.

He managed to inch down the hallway toward the bathroom holding his right side. Half way there he stopped and grabbed the wall while a wave of nausea washed through him. Codeine had never agreed with his system, but it was better than pain. An upset stomach was the choice of the day. Soon the hurt would subside and he'd move more freely.

In the bathroom, he relieved himself and sat on the side of the tub. How long before the pills kicked in? With closed eyes, he listened to the pouring rain and raging wind as it lashed the vintage cabin. The old building must have seen many such storms and it still stood strong. Could he do the same? Stand sturdy and not let his need to shelter with Emma take him off his objective?

Testing the strength of the meds, he drew a breath, an ache, but not excruciating pain. In the vanity drawer, he searched for the small screwdriver he'd placed there three years earlier. If it wasn't there, he'd be the one who was screwed.

"Yeah," he whispered when his fingers wrapped around the plastic handle. Even in the small beam from the nightlight, he knew it was the one he wanted.

Without too much trouble, the fake outlet opened showing the small box made for belongings, a good place to hide jewelry from a thief. This one concealed house and car keys, twenty hundred-dollar bills, and a few twenties. That would keep him until he could get to his next stash of cash. He shoved the money and keys in his jeans, put the cover back in place, and left.

In the bedroom, the medication had started working because, though he fought to stay awake but was losing the battle. *Shouldn't sleep. Too much to do.* Still, he adjusted the pillow under his head and let the dreams capture him.

"Come to me." A blue-eyed angel raised her arms to him. "Let me hold you. You've done enough. Just relax and come to me."

She tempted him to give up the fight and stop the anguish of his current life. "No. I can't. People are depending on me." He struggled to wake up—no good.

"Why is it so hot?" He was burning up until a cool hand touched his forehead.

"Hush, Webb. Don't worry, it's all right. Rest." With a gentle hand, the angel coaxed him to lean back in bed. "I'm here. You don't have to do anything but sleep. I'll do everything else."

"I've got to…"

"Yes, but later, after you sleep. Then you can go." She tenderly stroked his brow with a cool cloth, his tension abated, and his eyes remained closed.

***

He woke with a start. A beginning of the day, except it wasn't morning coming through the window—the light was waning as night fell. He must have slept around the clock.

His side wound ached as he stood, but the swelling had gone down and a clean bandage replaced the bloodied one he remembered. The bedroom was empty. Emmy no longer sat vigilant in the corner chair.

In the hall, to his surprise, the aroma of pancakes floated in the air. He took a deep breath and was rewarded with twinge in his right side. Still, his stomach growled and acid from hunger gnawed at him.

Emma, dressed in gray sweat pants and a pink T-shirt, her hair pulled up in a ponytail, held a spatula, ready to flip a pancake. With the ease of a short order cook, she sent food into the air and it landed back in the frying pan.

Suddenly, he was aware what an ordinary life looked like and remembered the many Sundays he'd spent with her. A time when he'd thought there was a chance for him to turn his life from secrets and lies to living with a wife, kids, station wagon, and a dog. Some men ran away from it, but he'd wanted the life. Until—he didn't want to remember.

"Webb, you're awake."

His mind quickly returned to the present. Her expression looked friendly, no malice in it.

"Sit down." She carried a platter of hotcakes to a table which had already been set for two. "Sit and butter them before they get cold." She motioned to the chair nearest the backdoor. "How do you want your eggs?"

"What?" He was having trouble focusing on the conversation. He'd been remembering the deaths that had torn his brother's life apart, while she was blithely jabbered on about eggs.

"Scrambled or fried?"

"Fried, easy," he said. He was tempted to say hard because that's what this was, hard pretending to have an ordinary conversation with his wife in what had once been their honeymoon cabin. Damned awkward.

"It must feel like morning to you, so, I decided to make breakfast."

"Yeah. Okay." He wasn't in the mood to play house. If she asked if he wanted one or two eggs, he was going to leave the room hungry or not.

"When we've eaten, you can get cleaned up and then we need to talk." It didn't seem to be a demand, more a statement of fact.

She nibbled on the one egg and a small hotcake she had on her plate. "Sorry, there's no syrup. I only have strawberry jam. I brought it for peanut butter sandwiches."

He wolfed down the four pancakes and two eggs she'd given him and wished he had more. She, no doubt, was waiting for him to talk. That wasn't happening. He wanted to kiss her, bed her, and leave her. Hell, she wasn't supposed to be at the cabin.

Finally, he said, "I'm not going to apologize for leaving you. But you deserve a few answers."

Chapter 3

Webb pushed back his plate and drummed his fingers on the table. "I'll tell you the truth."

Stunned, Emma didn't respond. Did that mean he hadn't told her the facts during their marriage?

"You're not going to like what I say." He stood up.

"Are you leaving?" She grabbed his hand.

"I'm turning on the light." He pulled away. "It's almost dark."

"Oh." Embarrassed, her cheeks burned. "I thought—never mind."

In the quiet room, she heard the rain hitting the roof.

"The first day in San Francisco was my fault."

"What?"

"Emma, we should never have met."

"Why?"

"Because I knew what I was. You had no idea."

"Dear God, you're a bigamist."

He laughed, then grabbed his side and grimaced. "I wish it was so simple."

"Damn you. I don't see anything funny."

"You're right." His smile vanished.

"What were you going to say?" She'd better get her emotions under control or he might not continue.

He hesitated, then said, "I saw you for the first time and you were so damned beautiful, sweet, and innocent. Such a counter point to my life—I was selfish." He paused. "I didn't work for a computer company in their IT department, like I told you. It was all a lie."

"But you…"

"I needed a story to convince you it was okay to go out with me. I never thought our relationship would go as far as it did."

"Nothing you told me that day was true?"

"Not even my name. I'd been trained to improvise. In the bookstore, I was standing next to a Webster's dictionary. Craig was a childhood friend of mine."

"You're kidding?" His eyes told her he spoke the truth. "If you're not Webb Craig, who are you?" She remembered the name on the bottle of pain killers. "Ethan Lancaster?"

Silence.

"You fib to strangers. You lied to me from day one?"

"It comes in handy sometimes. I worked, still work, for a black ops group. We're employed by the U.S. government. We're off the books, under the radar, doing the bidding of the U.S. when deniability is needed."

"I don't understand."

"Have you ever wondered how western democracies get rid of problems discreetly? How they take their enemies out, or monitor what's going on in countries where there is no embassy?"

"Not really."

"Most people haven't. They go about their lives with business as usual. Oh, they understand lone wolf attacks, bombings in foreign countries, and the like. But people don't know all the wars, terrorist assaults, internet hacks on our voting operations, banking systems, that were averted. Something that didn't happen is hard to quantify."

How many nights had she seen him bent over the keyboard of his iPad? She stared at the handsome man sitting before her and realized he was a stranger. He appeared calm, normal, but he must have lost touch with reality. "You don't work with computers?"

"I can if I need to. I'm trained in IT, but that's not my mission."

She blinked and shook her head. "Mission? Like Mission Impossible, the movies?"

He stared at her.

"Webb, I don't believe you for a second—what does any of this have to do with me?"

"I'd hoped you could understand my position during our marriage and give me some slack." He rubbed his chin then looked her in the eye. "You're right. It doesn't have anything to do with you. It's not necessary for you to appreciate my motives, just understand I never meant to hurt you."

"Really? You lie to me, marry me under a false name, then disappear without so much as it's been fun. Now, you want me to believe some bullshit story about secret missions?"

"Emmy..."

"Is that the best you can do? Invent some crazy ass story about being a super spy." She grumbled. "Give me a break. Are you saying you're hiding until you can get to your *secret* home base?"

"Something like that."

"Shit, Webb, I've seen that movie. Do you have a secret decoder ring and a hand shake?" She wanted to laugh, but under the circumstances it was hard to find humor when anger swelled in her. "When you walked out, I spent days calling the police departments and hospitals looking for you. Do you have any idea the horror I went through thinking of you bleeding somewhere in a ditch waiting for help and it didn't come?"

"I—no."

"And you think I should believe you?

"Emma, what do you want from me?"

She faltered. How could she answer? Did wish he'd declare his undying love and beg her to let him return to her arms?

He walked to the stove and picked up the coffee pot. "Want a cup?"

"No."

At the table, he sat heavily onto a chair, still favoring his right side and sloshing coffee onto the table. He moaned softly, his skin tone turning pale.

Not wanting to see his pain, she glanced out of the window. She wasn't going to empathize with him. "Why are you at the cabin?"

"I needed a place to rest and recoup. I've paid to have the place kept in order and stocked with food in case I needed it. Em, you haven't been back in years, so, I thought it was safe from you."

"You've come here before?"

"Once. I was informed, by a reliable source, you never visited." He finished his coffee and went back to get more. "Want some?" He held up the pot.

She shook her head. "This is the first time I've been on the property since you left me."

"Why now?" he asked, consternation in his voice.

"I'm selling the place. I came to get it ready."

"Oh."

Was that expression sadness, or could he be upset there'd be no hideout from his imaginary enemies? "Did you expect me to keep this place as a remembrance of you?" It was her turn to stand and move away from the table. She carried the dishes to the sink, thought about washing them, but instead she set them down.

"Ok. I'm going to bite. Why did you have to hide?" She adjusted her T-shirt and sat down.

"I have a link to a list someone wants and I'm not about to give it to them."

"Call your boss. Take the note to him? Why come to the middle of nowhere?"

"It's not a note, and I need to recoup first—it's a long story."

"Yeah, I bet it is. Need more time to make up the fairytale?"

"Hey, I admitted I was a jerk, but I'm leveling with you. It's the least you deserve."

"You got that right." She hated to agree with him about anything.

He groaned and his skin had a sallow hue to it again. How much blood had he lost from his wound?

"You need help."

"I can't use a cell phone to call my boss. It could be monitored. I don't use tech, too easy to leave a trail."

"Well, there is no signal anyway. So, Webb, you use carrier pigeon, no doubt," she scoffed.

"You laugh at me, but anything on a computer, a cell phone, or a cloud can be hacked. The Russians have gone old school as well to protect their info and their agent's names."

"How would you know what the Russian government does?" She tried but couldn't keep the disbelief from her voice. "Call the police, FBI, CIA, or whatever."

"You don't get it. I can't call anyone because I don't exist. My history has been expunged, wiped from the records. I was never born. The Task Force went to extensive efforts purge my files to make sure I don't."

"The task force?"

"A branch of RAT, Rapid Advance Team."

"I've never heard of them."

Then they've done their job. No one should be aware of their existence."

"But what about Ethan Lancaster? Is he's real?"

"Emmy, I'm on my own right now." He ignored her question. "I can't take the chance of contacting the team until I understand more about what is going on. I tell you because you could be in danger, because you're involved with me."

Their eyes met. "You're certifiable, Webb. I don't buy any of this for a second."

"Emma, I'm going to get cleaned up." His annoyance at her statement was marked by the slamming of the kitchen door when he left.

She startled, but resisted running after him to yell something rude.

***

The rest of the evening, she spent vacuuming and dusting the living room. She plugged in the vintage AM radio, found tucked away in the second bedroom closet. It surprised her when the thing came to life with a crackle of static. An oldie station, broadcasting miles from the cabin, came on. She turned up the volume as she cleaned the bathroom and washed the kitchen floor. With the vacuum and cleaning items stored on a shelf on the back porch, she made a mental list of what else needed to be done before the place was put on the market.

The whole time, Webb didn't come out of the master bedroom.

Later that night, she made pasta with red sauce and set a bowl of it in the fridge for him. She was tempted to peek in the bedroom to check if he needed anything but decided against it. They hadn't spoken since he'd slammed the kitchen door behind him. No need to start the argument again.

Alone in the guest bedroom, she wondered if anything he told her could be true. With a shake of her head, she lay down on the double bed and stared into space. Cobwebs hung from the ceiling making shadows in the dimly lit room. A harmless spider hung from an open rafter. The creature was unaware it would be homeless when she finished cleaning the house tomorrow.

The rain continued and lightening lit the sky. She shivered and counted the seconds until thunder struck. *You're not a scared kid anymore. The storm can't hurt you.* Even so, the memory of her father's death, lost in a tornado, was dredged up with every strike of thunder. She worked to control her rising fear. With Webb back in the picture, she missed having her father even more acutely. The loss of her parent haunted her even now, years later.

***

The next morning, showers threatened and mist hung in trees, but she grabbed a windbreaker and hat, then went to pull up the dead perennials planted two years earlier. A symbol of her enduring love for her husband, they had withered and now lay rotting in the cold rain.

With too much time to think, she'd begun to wonder who she'd married, Ethan, Webb? Was he the young man who'd grown up in a series of foster homes? A kid who found it too painful to talk about his past so he didn't say much about it? Was that true or another story invented to get her sympathy? Maybe his real family still lived somewhere in another state. Did it really matter now? She shrugged and took the pile of weeds she'd pulled to the compost barrel and tossed them in.

Her hands were muddied, her nails broken, and yet she continued to work. She yanked every flower and weed out until only mud remained in the garden in front of the cabin. Finally, exhaustion and the increasing rain sent her inside.

Dangerous Web

When she entered there was evidence Webb had been in the kitchen, most likely waited until she was outside, so he didn't have to see her.

She sighed, relieved. What could she say at this point? Better not to talk at all. Sharp words sprang too easily to her tongue. If left unsaid, she wouldn't regret them later. Her plan was clean up the place, put it on the market, and move on. Simple to say, she hoped to have the strength to accomplish the plan.

Once the cabin was sold, half the money belonged to Webb, if she knew what name went on the bank check and where to send it. If he didn't tell her, she'd deposit the funds into a high interest savings account and wait until he came thru with the information. It wouldn't be said she'd kept his fair share, regardless to his betrayal of their marriage vows.

With that settled, she took a deep breath. The windows needed to be cleaned, the stove as well. She went to work. The goal was to be worn out so sleep would come uninterrupted by nightmares if the thunder returned.

The cupboards were scrubbed, the stove, the oven, and the bathroom. She cleaned anything else she could think of, then rearranged the furniture in the living room and set logs in the fire place. A homey touch showing what a family cottage could be, something she'd never experience again. She swallowed slowly and tried to avoid the sadness brought on by the demise of her life with Webb. It was gone years ago, no point in reliving the agony again.

In the days that followed, she continued to make food for each meal and leave it in the fridge for Webb.

He took it but avoided seeing her. He too must be grateful not to carry on obligatory conversations.

On the fourth day, the rain stopped and the sun came out. It was a welcome sight as she was coming down with cabin fever. The small radio had stopped working and though the only station it received hadn't delivered any real news, it had been company. Until now, she hadn't realized how reliant on electronic equipment her life had become. Out of touch with the world and her friends, she longed to check Facebook and look for tweets or talk to friends on her smart phone. Not to mention, it was getting harder to avoid Webb in the small cottage.

Though she dreaded the idea, they had to speak and come to an understanding on how to move forward. He had to agree to a divorce. Even if it was a union made under a false name, all her legal documents were under his name, valid or not.

His 1967 British Racing Green Austin-Healy sat in her garage. At the time of his disappearance, it had been proof something terrible had happened to him. He might leave an inconvenient wife, but he'd never leave his sports car—his baby.

Wrong.

"Hi."

Standing tall, eyes clear, chin without stubble, and hair combed back, Webb entered the room looking like the man she'd fallen in love with years earlier. Her heart stumbled, then began to beat faster.

Chapter 4

Jon Lancaster stared out the window of the rented eighth floor condo in San Francisco, and noticed how small the cars appeared from this vantage point. Soon the lights would go on, turning the city by the bay into a jewel.

Frustration gnawed at him. It wasn't like Webb to stay out of touch for this long. He'd checked his private email for messages. Nothing. They worked independently but always maintained contact even if it was only a random text. Time was of the utmost importance and for days he'd had no word. A deadline loomed and the two of them had to formulate arrangements.

He rubbed the back of his neck and grumbled under his breath, "Call, damn you." He tried but couldn't stop worry from spreading through him.

Clouds filled the sky, changing the deep blue to a pale gray. Rain was on the way just in time for the commute traffic, making it impossible to get out of the city quickly. Forget the Golden Gate Bridge; it was gridlocked by now.

He couldn't prove it, but the tension in his back, and his training told him he'd been followed when he arrived here. If he was going to search for Webb outside of San Francisco, particularly in the North Bay, a decision must be made as to how to leave the city and not be tailed. He'd head south to throw off anyone following him and cross the Dumbarton Bridge, go back up the East Bay to the Richmond Bridge, and on to Marin County.

It would be a pain in his rear to add miles to his journey because traffic would be at a standstill, but a good idea to be on the safe side. Easier to lose any tail in the congestion, something he was good at, particularly in the East Bay. There had to be some reassurance he didn't lead anyone to his brother's location. Even though it was risky, they were both convinced, they had to meet.

His cell rang. He didn't know the number, but that was often true when Webb called. He grabbed for it too fast and almost disconnected the call. With the recovered fumble, he shouted, "Webb?"

"Well, you've answered my question, Jon. No word from him yet?"

He recognized his boss and the slightly higher pitch of irritation.

"No."

"Shit, he had a simple job, track the group's movements when they crossed the border and report back. He must have blown it. If this all goes to hell, it will be on his head."

"I…"

"Get your ass out there and find him. I need the information or his body—yesterday. Got it?"

"Yeah."

Dangerous Web

No one was better than Webb at finding, tracking, infiltrating terrorist, criminal, and other groups who entered the U.S. illegally. Why his silence?

Jon was damned concerned. He left the window and searched the pocket of a jacket in the closet for the car keys. Ready to leave, he wondered if he'd find his brother dead or alive.

***

Back in the Bay Area with Webb in the passenger seat of the old sedan, Emma drove to their small west coast bungalow and parked in the driveway. A memory of the first day she saw the home, with the for sale sign out in front lawn, taunted her. Would he remember too? She didn't dare check to see if he appeared moved by the sight. What difference did it make now?

There was an almost imperceptible pause when he entered the place. Yet, his stoic expression didn't change as his hand raked through his thick dark hair. He scanned the room, pausing on the Danish furniture they'd picked out together. However, his deep brown eyes gave no indication of his thoughts. He stood tall, strong, and in command and she couldn't help admiring him. *Damn it.*

"You know where everything is. I'm going to take a shower. It was a long hot drive."

She rushed to the master bedroom before he could answer. Why did she bring him to their home? Too many uncontrollable feelings were bubbling to the surface.

What would he think when he noticed his clothes were the way he'd left them? She'd kept telling herself it was time to throw them all out or donate the bunch to a needy cause. Somehow, she hadn't been able to do it.

Before long, he'd pick out some of his things from the dresser and maybe take items from garage, then walk out. The marriage would be over. It couldn't come too soon. She'd been able to manage her emotions while they were at the cabin, but being near him in their house threw her off balance. Without equilibrium, her life had tilted out of control. She had to get her day-to-day life in balance, ASAP. Their relationship was dead and she'd carved out a new fulfilling existence. She had to hold on to that realization.

In the bathroom, she undressed and tossed her clothes into the hamper.

The spray of cool water lowered the temperature of her heated body, and the aroma of the coconut shampoo soothed her. She closed her eyes to enjoy the fact she was okay, and he'd be gone soon. When he left, everything would return to the "new" normal.

Out of the shower and wrapped in a pink bath-sheet, she dried her hair with a hand towel.

"I don't mean to get into your private space, but I need a bandage. I'm bleeding again." Wearing only boxers, he came into the room appearing way too appealing even with the wound in his side.

"Shit." She held the bath towel tightly to her. "Uh, I think there are some in the plastic box under the sink."

"You don't have to protect yourself so carefully. It's not like I haven't seen you naked before."

She bent down as he came forward. Her line of sight was at his crotch. Involuntarily, she caught her breath and quickly searched for the first aid container.

"Here's some gauze and tape." She cleared her throat. "That should do."

Was it the steam from her recent shower or could he be making the room hotter?

"Thanks, Emmy. If you don't mind, I'll get cleaned up now."

She was barely able to grab the hairdryer, when he dropped his boxers. She ran into the bedroom, but heard him chuckle as she slammed the bathroom door.

***

Webb sauntered into the galley kitchen wearing the pale green polo shirt she'd bought him for Christmas the year before he'd disappeared and a pair of black jeans that fit too damned well.

"I made a couple of cheese sandwiches."

"Good. We can take them with us. Emma, go pack a bag."

"What do you mean? I'm not coming with you."

"You have to."

"Why?"

"It's not safe here. I can't secure the place, too many access points."

"I don't need protection in *my* own home," she said pointedly, not their house.

"Put a few things together. You've got five minutes."

She plopped into the nearest chair and crossed her arms. "I won't. If I were leaving, it would *not* be with you."

"Emma, we don't have time to argue."

"What can't you understand about I'm staying?"

She took the tray of food and the iced tea into the living room and set it on the coffee table. "Webb, be reasonable."

"Okay. I'm willing," he said, following her. "I'll listen." Nevertheless, his body language was tense and he didn't sit.

"You say I'm in jeopardy. Until you came back into my life, the only danger I had was the risk I'd miss a bus and be late for work or the possibility the grocery store would be out of crunchy peanut butter and I'd have to settle for creamy."

"Be serious, Emmy. I've explained the situation. I'm trying to protect you."

"Webb, you live in some weird scary world. I was miserable when you left me, but I was never in danger. I'm not in jeopardy now."

"Any strangers hanging around, things in the house gone missing, or out of position while you were at work?"

"No," she answered without taking time to think about his question. "Take the sandwiches, your clothes, and whatever you want, then get out."

He rubbed his forehead as if he had a headache. "Let me think."

"Okay, but it's not changing the situation. I'm going for a walk. Webb, don't be here when I get back."

She didn't hear what he shouted at her as she left the house because she wasn't listening. He didn't exist anymore, not to her. Two years ago, he wanted out and broke their marriage contract by abandoning her. He couldn't waltz back and tell her what to do, not now, not ever. He'd lost the right, tossed it in the garbage as if a vow was merely a lie of convenience.

Would he come after her?

Calm down.

To her relief he didn't.

Her car was needed only on days she had clients to take around the city to view properties. Otherwise, she took the bus because it was too costly and hard to park in downtown San Francisco. She sat at the bus stop. The diamond wedding band she still wore, sparkled on her left hand. She sighed. Why hadn't she taken it off? Karen, her boss, was right, the thing should have been thrown away long ago. Twisting to get it off, she took a deep breath. It wouldn't budge.

Webb was certifiable, paranoid, thinking his imaginary villains were chasing her too. She'd be lucky to finish with the sham marriage. So, why did nausea churn in her stomach and regret spiral though her veins?

As she took the thirty-minute bus ride to San Francisco, she realized the rest of the world hadn't gone into an insane alternate universe. She nodded to the middle-aged woman she saw most days and the young woman she knew, was still pregnant.

"How are you?" Emma asked as she took a seat across the aisle from them.

"Fine." She patted her stomach. "Not long now. This is my last week at work."

Emma listened to the possible names her friend considered for the baby and suddenly realized motherhood was no longer an option for her. Not without a partner. Others might cope without one, but... She swallowed a groan, but managed to smile as her friend talked about narrowing her name choices.

With a wave, she left the bus and walked the short distance to the Palmer Real Estate Office. The door was closed. Surprising. Karen, the owner, wanted it open all day to welcome any prospective client who might wander by.

She pushed the door open, entered. A couple of years ago, Karen Palmer had been the only person who'd given her a chance to work, when she'd come into the office with her new realtors' license in hand. She'd be eternally grateful to her boss. Without the job, she'd have lost her car, house, everything after Webb disappeared.

Karen's pink suit jacket hung on the coat rack as usual and her Louis designer handbag sat open on her desk, but she was nowhere to be seen. The phones were quiet, no surprise there. Emma guessed business hadn't picked up in the days she'd been out to the office.

As she got closer to the row of desks, she stepped on a broken shard of glass. A coffee cup lay in pieces and liquid had splashed on the linoleum floor. Her friend must be in the bathroom looking for something to clean up the accident.

An anal person, her boss would never leave a mess for long, as a client might trip and fall.

"Karen." She walked toward the back of the office. "Are you in there?" *Maybe she cut her hand.* "Can I help?"

Something crashed and she threw open the bathroom door. In the windowless room, it took a second to see. But she heard a groan and flicked on the light switch, then screamed.

The realtor lay on the floor, bloody and moaning. "Emmy, run. He thought I was you." Karen coughed.

"Who did this do you?" Emma was shaking so badly she struggled to pull her smart phone out of her bag. She dialed 911. "My boss was attacked. please send help, an ambulance, and the police."

She gave the address and knelt next to her friend. "What can I do?" She closed Karen's torn blouse and wiped blood from her lip with a tissue from her pocket. A bruise had formed on the woman's cheek. "Oh, Karen, I don't know what to do to help. Do you want to sit up?"

"No! Don't move me. It hurts. Go before he comes back," She moaned again.

"I won't leave you alone."

"You have to." She winced. "I…"

"Don't talk. The ambulance will be here soon." *Please God, let that be true.* "It's all right. Stay still. Everything's going to be fine."

"Water, Emmy, please."

She found no glass in the bathroom and went to find a paper cup in the small cupboard near the coffee maker.

As Emma stepped out of the bathroom, a man grabbed her from behind and covered her mouth so she couldn't yell.

"Gotcha."

Chapter 5

Stunned, **Emma froze in the hallway** of the real estate office until the stranger pulled her toward the exit. When she resisted, he lifted her, carrying her in his arms. Her heart beat swiftly as she twisted and clawed at him. His grip tightened.

She grabbed the only vulnerable place she could reach. Yanking downward and twisting his crotch hard.

"Son of bitch," he yelled, relaxing his hold slightly.

She slid from his arms and ran toward the backdoor.

***

Webb parked in the alley behind the real estate office in the hope anyone watching the building wouldn't spot him.

The lane was marked for commercial vehicles only. Perhaps it would discourage others from entering. He parked his green Austin Healey behind a white delivery van. Nice of Emma to keep the car gassed and the battery charged. He pulled up the convertible top and snapped it in place. Wishing he'd thought to bring a jacket, San Francisco, the air-conditioned city, sent a gust of wind to remind him to be more careful the next time he crossed the bridge from sunny Marin.

The backdoor to the real estate office wasn't marked, but he'd counted the number of offices from the corner of the building, and door number four had to be the one. The door crashed open and Emma fell into his arms.

"Help me," she gasped.

He pushed her behind him. For a second the stranger chasing her slowed, stared, then slugged Webb. He flinched, but counter-punched, sending the man back into the office hallway. The thug swore and planted a powerful blow to his ribs. With grunts, they continued to fight until Webb hit the man one last time and the creep fell backward slamming his head on the cement floor with a loud crack.

Webb faced his wife standing behind him. "Who is this asshole?"

"I don't know, but Karen's hurt—my boss."

When she turned to go back into the office, he grabbed her arm.

"Let me go."

"I'll call 911."

"I did, but she's hurt. Webb, please." She glanced at his hold on her.

"Emma, it's not safe."

"Please, I have to."

"Go, tell your boss you're out of here." He tapped the foot of the man lying on the floor. "I'm going to throw a couple of zip ties on this creep, in case he's not dead. That's all the time you have. If his armed buddies come here, I can't protect you." He released her. She shivered and this time didn't mock his words about being in jeopardy.

While she ran to her friend, he tied the hood's hands and feet, then rolled the man over and checked his pockets. No ID, driver's license, or wallet. But in his back pocket, he found a cheap cell. Probably a burner phone, to be used for this job and discarded. There wouldn't be much info on the damn thing. Even so, he took it. Any number was more information than he had at this point. He looked at the stiff, the man had planned for all contingencies, except Webb.

What would've happened to Emma if he hadn't arrived in time? *Don't think about it.*

He hoped her friend would be okay, but perhaps it happened for a reason. Em now understood she was at risk. She couldn't comprehend the full extent of the situation without more information, but she didn't need to know more. She was already overloaded. The last thing he wanted was for her to have a complete meltdown. If he told her the truth, she'd be convinced he was insane and would run from him. She might remain with him as long as fear of the unknown men ruled her emotions. He hoped that would be long enough to do what must be done.

The blare of sirens sent him further down the hallway toward the office, but not all the way. No need for Karen to see him. The less she knew of him the safer they'd both be. He didn't want her giving a description of him to the police.

"Emma, we have to go." His English accent exposed, something he'd worked hard to suppress especially under stressful situations. Between his wound and his concern for his wife, it came out after the most rigorous preparation to curtail his accent.

Damn did she recognize it?

"Webb, give me a little more time."

"Now!" he said in his best American, much the way a United States commander might talk to a disobedient soldier. "The sirens are close. The medics will be here for your friend," he said when she appeared, her face pale with stress.

"We better leave before they arrive or we'll be stuck making statements to the police. Neither of us want that. Not when the men looking for you could be watching or will be searching for him when he doesn't call in."

"Oh, God." She trembled and leaned against the wall.

"Where's your other high heel?"

She glanced down at her feet. "I—guess it fell off when the stranger picked me up."

"Find the shoe." His voice sounded harsh even to his ears, but he didn't have time to sooth her. He needed to hold her in his arms and tell her nothing bad would happen again. Damn. He couldn't make a promise when he wasn't sure he'd be able to protect himself let alone her.

Without a word, she rushed to the office and came back wearing both pumps. She carried her handbag as well.

He kicked the thug out of the way and held the back door open for Emma. "The Healey is parked in the alley."

Once she settled in the seat and strapped on the seat belt, he started the engine. "Thanks for keeping my car in running order."

"I never gave up hope you were alive and would come home."

He cringed and guilt ran though him. He never should've married her. He acted like a self-centered shithead for doing it. Never the less, the truth wouldn't make her feel any better.

She didn't ask where they were going. He guessed Em was no longer speaking to him. Lucky because she should be giving him hell. Somehow, her silence was worse.

Before he landed the knockout punch to the stranger, the man's beefy fist had slugged him hard. The creep appeared to understand where to hit him to do the most damage.

His pale green shirt became red with blood. His old wound was open again. Pain pulsed through him and radiated to the lumbar region of his back. He sucked in a quick breath.

Did Emma notice? Again, he remembered he should've brought a jacket to cover his shirt. She had to believe he was in charge and could take care of all threats that might assault them.

"Webb, what's wrong."

"Nothing."

"Tell me."

He grimaced.

"Shit, you're bleeding! Pull over. I'll drive."

"You can't handle a stick."

"Since you left, who do you think has been using the Healey these last two years? Webb, pull the damn car to the curb."

***

Webb didn't tell her a destination, so she drove out of the city heading toward Marin County.

Before pulling onto the Golden Gate Bridge, she took a glance at him. His eyes were closed and, for a second, she thought he was asleep.

"Where do you think you're heading?"

She jumped surprised by his question. "Home."

With a grimace, he sat up. "No—the last place you should go. The first location they'd look for you."

"Who are they?"

"Wish I understood. Look, at this point, it doesn't really matter. All you need to comprehend is they will hurt you to get info on me."

"What can I tell them? It's been two years. I have no idea what you did while you were away."

"Exactly, you couldn't inform them."

She maneuvered to the slow lane and thought about what he was saying.

"Emma, they won't believe you can't help them and they won't let you go until you give them what they want."

"But I don't have it."

"No, but the danger to you is real. Your life has changed, at least for now."

Go to hell. She bit back the words and continued the journey in silence, unsure where either of them would end up.

When the exit sign for San Rafael appeared, she flicked on the right turn signal.

"Don't. Keep going to Petaluma."

"Webb, I'm a stranger there."

"Good." He sucked in a slow breath. "No trail to follow, most people on the run go to a familiar place where they feel comfortable." He paused. "Shit."

"The bleeding's worse. I'm taking you to the hospital. You need stitches, or something to stop the blood."

"Not Marin General. Somewhere north."

"But…"

"Drive."

No use in arguing. At least Webb had agreed to get medical care, something he should've received days ago. What should she tell the doctors?

"Webb?"

"We better decide on a story," he said as if he'd heard her thinking. "No mention of the cabin or what happened today in the real estate office." He paused and pressed on his wound. "Understand?"

"Okay. Why don't you do the talking? I could stay in the car."

"I might need you in there."

"Me?"

"Hard to talk without pain. You may have to give my info to the doctors."

"Oh, God."

"Em, I need something to cover the wound."

"I think there are tissues in my bag." Though she struggled to control it, her voice shook.

He grunted while searching her handbag.

She wanted to help him, but instead, gripped the steering wheel, pressed on the gas pedal, and moved into the fast lane heading north on Highway 101, grateful the commute traffic hadn't started yet.

They rode in silence until he said, "You are Mrs. Johnathan Straight, married to a Canadian oil sands executive from Calgary, Alberta."

"Is that where you're from?"

"Never been there."

"But…"

"Just remember."

"All right, okay."

"In the glove box, I put a Visa card in Straight's name. Pay the bill if I can't."

"Don't say that. Why wouldn't you be able to…" She glared at him.

"Keep your eyes on the damned road or we will both be in the hospital."

"Shut up."

A couple of miles up the highway, he said, "Can you remember?"

"Visa, Mrs. Straight from—uh."

"Calgary, Alberta."

"Calgary." She kept whispering the place over and over, for so long she almost missed the sign for the Petaluma turn off.

At the hospital's emergency entrance, Webb was placed on a gurney and he disappeared into ER before she had parked and locked the sports car.

Air conditioned and uncrowded, the medical center at the level two trauma center had clear signage directing her to the admissions desk. A clerk, in civilian clothes, took the information for Webb and also copied the Visa card before returning it to Emma, no ID required.

In the waiting room, she tried to relax. *Webb is receiving care, everything's okay.* Not true, nothing seemed right. She'd never been good at lying, not to strangers or herself. *You're both in a shit load of trouble.*

Well-worn magazines lay on a table next to her brown plastic chair. Too upset to focus, she ignored them. A flat screen on the wall played a news channel. With the sound turned off, closed captions scrolled across the wide screen. The usual political news played at the top of the hour, followed by overseas wars and upheavals, then the stock market report. She was about to look away when the local news started. "A woman has been attacked in a real estate office in downtown San Francisco, motive unknown, the newscaster stated. The realtor was taken to San Francisco General in critical condition. Police would like to talk to any witness who might have seen what happened, anonymity is promised. A phone number for the police scrolled across the screen. She found her business card and rapidly wrote the number on the back.

Karen lay in a hospital bed in critical condition and it was her fault. She pushed back an anguished cry. All the woman had done to deserve this was hire Emma. If only she'd been at work instead of Karen.

Oh, God, was Webb in critical condition too?

Chapter 6

Two hours later, Webb was wheeled out of the treatment room of the Sonoma Hospital into the waiting room. He got up from the chair and walked toward her.

"We're out of here."

"Did they release you?"

"Signed myself out. Weaseled a couple of prescriptions that's enough."

"What about the bleeding?"

"Stitched me up."

He kept walking and she had to run after him.

She drove to a drug store down the street from the hospital and had the prescriptions he gave her filled.

"Webb, where are we going now?"

"A hotel."

The five-star hotel spa was located seventy miles north of San Francisco in the middle of the Sonoma County's wine country. The private lane appeared to go for miles before the huge beige mansion appeared in the afternoon sun.

"I'll go to the suite. They're expecting you. Talk to the front desk clerk."

A man, in casual attire, opened the car door. "Welcome to the hacienda. The bellman will take care of your luggage."

She cleared her throat. "It hasn't arrived yet."

"No worries." He smiled. "The staff will notify you when it does."

"Thank you." *That will be a cold day in...*

Casual but sophisticated California elegance greeted her in the wide-open lobby, decorated with flagstone floors, hand-carved mission furniture, and wrought iron chandeliers. Huge clay pots planted with indigenous flowers and native grasses helped with the indoor, outdoor ambiance so popular in the golden state. Vintage California landscapes hung on the adobe-colored walls, their gold frames shining as mother lode gold dug from the foothills by the forty-niners.

A cool breeze from the perfectly temperature-controlled air conditioner relaxed her.

At the desk a man dressed in a crisp white shirt, with a name tag that read Robert B, smiled. Could there be a Robert A?

"We have been expecting you, Mrs. Straight. We received your husband's text. His favorite suite is ready."

Webb had been there before?

The clerk copied the Visa much as the hospital billing department had done and required no ID.

She shuddered thinking of the cost of the trip to the emergency room and now the price of a suite in this five-star hotel. Why couldn't Webb be satisfied with a room? Why a suite? He said not to worry but...

Did the man see her hand shake when she gave him the plastic card? Earlier thousands of dollars had been charged to cover the hospital visit.

"Are you or your husband allergic to animals, cats or dogs?"

"No. We love animals." *An odd question.*

We have pet ambassadors who wander the inn. They enjoy attention and many of our patrons like interacting with them. The dog is a Golden Retriever called Skipper and the orange tabby is Butch. Interact with them whenever you like and if you'd prefer a companion on your walks around the many acres of trails, Skipper is always ready to go."

"Thank you. That's wonderful."

No key was needed for the suite. She chose a password at the front desk.

At the door to her rooms, she punched it into the keyboard on the handle. The lock released and she entered.

The suite with its painted white walls and plush carpet, designed for tranquility, was decorated with overstuffed sofas and chairs. A TV mounted discreetly on a wall could to be seen from any vantage point in the room. Like the lobby it was elegant, but possibly more luxurious. She glanced up at the open beam ceiling with the huge black wrought iron and crystal chandelier, then at a carved wooden mantel surrounding the fireplace.

Off the living room an office with everything a busy executive might need sat waiting. Down the hall was a kitchen, set up for one's servants and a simple bath in Calacatta marble. At the end of the hallway, she found a grand bedroom. A white king size bed on a raised platform gave the bed a look of a throne. The carved dark wood headboard reached toward the ten-foot ceiling. A white goose down comforter, pure white cotton linens, and pillows covered the mattress. A matching couch and love seat sat in a nook and a flat screen on the wall could be watched from the bed or the seats.

Webb wasn't there.

The bathroom. She rushed to push the door open to the master bath. A sudden chill ran down her back as she recalled finding Karen in the real estate store room. Afraid to look she stood for a moment with her head down. When enough courage filled her, she took a quick glance. No one.

Panicked, she was about to run out to search for him in case he'd passed out on the grounds or something, when the glass door to the deck slid open.

Webb. She ran to him.

"I take it everything went fine," he said.

"Where have you been?"

He shrugged. "Sizing up the area." He paused. "These stitches are driving me crazy."

He was still wearing the bloody shirt and she cringed seeing the dried blood. "You should rest. You don't look so good."

He sat heavily in an overstuffed chair, propped his feet up on the ottoman, and scanned her. "We look pretty rough. Take the charge card and buy some clothes. No insult intended, but find an outfit with a little fashion flare."

"What does that mean?"

"A successful business woman might be subtle in her dress, but never bargain-basement."

"You jerk! Do you have any idea how hard I've worked to keep the mortgage up to date and pay the house taxes in a rising market? They go up every year and I'm not earning a salary. No money comes in unless I sell a house or property."

"Hey, calm down. No criticism meant, but don't be fooled by the casual surroundings. This place is filled by movers and shakers of the world. The one percent. We need to fit in, at least for the moment."

"I'm not impressed. Any working stiff is worth twice what one of them is worth, when you add in good values, hard work and caring about the world..."

"Hush. This isn't about social correctness. Someone wants us dead. They won't think to look here among those who might have put a contract out on me."

"Dear God, what are you implying?"

"I want us to stay here and recover. While we are at the hotel, we might learn something, but only if we fit in. Understand?"

"No. I don't grasp any of this."

"Buy a dozen shirts of various types for me, in large. including a white dress shirt." He changed the subject. "And a few outfits, including, business, causal wear, and an evening gown, shoes, bags, and under garments. Oh, better snag some jewelry. Large diamond ear studs, a tennis bracelet and something that glitters for your neck to go with the gown."

"You're joking."

"Completely serious. If the sales clerk asks, though they should be better trained, let them realize you are waiting for your servant to bring your jewels and only need a few trinkets to wear until then."

"Trinkets! You're a man so you probably didn't see the brands or notice the boutiques off the lobby. It would take tens of thousands to buy what you describe." A headache bloomed over her left eye. She sagged into an overstuffed chair near him.

Webb picked up the room phone, placed it next to his chair and dialed, then extended it to her. She jumped up and grabbed it in time to hear a mechanical voice say, "Your available credit is…" She blinked and pressed number five to repeat the message, gasped and shook her head in disbelief when she heard the same number, seven figures. "Shit." *Who is this man who calls himself my husband?*

"Satisfied?" he asked, but didn't look pleased to give her the information. "Go do what I told you." He paused. "I need to sleep. The pain meds are making me drowsy."

She rubbed her forehead. Maybe humoring him was the thing to do. *Whatever you want dear. Rest honey, everything is going to be all right.* Then leave the room and run like the hounds of hell were after her. Problem: a person from Hades *was* chasing her. Webb, even crazy and injured, had proven he could protect her. If she left his side, who else would?

***

Instead of shopping, she walked for what felt like miles on the trails surrounding the hotel. Finally, her feet begged for a rest; high heels were never meant for jogging trails. She discovered a wooden bench overlooking the hotel's vineyard and sat and tried to admire the view.

Rows of grape vines fanned out over the valley, all evenly placed and well-tended. The sun was high and the clear blue sky devoid of clouds. She imagined it would be a tranquil setting for the usual visitor. But she couldn't focus enough to enjoy the panorama. Decisions demanded attention.

No matter how much money Webb had, there would be no buying expensive garments on his credit card. And if she stayed with him, she damn well needed to be told about his plans, goals, and who was paying him.

Somehow walking on the trails, with Skipper the pet ambassador, had cleared her mind. Earlier Webb appeared crazy. He wasn't. But he did have an agenda. A mission and he was willing to do whatever necessary to accomplish the deed. However, she couldn't understand the assignment. How would anything include her?

The dog nudged her hand with his head like he recognized her tension. She rubbed Skipper's ear. "It's okay boy. You're a good dog." He wagged his tail and then settled at her feet. She leaned back and closed her eyes. The Sonoma heat began to take the chill out of her bones and her body relaxed.

"May I join you?"

"What?" She startled, sat up, and stared at a man silhouetted by the bright afternoon sun. She shaded her eyes with her hand. Dressed in kakis, white polo shirt and expensive running shoes, the older man stood tall and commanding.

"Do you mind? These weary muscles need rest."

"Please."

He took a seat at the other end of the bench and looked out at the horizon. "Just arrive?" he asked without glancing her way.

"How can you tell?"

"Your heels and a business suit. Most are dressed more casually."

"Oh, of course. I got here this afternoon, I'm trying to relax and get into the vacation frame of mind," she said, surprised her how easily a lie came to her lips.

"Well young lady, give it a couple of days at least."

"You've visited the hotel before?"

"I've had the pleasure. What brings you here?"

The probing question alarmed her "Uh—In the summer, I like to leave San Francisco and see the sun for a few days." A half-truth, the city was fogged in most summer days. Of course, she'd never think of coming to this place, too expensive.

"Didn't someone say the coldest winter they ever spent was a summer in San Francisco?"

She laughed. "Well, if they did it wouldn't be far from reality. Between the wind and the fog, it can be pretty cold."

"I haven't been to San Francisco in years." He paused as if remembering. "When we were younger, my wife and I walked across the Golden Gate Bridge. I'll never forget the day."

The man stood. "Well, I came to stretch my legs. I'll be off. Nice talking with you—

He paused waiting for her name.

"Emma, Emma Craig."

"Enjoy your stay, Emma."

"Thank you." For the first time she really looked and recognized him, chief advisor to the president of the United States. He'd been on TV many times.

Before she could say anything else, he disappeared down the trail.

Stunned, she sat wondering if she should tell Webb. Or did he already have the information. Could that be why they stayed here? *No way.* Now *she* was thinking of crazy theories. Should she have told the guy her name? *Too late now.*

"Come on, Skipper, we better get you back to the hotel. I have shopping to do if I'm going to socialize in this place."

There must be outlet stores where I can buy a good pair of runners, some clothes, and use my own money.

Outside of town at a local strip mall, she discovered a designer discount store, entered and found the clearance rack. A slinky beaded black dress sparkled, probably discounted because it was las year's model, but the dress pattern appeared classic, nothing branded it as out of date. The fabric slithered down her body and clung to her as only a chic gown could. Glancing in the dressing room mirror, a sophisticated woman stared back at her. What would Webb think of her in this? *You shouldn't care.*

She checked the price tag. *OMG.* Yes, the third markdown from the first discounted price. Whether she had to or not at this price she wanted the dress. A silver clutch bag and a pair of shiny black leather sandals completed the outfit. Within under an hour, she bought several casual garments, underwear, runners and a nightie.

In the men's section, without emotion, she grabbed several Polo shirts, a couple of dress shirts, pants and underwear in Webb's size. Pushing back the memory of shopping for him while they were married, she rushed to the checkout counter and paid for the items.

On her way to the car a sign caught her attention, Going out of business. She peered into a jewelry store window before pulling open the door.

She browsed, then asked the clerk who made the jewelry.

"He is one of our local craftsmen. The guy's closing up shop and retiring," the store clerk answered. "Many items are one of a kind signed by the artist. Feel free to look around. Ask if you'd like to try anything on."

"How long is the sale?"

"Tomorrow is the last day."

"Oh—thank you."

She discovered an etched sterling silver choker, matching bracelet and silver and freshwater peal earrings, all signed by the artist. She also bought a long silver necklace.

In the car, she sat and closed her eyes. *Hold it together.* Pushing back the images of the man who had attacked her in the real estate office. *No tears.* She didn't cry when it happened. She wouldn't do it now.

Driving to the luxury hotel and spa, her hands shook holding the steering wheel. A man had tried to kill her and he died. Her boss was in the hospital, and she didn't even know which one or if she was alive. Unreal, Emma was trapped, in extravagant accommodations, but against her wishes with a man she hated. She hated Webb, didn't she?

***

Harold Lancaster sat in a club chair in Webb's suite and stared. "Son, you look like shit. What the hell happened?"

"I…" Webb grimaced in pain. *Don't call me son.*

"Ethan, you need a doctor." Mr. Lancaster stood and stepped forward, shoulders back, and head high. "No argument. It is not open for debate."

"I'm trying to keep undercover. Don't need anyone else being told I'm out of commission." Webb did his best to sit up straight. Something his stepfather, ex-military and current diplomat, always demanded from his adopted sons.

Mr. Lancaster texted on his smart phone then glanced up. "Done. A doctor will be here later tonight."

"Not necessary."

"Could have fooled me, you're hardly able sit up— when was the last time you shaved combed your hair?"

Before he could answer his stepdad said, "I met your lady on the jogging path. Not smart to bring her with you."

"Did you follow her?"

When Lancaster didn't respond Webb said, "Leave her alone. Emma has nothing to do with us."

"Really? You married her. If she has no involvement, why is she with you?"

"No choice, they found her at work. A man damned near killed her. What else could I do?"

Mr. Lancaster glared. "Who's after you, Ethan?"

"You know I can't say."

"You were wrong to marry the girl. You put her in danger." Father hesitated "You didn't introduce her to your family or take your vows in your own name. Ashamed of her or us?"

The words stung. However, what could he say to him. It was all true. He should have done better by Emma and his family.

"I've got the trust of the president." Lancaster's gray eyes narrowed. "But not my own son."

"It's not that." He paused. *You're my stepfather. Marrying my mother doesn't make you my dad.*

He coughed as the RAT oath he'd sworn echoed in his ears. Then the words of his boss: *There will come a time when you will disappoint your family and friends. They may call you a liar or be hurt by your silence. If you can't take it leave now. When you sign the oath of secrecy, there is no going back.*

"Shit, Ethan, what the hell are you involved in? If you need a good lawyer…"

"No. I can't talk about it, even to you. Not without breaking my word—I understand you'd never want me to do that."

Checkmate.

The expression on his stepdad's face led him to understand the man knew the truth of the statement. As far as Webb comprehended, Lancaster had never violated any vow he'd ever made.

"Ethan, it is time to grow up and stop playing kid's games. You'll be thirty-one soon. Is this your way of rebelling from the proper upbringing we gave you?" Harold Lancaster paced the room, then stopped. "I suppose you have a secret decoder ring too."

"Give me a break, Dad." He added dad knowing how the man hated being called that name. "Why is everything in relation to your life? Can't you understand I want to do something on my own without your involvement."

Mr. Lancaster recoiled from him. "Think of your mother and if you won't consider her, what about the girl? Reflect on what this does to her."

Webb resisted correcting his father and reminding him Emma was not a random girl, but his wife. "I'm doing this for her and everyone in this country."

"A dramatic statement. I hope I didn't raise a child who is prone to exaggeration." He shrugged. "Well, I'll take your word. I brought the file you asked for." He handed Webb a paper folder. "Burn it when you're finished." With his hands in his pocket of his well creased slacks, Lancaster surveyed the room.

"Thank you, for bringing it."

"Eat and get some sleep. I'll talk to you in the morning." With his hand resting on the doorknob father continued, "I ordered a nutritious meal for you and your girlfriend. Buy her some decent clothes. She looks like a waif."

By his stance it appeared something more was on his mind. Yet, the silence continued. At last, he asked, "May I give a message to your mother?"

"Tell her I send my love."

"Demonstrate you care by calling her once in a while." Lancaster cleared his throat. "Mend quickly. I need you out of this place. The public relations department reported the president is enjoying a week at Camp David, but he will be here tomorrow. He doesn't need the added danger of the thugs who are after you entering the hotel.

The man turned to face him. "Even if you aren't using my family name, I gave it to you when I adopted you and you are known by that surname, don't besmirch it." Carefully closing the door behind him, his stepfather disappeared.

Webb let out the groan he'd been holding since Lancaster arrived. *Damn. Where did I put the pain killers?* The thought of getting up and searching seemed daunting. He leaned back, trying not to breath too deeply.

***

The slim older man she'd seen on the trail exited her room. She almost yelled at him. *Hey, what are you doing in my room?* Almost. Something about the man intimidated her.

He walked quickly in the opposite direction. *Damn.* Why was he there? Webb's room too, she corrected, again reminded how little she knew about her husband. Oh, he'd told her a story. That's what he did best, weave outlandish tales.

Time for answers.

Her hand shook as she opened suite's door. Though the sun was setting, no light was on in the quiet room. Webb sat slumped in a chair. The same place he'd been hours ago. His eyes were closed. Asleep? He hadn't changed clothes or combed his hair and stubble grew on his strong chin.

She entered as quietly as possible but fumbled with her packages.

"Where have you been?"

She startled, expecting to go into the bedroom unnoticed and let him continue to snooze.

A reasonable question, but it still irritated her. He'd left for two years without a word and now he demanded to know where she had been. "I went shopping as you ordered."

She threw the bags onto the nearby sofa.

"Who was the man?" she challenged.

His eyes flew open and a grim expression spread across his face. "No one you need to meet." He tried to straighten up in the chair. "Hell. Where did I put the pain meds?"

She glared and thought of denying the information he wanted. Instead, she huffed and moved toward the bathroom where she'd last seen the bottle of pills.

With the medication and a glass of water set on a table next to Webb, she sat across from him. He looked pale and the strength he's shown when he took on her attacker was gone. Grateful to him but angry, conflicting emotions swirled in her. She started to ask a question, when there was a knock on the door.

She had just pulled it open when Webb shouted, "Don't answer."

A man in a white polo shirt and white pants entered. "Where's the patient?" A stocky guy in his middle years and carrying a leather bag, moved quickly into the room. "Ethan, heard you are in a mess again." The man smiled as if this was a usual occurrence. Without waiting for a response, he continued, "Stick this under your tongue and take off your shirt."

To her surprise, her husband did what he was told without objection.

"You have a fever and I don't like the look of the wound. You probably should be on IV antibiotics." He held up his hand against anything Webb might say. "I understand there's no way you're going to the hospital." He scanned the room. "I could do it here." The man wiped the tip of the digital thermometer with an alcohol swab.

"Not happening, Doc. Do what you can now."

"I don't recall you being allergic to anything."

"Not as far as I remember."

"Good. Let me help you into the bedroom. I need to work on your lesion. It has to be drained, cleaned and sutured."

"Miss, turn down the bed."

"Mrs.," Emma corrected him."

"Really."

A statement or a question, she couldn't tell, but she stupidly hoped being Webb's wife might cause the doctor to show her some respect.

"Hurry up, girl," the doctor said.

Girl. She was liking the doctor less and less but had to depend on his expertise to help.

With Webb resting uncomfortably on the king-sized bed, the examination started.

The physician had him remain still as he examined the injury while talking the whole time as if he was visiting a friend.

"Your father tells me you've got yourself in another fix. I remember your days in Uni. I flew to England back then. A few nasty scrapes and a black eye back in the day but looks as if you've done more harm this time."

Webb's dad was alive? She'd been led to believe his parents were dead and he had no other family.

"No strolling down memory lane." He coughed. "I've got to get back on my feet—now."

"Whatever you say, dear boy. Lancaster mentioned you were in a dour mood. Can't say I blame you. Must hurt something fierce." He grinned. "I'm going give you an injection of antibiotics, and then one for pain. It's going to make you drowsy, but your little lady will bring you whatever you need. I'll clean out the wound and add a few of sutures." He searched in his bag. "Tomorrow, swallow these wide spectrum antibiotics as directed until they're finished." He tossed a container from his open satchel to Emma. "Ethan, stay in bed and rest for a couple of days."

He paused focusing on finishing the stiches. "For once do what I tell you to do and you'll start to feel more like your old self. I will leave a prescription for pain." The doctor cleaned up and motioned Emma to follow him into the living room of the suite.

"Young lady, I've left the medication and directions. Make sure he doesn't stop the antibiotics before they're all finished." He hesitated. "I'm going to trust you to think of Webb's best interest."

"Of course."

"Here is his father's cell phone number. This is private information, extremely confidential, not to be shared with anyone and I mean no one. Use only if Webb is in dire straits. You understand what your husband is doing and how important it is," he said apparently taking for granted she was in the loop and comprehended the high stakes. "Memorize the number and then destroy the note. Burn it, if possible. There is no name on the paper. Don't add one."

He picked up his leather bag and left the room without a goodbye. The sound of the door closing reverberated in the suite and she was left with her mouth open and questions unanswered. She didn't have the doctor's name, let alone the name of Webb's father or why she would need to call a stranger.

***

Webb was sleeping when she checked on him. Back in the living room, she moved her shopping bags from the couch sat back with a sigh, then turned on the flat screen for local news, hoping to hear about the man who had attacked her. Nothing. And no information about her boss either. What would Webb say if she called the San Francisco hospitals to find her? A friend in need, she couldn't forget Karen. Something should be done to help her but what?

Emma paced the room wondering whether contacting Karen would help or put her in more danger. She stared out of the sliding glass door at the well-lit grounds surrounding the hotel and spa. A middle-aged couple, casually, but expensively dressed, strolled toward the open bar near one of the swimming pools. When the man spoke, the sound of the woman's lyrical laugher drifted upward on a warm gentle breeze.

If only that was her life. *Shit*. What next? Go along with whatever Webb suggested or run for her life? She slumped into the nearest chair.

She must have fallen asleep because she woke with a start when the TV news announcer said, "Breaking News, well-known realtor Karen Palmer of Palmer Reality has died from injuries received from an attacker in her office. Theft is assumed to be the reason for the assault. Cash was often kept on the premises."

"No!" Emma screamed. "Karen can't be gone!"

Chapter 7

Webb rushed to the living room unsure what he might see and found his wife on the floor screaming.

"Emma, what's wrong? Are you hurt?"

No response.

"Damn, talk to me."

"It's your fault Karen's dead. It's because of you."

Stunned, he stood trying to understand. "Who died? What are you shouting about?" He muted the TV and moved closer to her.

"My boss, Karen Palmer. You don't have any idea what it's like to lose your best friend. Karen would be alive if you hadn't come back into my life. I hate you and all you stand for." She tried to hit him, but he moved quickly out of range. His movements were too fast and the reward was a shooting pain in his abdomen. *Shit.*

"Em, I…" What could he say? She was right. He exhaled. No way to fix things now.

"Get up." He stopped short before adding *honey*.

No response.

He understood Emmy's anguish. He had watched his brother, discover his family slaughtered. Jon's three-year old son and pregnant wife were gone. Webb winced as the memory of that day depressed him. He was powerless to change what happened back then, and now his wife, Emma, had suffered a terrible loss. He ignored the agony of his physical injury and knelt down to hold her and rock her in his arms.

In the darkened hotel room with only the glow of the television to illuminate the room, he debated what to do next.

It *was* all his fault. *No.* If he hadn't returned to the real estate office, there might be two dead realtors reported on the local news tonight, Karen and Emma. He shivered at the thought.

"Please let me help you get up. Sit on the sofa." The desire to protect her almost overwhelmed him. "Come on."

She glared at him.

"I won't touch you, Emmy." With his hands up, he backed away. "When you're ready, I'd like to hear about Karen. I wish I had known her."

His wife struggled to her feet. He gasped when she stumbled, but she managed catch her footing, then collapsed on the sofa.

An occasional laugh from the partygoers outside broke the dark mood in the room. Webb sat in the overstuffed chair where he'd spent the afternoon dozing. The day had come full circle. Nothing accomplished, merely pain.

The injection Doc had administered had worn off. But Webb wouldn't leave the room in search of pain killers, not when Emmy suffered agony medication couldn't cure.

"I was happy until I met you."

She stared at him and he felt hatred. He couldn't contradict her because he understood the truth of her statement.

"Your love is poison. It destroys everything it touches," she sobbed.

Damn, he'd chosen the life he was living. Even when everything went to shit, he understood why and the penalties. Not Emmy, she thrashed against the only person she saw hurting her—him. He rubbed his eyes and stared at the muted television, then glanced at his wife. Curled into a fetal position, she had fallen asleep on the sofa.

Relief for her. The pain would return with the dawn, but for now…

How long had it been since he'd felt safe enough to hold Emma's hand and watch the sunset with her? With a grunt, he shut off the flat screen TV and in the dark, he limped to the bedroom to hunt for his pain killers.

*****

Emma woke in the living room, covered with a blanket, but didn't remember finding one. She glanced at a clock near the TV, four in the morning. She closed her eyes again. Memories of the evening threatened, but she pushed them down. No reason punish herself and recall things that couldn't be changed.

The night's silence was broken by the sound of something falling in the bedroom and Webb swore under his breath.

The bedroom was dark when she entered and turned on a small nightlight. He glanced at her. "What are you doing here?"

"I heard you fall. If you're searching for the pain meds, they're in the bathroom. I'll grab them."

"I can manage."

"Webb, sit on the bed. I'll do it."

He sat, grunted, and held his side.

When she returned from the bathroom, he swallowed the pill she brought him and nodded his thanks.

"You okay now?" She rubbed her eyes. "If you don't need anything else, I'll let you rest."

"Don't leave. We need to talk."

She sat in a chair across the room. "What's there to say? I can't go home."

He struggled to sit up and grimaced. She saw his suffering wanted to do something to comfort him. What?

"You're right, Emma, no going home. I tried to explain. You weren't ready to listen." He coughed and held his wound for a minute before talking again. "They know who you are and understand your usual movements. You mustn't fall into your usual routine. They'd expect it."

"How long before I can go back?" She couldn't hide her irritation.

He looked away from her. "Until it's over." He paused. "I'll do the best I can to give back your life without me. I can't predict when."

"What now?"

"We'll attend a cocktail party here at the hotel tomorrow night. Why else did I ask you to buy some decent clothes?"

"Damn. I'm trying to trust you. And you talk about parties. You *are* crazy.

Shit. Why do I try to deal with him?

"Seems weird, Emmy. I get it. Wonder why I'm here of all places? Not to enjoy the wine country," he said sarcasm in his voice. "I hope to make contact with my partner."

"Thought you worked alone."

"For the most part, I do. This case is too important not to secure backup. The phone and the internet aren't safe. In person only. Even that's dangerous." He took a shallow breath.

"But, Webb, I…"

"This place appears to be a nice upscale resort. He swallowed slowly. "The hotel is a fort. An outpost, discreetly guarded. Safe enough for the president to visit."

"You aren't kidding."

"No. There are people I need to see at the party. The thing starts is at seven pm. Be ready." He shut off the light and left her in the dark. "Go to sleep, Em. Morning will come soon enough."

Dismissed as if she were a child, she left the bedroom, slamming the door behind her.

***

Webb spent most of the day in bed, rousing only for meals. They didn't talk. She searched for news about Karen's case, not much information from the local news.

Her frustration grew.

She glanced at her smartphone, seven pm already.

Her hair done and makeup applied, she dressed in the black jersey cocktail length dress she'd bought yesterday.

Her zipper stuck. The more she pulled the worse it got. The fabric was snarled in the side zipper. She twisted to see how to loosen the material.

"I'll help," Webb said as he entered the room.

She squirmed as he touched her ribcage trying to free the fabric from the clutches of the metal zipper. The mere brush of his large hands sent heat to spiral though her, how easy it would be to turn and be in his arms. And how damned discouraging that such a thought could pulse in her. She wanted to touch him, run her hands through his perfectly combed hair, but resisted. "Can you fix it?"

"Give me a second."

"Don't pull too hard. You'll break it."

"You want me to fix the thing?"

"Yeah."

"Stand still."

"It's delicate."

"Quiet. I used to help my kid sister."

"You have a sister?"

"A sister and brother."

"You tell me that now?"

He yanked the zipper.

"Ouch!" She rubbed her side.

"Don't move, if you don't want the fabric to tear."

She froze at the coldness of his voice.

"Done." He walked away from her and slipped into his suit jacket that hung in the bedroom closet. Showered and shaved, she barley recognized him. A handsome stranger, tall with shoulders back, and outfitted in a dark European cut suit and a white dress shirt, he stared at her. He pulled at his cuffs and the black onyx gems of his cufflinks shone against the white shirt. She bet his leather shoes were Italian made.

She needn't have wasted money buying a shirt for him. Webb and told her to use the hotel store. Apparently, they had whatever he needed, judging by his appearance.

"You good to go now?"

"Almost."

The sling back sandals sat near the door. She grabbed her wrap, clutch purse, and stepped into the shoes.

Why had he hidden her from his family? She wanted to blame him for not caring enough. A little voice in her brain said he was protecting his family and her. She began to see the tightrope he walked.

"You look just right." He hesitated. "Beautiful." He started to walk out of the door, then stopped and waited. "You coming?"

"Yeah." Her hands tingled. *Nerves.* What was she walking into, a part to play in a bizarre event?

"What became of the kind and gentle man she had married, the local guy who hoped to make good? Webb was a stranger. She almost needed an introduction. The good man she'd given her heart and body to didn't exist. Never did. She'd married a lie.

***

Emma sat at a table by the arbor outside the conference room where the party was being held. The night's warm breeze caressed her, a relief after the rush of introductions and the blur of faces as she met the people who apparently populated her husband's life. Famous men and women she'd seen on the TV news. Congressman this, ambassador that and the gentle lady from wherever, she didn't try to keep track of any of them. They weren't involved in her life. She had no lofty goals and only wanted a traditional life like her parents—marriage, kids, career. Nothing wrong with that. Right?

Emma Craig was her name. She flinched every time someone called her Mrs. Lancaster. Who the hell was that?

Ethan did thus and Ethan did so, they'd told her, with a smile. The people talked as if she shared the secrets from his childhood.

"So nice to finally meet you, dear," the UN ambassador had said. "Don't you and Ethan be strangers now, you hear?" Before Emma could answer, the woman strolled away to smile, her lovely southern grin, when she saw a VIP who needed her attention.

Emma surveyed the courtyard near the pool where soft lights, illuminated the surroundings. Fresh flowers set in urns around the area sent a delicate floral fragrance to permeate the air. Soft voices of the well-heeled and gentle sounds of feminine laughter wafted from the party. The rich did exist in a different world from the rest the people. No hustle and bustle even when a crisis emerged. By Webb's situation and what she'd personally seen, a disaster was about to befall all of them. Were they aware?

After a sip, Emma set a stemmed glass filled with champagne on the patio table. French or Californian? In her life, she hadn't drunk enough of the bubbly to be sure. However, it went down easily, light and frothy. Had circumstance been different, the glass would be empty. However, she needed her faculties sharp tonight.

"May I join you?" a tall, slender man with Nordic features, blond hair, and intense blue, seen even in the low light, spoke. When she didn't answer he continued, "Are you waiting for someone?"

"Well—I came out for the fresh air."

"Good." He sat near her. "A lovely evening."

"Yes." Not good at small talk tonight, she cleared her throat.

He leaned closer. "Tell Webb…"

"What!" No one knew him by the name that name, except her. She jumped up and was about to run when he caught her arm.

"It's all right. I'm his partner." He let her go. "Sit. Please."

Something in his intense eyes made her do what he asked. But one hand remained on the crystal glass to use as a weapon if needed.

"The message is landing two, ten am, ferry south, Miranda."

"Are you a nut job?"

He laughed, a baritone chuckle as his lips curled in amusement. "No. Definitely not a nut. Repeat it. Landing two, ten am, ferry south, Miranda."

"You're serious."

"Dead serious."

He stared at her and a shiver ran down her spine. Her voice shook when she repeated his words.

"Good—enjoy your evening." The man stood and slipped into the darkness and disappeared.

She repeated the message, burning it into her brain.

Would Webb understand the meaning?

She needed to find him ASAP.

***

She located Webb standing near the buffet table. "I have a message for you." She whispered into his ear.

"Okay. I'll say good night and we can leave." She stood next to him and did her best to smile while he said their goodbyes.

In their room, Webb dressed in blue jeans and a plaid cotton shirt. "We've got to get out of here. Pack. Five minutes."

"Why?" She slipped out of her sandals, relieved to be out of the pretty, but not very comfortable shoes. "I'm not going. I'm sleeping in the bed tonight. *You* can stay on the couch."

"No. POTUS is on the way here."

"What's a POTUS. A disease?"

He laughed. "President of the United States."

"You're kidding."

"Four minutes and we're gone. When he is on the premises, the place shuts down tighter than an oyster protecting a pearl."

***

Ten minutes later, on the road about a mile from the hotel, a line of white vans sped by them heading toward the hotel they'd just left. Webb pulled over on the narrow street and let them occupy the road. "Now, no one will be in or out of the place tonight," he said.

The small MG shook as the vehicles passed. She turned to make sure the caged dove in the jump seat was okay.

"You really use a dove to send messages?" she asked.

"Pigeon, homing pigeon."

"Where do they go?"

He shrugged. "The less we know the better. The important thing is I trust the man who brought the bird to us. If I'm caught and tortured, I can't tell where the bird is heading because I don't know."

"Oh, dear God."

When the last van went by, he drove back onto the road. "Name a small town."

"What?" She was still imagining the president entering the hotel.

"A rural burg," he repeated while negotiating a sharp turn.

"Healdsburg."

"No. A town out of the Napa, Sonoma Valley."

"Why?"

"Just do it."

"Boonville."

"California?"

"Yeah."

"Ever been to the place?"

"No. I saw it on the map and wondered about the town. At different times of the year, there's a beer festival, a wool-growers' barbecue, and sheepdog trials. I thought it'd be fun to go."

"Let's find out."

Chapter 8

They grabbed a cup of coffee from a pot near the checkout counter at a rest stop. She took the drink back to the car. She forced the stale, but warm liquid down her throat, leaned back in the passenger's seat, and closed her eyes.

An hour ago, she been at a gathering of the powerful players in the United States government. For all she knew, movers and shakers and highly placed political players, from both parties, might often mingle. However, the vibe from the group tonight seemed tense rather than congenial. The music and food gave a celebratory impression, but the atmosphere was definitely not festive.

Virtually ignored after she was introduced as a wife, she viewed the participants as if watching a movie. The wealthy dressed in their best garments, frowned while they downed their expensive wine and imported vodka. They kept their voices low as men and women passed from one small group to another. The buzz in the room was like a hive of troubled bees. The government at work or a dire response to an unknown threat? If only she'd heard what they were saying.

She'd tried to eat a few hors d'oeuvres, but her stomach had objected. Now bitter coffee churned and she held her hand to her mouth to keep bile from coming up. She should have eaten regardless of the situation.

She startled when Webb entered the MG and squeezed her hand. He tossed a packaged cheese sandwich and a small bag of chips into her lap. "Better eat. It may be a while before we get another chance." He hesitated. "Emmy, thanks for not asking too many questions tonight. You must be miffed about being told what to do without really understanding what the hell is going on."

You have no idea. She didn't respond.

He continued, "What do you want to know? I owe you."

Where did she start? She wouldn't ask about their relationship. The marriage was over and didn't matter anymore. But something had happened at the party and Webb understood.

"Who's the guy, and what did the message mean? Landing two, ten am, ferry south, Miranda."

Webb groaned at the name. "Some codes are complicated and need a key, perhaps a specific book to decipher them, a novel or the bible, etc. This is one is quick and understood by the person who sent it. Number two means number one, POTUS, ten am is pm the time of his landing. Ferry south means I go north.

"Who sent the communication? Can you trust this guy? You didn't ask for a description of him." She started to describe him.

"He is my brother."

"What! You sure? The man's hair was so blond and…"

"I understand because he used the name of his murdered wife," Webb interrupted. "Not her legal name, Julie, but her nickname, Miranda." The pain in his expression sent a need to comfort him. Then his eyes narrowed and a look of determination changed his features. "Miranda was the kindest, most gentle person I've ever met. After this is over, I'm going to find the man who took her from my brother."

She cringed. Instinctively, she understood once he found the man, he'd kill him. She swallowed hard and left the sandwich uneaten.

Later, Webb pulled up to a motel and parked in the parking lot behind the building away from the view of the freeway.

She rubbed her tired eyes and glanced around. A few cars were parked in the dimly lit spaces. None appeared suspicious. Not that she understood what to look for.

"I'll check us in."

He left before she had a chance to answer.

Her stomach growled and she picked up the wrapped cheese sandwich. *Better eat before you're sick from hunger.* She hadn't consumed a decent meal since the recent events began to unfold.

The soft bread and cheese were tastier than she'd expected. She needed something to drink, even so the last bite slid down her throat. Despite the looming problems, she felt better.

"We got a room," Webb said as he opened the passenger's door. "We can stay for a few hours and get some shut eye. We'll be driving the rest of the day and into the night."

"Where are we going—never mind." Things were out of her hands. At this point, what else could she do but go along until other options presented themselves? *You're exhausted. Don't think anymore.*

The bland room, with no theme or recognizable décor, looked clean enough. With relief, she noticed two queen beds. She sighed and dropped onto the soft mattress of the first bed and pulled a pillow under her head.

Webb brought the caged bird into the room and placed it in a quiet corner.

"Rest. I'll wake you when it's time to leave." He yanked the blackout drapes closed and settled on the other bed. He moaned and she wondered if his wound had opened up. Should she ask to see it? After consideration, she decided against the idea. He'd probably tell her to mind her own business.

Webb turned his back to her and soon she heard his even breathing as he slept. If only she could do the same, shut out the world and ignore the fear of the unknown that plagued her.

Apparently, his job trained him to separate his feelings, and sleep, if he had any emotion at all. Was it fair to think the ability to feel was not part of his makeup?

Some of what he told her could be true, right? After all, he mingled with important officials in the United States government. He must be of some use to them. Never mind. It didn't matter. She wanted her life in San Francisco with a career in real estate, nothing else. These officials meant zero to her.

Emma had to think of her life now. Karen Palmer died and the man who'd hurt her did too. Case closed. But her friend's business needed tending. She owed Karen that much and more. With a sniff, she wiped a tear. *I'll keep her name alive through her company.*

The cabin continued to be for sale under the Karen Palmer Reality banner. Em had a meeting with an interested client asking to view the property. If she made that sale it would keep her and the office running for some time. Other clients could be lined up. She'd check the office log. She let out a slow breath. There's a plan, life might once more begin to come back to a normal, as much as possible given the loss of her best friend.

***

At the low-end motel, Emma slept on the other bed, rather than join Webb. As she moved, the sheet slid to her waist. Even in the dim light, she was beautiful. Her luscious lips parted and he wanted to kiss her. No. She detested him for lying and making her life hell. He deserved her disdain, but it didn't make being near her easy. Still, to keep her safe, they must stay together, at least for now.

He rolled to a sitting position. With no air conditioner in the room, sweat beaded on his body. He tore off his T-shirt. *Damn, going to be a scorcher today.*

He grimaced and swallowed a pain pill, forcing the medication down his dry throat. Careful not to waken Emma, he got out of bed and with his shaving kit and supplies, moved toward the bathroom. He needed a cool shower if he was going to manage his desires.

Was it seeing her in bed? He wouldn't say, but as he stood in the shower, he remembered their wedding night. His hands tingled with the need to touch her as he had that night.

After they'd made love, they had showered together. He'd gently washed her, giving special attention to her pert breast. Then coaxing her legs open, he'd entered her again.

Enough! Thinking about the past helped no one. Once this assignment ended, they would go separate ways.

He turned off the water and towel dried. With a gauze bandage in place on his wound, he found clean clothes and dressed in blue jeans, navy T-shirt, and running shoes.

He woke Emma. She went to shower and he jogged next door to a local restaurant and ordered scrambled eggs, toast, and coffee for two.

Back in the room, he set the food on the table near the window and pulled back the curtain. Not much action in the small parking lot. Nothing suspicious. He relaxed in a wooden dining chair, took a sip of coffee, and didn't allow thoughts of his wife in the shower, water caressing her. No longer his spouse, he should stop thinking about her as his partner.

The sound of the hair dryer stopped and soon Emma joined him at the table, her long dark hair flowed around her shoulders, a pink shirt hugged her breasts.

"It felt good to shower." She sat down and eyed the food. "Thanks for the breakfast."

"Yeah."

They ate without speaking further. He couldn't be sure, but maybe each waited for the other to break the silence.

At last she said, "Tell me about the man I married."

"That's a strange request." He shrugged. "Ask me something."

"What is your real name? The name I should've had."

He set his coffee cup down and stared out of the window. How much did she need to know?

***

Would Webb answer the simple question? If not, what was the point in demanding to know more? She forced a bite of egg down her throat and coughed. She stood from the table.

"You okay?"

"Yeah. Answer the question."

By his expression, she understood her voice was harsher than she'd realized.

He crushed his empty paper coffee cup. "Most of my life I've been called as Ethan Lancaster." He paused. "I prefer Webster Craig."

"Only part of your life?"

"Lancaster is my stepfather's name."

"So, the man I met at the spa hotel is your stepdad?"

"Yeah."

"Is your father alive?"

"No, killed by a hit and run driver when I was a teen. My mother married Lancaster a year later." Pain flashed in his intense eyes. "My kid brother and my little sister didn't mind. They were too young to hold

88

on to the memory of our father. I remembered and resented Mr. Lancaster."

"I'm sorry."

"Don't be. To be fair, he tried to be a good parent, but I didn't want anyone taking my dad's place. This has nothing to do with you."

Whoa, she was nothing to him, just an existing duty to be considered. She tried to finish eating but couldn't swallow. Did she dare to bring up a question dogging her?

"Why didn't you introduce me to your family? Ashamed of me?"

"Don't be ridiculous. I wanted to protect you. You're aware of what happened to my brother's wife and son. They were slaughtered in their own home. I didn't want you harmed."

"Oh, God," she gasped and pushed back a cry.

"The people my brother, Jon and I deal with are ruthless."

She trembled and couldn't think what to say. "I— I'm sorry."

"Stop saying you're sorry. You didn't do anything. What's important now is to get you back to your normal life and away from me as soon as possible?

She trembled.

He stretched and walked to the window and stared out. "Are you ready to believe me if I tell you the truth?"

"Yeah."

"Okay." He sat down again and stared at her. "I told you where I work, RAT, Rapid Advance Task Force, a clandestine operation that gives the U.S. government deniability if a mission goes wrong. I realized the risk when I took the job. At the time I didn't care, thought it was exciting." He took a deep breath. "Damn, I wish had another cup of coffee."

"You can have the mine. My stomach can't take the acid today."

"You sure?"

"Yeah."

He took a gulp of the liquid and swallowed hard. "The current job should have been easy. That's why I was sent alone. I had to retrieve a file, read it, and burn the paper. But I was waylaid and this whole assignment has been anything but rapid. The job won't be over until the damn dossier is in my hands and I absorb the info and destroy the thing."

Was Webb hurt trying to discover the file? "Can someone else pick it up?"

"The task force team lost a couple of our best men and even if they were available, there isn't enough time to brief them and transport the guys here. It's my assignment. I won't fail."

He hesitated. "Emmy, don't roll your eyes when I say this. I don't know who to trust anymore, and even if I could be sure of the police or sheriff, they'd need a top-secret clearance to receive this data." He drank the rest of the coffee and stared at her. "I believe Russian agents infiltrated major companies and the U.S. government at high levels. Without the names in the folder, the country can't be properly defended." Webb ran his hand over his chin. "At the moment, I trust my brother Jon, Harold Lancaster, my stepdad, and I trust you. I never meant to involve you, Emmy, but I need your help."

***

In the parking lot outside of the motel, Emma smiled at the pigeon soaring in the summer's azure sky. "Have a safe flight and carry your message home," she whispered. "If only I could go with you, but my house is out of bounds."

"Let's move."

She startled at the sound of Webb's gruff voice.

"Where?" She pulled her hair into a ponytail holder and took sunglasses from her purse.

"Anywhere. It's not good to stay too long in one place. People are searching for us. You take the wheel this time. Drive south until you reach Highway Thirty-Seven and drive east toward Sacramento." He tossed the last bag in the in the jump seat.

"What about the bird cage? Aren't we taking it?"

"No need for it."

What message was in the note the bird carried? She wondered but didn't ask. If Webb wanted her to know, he'd tell her.

He handed her the ignition key and got in the passenger's seat. "I need to reconnoiter."

"I love driving." *Feels good to be in control even if it's only of the car.* "What a glorious day. I wish we were going on a picnic."

"We're not," he said bitterly.

"I understand." She hesitated. "Remember the road trip we'd planned. You found an old paper map of California and a red pen and we drew our route, first to the wine country and on to the gold country. And maybe Lake Tahoe and Reno." She glanced at Webb. His cold expression chilled her.

"I shouldn't talk about the past. Sorry," she said.

"Don't be."

"I don't understand why I thought about that now."

His features hardened as he focused on her. "Doesn't matter. The best laid plans…" He shrugged.

"Webb, remember we bought pans to look for gold? I dreamed of finding enough to make us rich." She laughed. "Dear God, I was young and naïve two years ago." If she expected him to contradict her declaration of being immature, he didn't.

"We were both younger and unrealistic. The world has a way of wising people up," he said with a hard edge to his voice.

The discussion had taken an unexpected twist and his grim expression let her understand he'd had enough. No need to reminisce about what might have been. She couldn't deny their past, but there'd be no more talk about it.

A breezed blew into the old Austin Healey as she pressed on the gas pedal, steered out of the parking lot, and headed toward the freeway. With a quick glance, she saw Webb lean back in the seat and close his eyes.

From now on, she'd do her part and stay in the present.

As the miles rushed by, she kept the car at the posted speed. No need to invite the attention of a California Highway Patrol officer.

A baseball cap over his eyes, Webb appeared to nap. So much for reconnaissance.

Later, a black Lexus stayed behind her car when she slowed down. To let the vehicle pass, she pulled into the right lane, but the SUV decreased its speed too.

It was a beautiful day, so why wouldn't people drive leisurely and enjoy the trip? Did she believe that? In the rearview mirror, she saw the car's windows were tinted, her view of the driver obscured. No big deal. Right?

At last, the black Lexus pulled out from behind the Healey, sped into the fast lane, and disappeared. She let out a sigh. Okay, the driver wasn't tailing them. Maybe she'd seen too many action films. She laughed. *Don't let your imagination take over your good sense.*

She stole a look at Webb. Thank goodness, he was sleeping. He didn't need to know about her stupidity.

At a truck stop outside of Sacramento, she filled the gas tank, then parked near the covered patio area next to the station's convenience store.

She entered the building and paid the for the "fill up" then bought lunch, pleased to find, fresh fruit, homemade sandwiches and bottled water.

Webb joined her at a patio table. "Guess I fell asleep."

"No worries. Turkey and cranberry or mozzarella and avocado?" she asked.

"You choose." He grimaced when he sat at the table.

His wound must be bothering him.

He grabbed a bottle of water and took a bite of the turkey and cranberry on rye bread. "Thanks for driving. If you want, I can take the wheel after we eat."

"I'm good."

"The list we want is in a home in the Sierra foothills. It's in the master bedroom in a hidden safe in the closet. I have the combination. Easy. When we get there, you can wait outside and I'll be in and out in minutes.

"Then what?"

"I'll memorize the list and burn the damn thing."

***

In San Francisco, Smith surveyed the office he bought on the tenth floor of the expensive financial district building. He wanted the penthouse, but that was out of the question given his current financial circumstances.

It was irritating to realize he'd become overextended. In New York and D.C., his office and home might be in peril if this current transaction stalled. He shouldn't have bought the high-priced mansion in Georgetown or the condos in New York. Still, the easy financing from a foreign bank had been too good to pass up. Now the recent precipitous drop in the stock market was straining his situation.

Even so, his wife had brought in a New York designer to work on the San Francisco office and, with a healthy budget, had turned the modest work space into one of elegance and authority. A person entering his agency would never wonder about his economic standing. He appeared rich, powerful, and part of the one percent.

Where the hell was his employee? The fellow promised the tracking devices he installed on the autos in the alley near Emma Craig's office were working. Soon, they'd locate the Lancaster's vehicle and catch him.

He glanced out of the window to the sky. The midday blue changed to gray. *A storm is on the way.* Not an omen of things to come, he hoped. He pulled his hands through his annoyingly thin hair and closed his eyes. What happened the to the eager young man who came to Washington, D.C., college degree in hand, ready to save the world? He'd been an honorable guy with a promising future. He might now be the president or at least a senator, but not without money from the rich and power mad. Maybe money *was* the root of all evil.

He needed a drink. No. He stretched his aching back muscles. Better to go to the gym and soak in the spa before the lumbar pain caused him to walk like an old man. His much younger wife needed a viral man she could open her legs to and let him hump her until her cravings were satisfied.

Shit. Served him right. He didn't need to marry again after his first wife died. *Too late.*

He must find Ethan Lancaster and squeeze names from him or he might add his high maintenance spouse to the list of items he'd lose. At sixty, he'd kiss the devil if that's what it took to keep his money and his new wife.

His office phone buzzed.

"I don't want to be disturbed."

"Excuse me, sir," a female voice said. "Your two o'clock is here."

Hell. "Send him in."

At the sound of the opening door he shouted, "Tyler, you better be bringing good news or you can look for another job."

"We got a lead on Lancaster." An eager young Caucasian male moved toward a club chair located near an ormolu and mahogany desk.

"Where is he?" Smith demanded.

"Northern California, outside of Boonville."

"What the hell is in Boonville?"

"As far as we can tell, not a damn thing." He started to sit down.

"Don't. You won't be here that long. Get your ass out there and find Lancaster."

"Roger that."

"If you grab him and the list of names there's a bonus. If not, I don't want to see your ugly face again."

***

Emma parked in front of the turn of the century mansion in the small Sierra Mountain town off of highway eighty-eight. The remodeled Victorian "painted lady" stood proud in the afternoon sun. An "open house" sign welcomed visitors.

"Damn. I expected the place to be empty." Webb sat up.

"Should I drive away?" She put the key back into the ignition.

"No." He paused. "Here's our story. We're a happily married couple with kids, searching for a new home for our brood. You keep the realtor busy while I run upstairs and get the what I need. Can you do that?"

"I guess. Uh, yeah."

"Let's get this over with." He slammed the car door and moved toward the front stoop, then stopped and turned, "Smile."

Her hands shook and as her stomach churned, she wondered if she could keep breakfast down. *I don't think I can do what he wants.*

With a smile pasted on her face, she entered the Victorian. Under different circumstances the beautiful home would be a joy to view. However, her only thought was to do what was expected and leave as soon as possible.

A middle-aged woman dressed in a gray suit and pink blouse with salt and pepper hair welcomed them. "I'm Mrs. Joyce. Isn't it a lovely day?"

"Yeah." Emma accepted the brochure and business card from the woman. She listened to the history of the home and the all the updates that had been completed to bring the grand old place into this century.

"Honey, take a look at this craftsmanship." Webb took her hand and walked to a carved staircase. "Remember to keep the realtor occupied, and away from the upstairs," he whispered in her ear. "Babe, why don't you glance at the kitchen while I scope out the bedrooms? She's a marvelous cook, Mrs. Joyce. I want her to have the best."

"Of course, you do. I see how much in love you are." She hesitated. "We're a small town, I don't believe I've seen you around. New to the area?"

"We plan to relocate," Webb answered quickly. "We want a good place to raise the kids."

"Well, you can't do better than our community. The schools are small, but excellent."

"Perfect."

Emma almost choked when he said, "We've got four kids and twins on the way."

"Really, you're such a young thing." She smiled at Emma.

"Well, I…"

"Never mind, dear. Let me show you the kitchen."

The realtor led the way into the huge room with wide plant dark oak floors, golden oak granite counter tops, and gleaming stainless-steel appliances. "You're going to love the sub-zero refrigerator and the six-burner gas range with a griddle, not to mention the double wall ovens." The realtor beamed. "Nothing has been left undone."

The woman was good at her job. Giving the important elements, but not overselling the remodel. It was awful to give hope to the woman who worked on commission. How many times had Emma gone through this routine all the while understanding the people were probably looky-loos. Still, she did her best to show interest in the appliances and ask appropriate questions as she talked about the gorgeous home. Still, her mind was on Webb. How long would it take to retrieve the list?

Her cheeks burned with embarrassment when Mrs. Joyce inquired about the ages of her children and the due date of the twins. With the ages of her imaginary kids stated, she did a hurried calculation of the birth of twins who would never exist. Nervous, would she remember what she told the realtor, should she ask again.

"I asked their ages because the elementary school is close enough to walk to. You might drive by on you way out. I'll give you directions."

"Thank you. I'd like to," the lie spewed from her mouth. *Damn, Webb hurry up. I can't lie to this kind woman anymore.*

The sound of children's laughter echoed in the entryway. The realtor looked toward the noise. "Please excuse me. Wander through the property and let me know if you think of any other questions."

Relieved to be alone, she went out to the backyard and sat at an umbrella covered patio table. A warm breeze sent the aroma of pine from the forest on the property. The sun played among the color spots that lined a pergola near the swimming pool. This might be someone's dream home. Why had a nightmare ensnared the peaceful oasis?

"I'm done." Webb stood next to her, appearing cool in the hot sun.

"I didn't hear you come outside." Emma shaded her eyes from the glare and stared.

"Mrs. Joyce is busy with another family. Go to the car. I want to be gone before she's finished with them."

Emma tossed the car keys to Webb and sat in the passenger's seat, too aggravated to concentrate on the road. He drove off without a word about where he was going, too often his modus operandi.

"You were good with the realtor. Just the right amount of interest in the place," he shouted over the roar of the engine.

"I hated lying. It might be normal behavior for you, but not for me. The experience made me sick." She paused. "My whole life, I've prided herself in doing the right thing and never being dishonest. Today, I grinned as lies spewed from my lips." *I'll never forgive you.*

He stomped on the gas pedal.

Her tension increased and the speed of the sports car didn't help. She held her breath as he down shifted and maneuvered a hairpin turn. When the Healey straightened out, he said, "You think I'm happy about any of this?" Before she could answer he continued. "I didn't plan on using you. I do what I have to and make the assignment work." His expression hardened as he glared at the winding road.

"Really, Webb, four kids at my age and twins on the way?"

"Guess I laid it on a little thick."

"You think?" She wanted to remain angry, but the image of her with six unruly kids caused her to laugh.

He joined in and the sound of his amusement relieved her tension—somewhat.

"I generally work alone. I'm not used to thinking on my feet about domestic issues."

Another turn came into view and he down shifted again and handled the curve with ease.

"Did you get the list?"

"No list." He glared at her, then returned his attention to the road. "Nothing but another place to check out. I hope we're not getting the run around."

"You'll go there?"

"Have to, no other choice. Someone's playing a devious game with the Rapid Advance Team. I've got to untangle what's happening with the team before it's too late."

He had a mission. Was it her job to do whatever was necessary to help him? Maybe, but inquiring about things she didn't need to know wouldn't do any good.

As Webb continued the drive, a vista of sugar pines rose up before her, shading the sun. She leaned back and tried to enjoy the trip, because as he'd said, she had no option.

"Emma, hang on!"

She reached for the grab bar on the dash as the Austin Healey was hit from the back. "What the hell?"

Webb struggled to keep the car on the road.

With a bang, the black SUV struck again, and this time it shoved them on the wrong side of the road. A logging truck honked. She screamed as the semitruck and trailer barreled down on them.

Chapter 9

Did I black out? The Austin Healey's horn was blaring when Webb opened his eyes. He hit the wheel with his fist and the noise stopped. Rather than strike the logging truck, he'd driven off the road and down a slope that turned out to be steeper than it first appeared. The Healey slid to a stop just short of slamming into a giant pine. The vehicle was tangled in the underbrush but the engine revved. He reached to turn it off. With a groan, he released the tight seat belt. His hand came away with blood from his reopened wound. "Shit."

"Emma." Held against the passenger seat by the safety belt, she didn't move. "Emma, wake up." She looked too pale, but he couldn't see any obvious injury. Of course, internal wounds wouldn't show. "Talk to me." He pushed hair out of her face and caressed her cheek. "Are you hurt, Emmy?"

"What happened?"

"Thank God." He let himself breathe again. "You scared the hell out of me. You okay?"

"Where are we?" She sat up and looked around. "I thought we were going to slam into the semi." She started to take off the belt. "It's stuck. I can't open it."

When he leaned over to yank on the latch, the car slid further down the incline. She screamed and he glanced down the bank. About thirty feet below a river flowed rapidly over a rocky outcropping.

"Don't. Quiet." He reached for her. "Yelling doesn't help. Calm down. We'll get out of this."

"Yeah. Okay."

He undid her seat belt. "Emmy, open the door and jump out. I'll follow you."

"I can't. If I do the car is going to plunge into the river."

She might be right, but he didn't see any other choice. How long would the underbrush keep a twenty-five-hundred-pound sports car, people, and luggage, from falling?

"Move!"

When she opened the door, he pushed her out and tumbled after her. The Austin Healey slipped downward, rolled over, bounced on the rocks below, and landed in the shallows of the river.

"We would've been killed," she gasped. With a shaking hand, she brushed leaves from her hair.

He resisted taking her into his arms. Instead, he asked, "Can you hike back up to the road?"

"Webb, what about your car?"

"I'll deal with it later. We need to find a place to stay, then we'll decide what to do next. Emmy, are you strong enough to climb to the road?"

"I think so."

Her voice was determined, but she sat down and closed her eyes.

"What hurts, Emma?"

"Nothing. I'm fine. Must be the shock of the accident, I'm trembling."

"Rest for a minute."

"A black SUV slammed into us."

"Yeah."

"Webb, I noted the license plate when it came up behind us."

"You did?"

"I saw the vehicle earlier and for some reason memorized it."

"You mean a similar one."

"No, the exact car. I thought it followed us this morning. I almost woke you, but the darn thing passed the Healey and drove out of sight."

"And you didn't mention this until now." His voice sounded too harsh. She'd had no way to understand how important the information might be. Anger rose in him, more toward the unknown person who forced them off the mountain road than at her.

"I'm sorry, Webb. I should have…"

"You're not responsible, Emmy. Sit here and rest. I'm going to the car and retrieve what I can."

"No. You'll get hurt. Things can be replaced, but you…"

"Don't worry. I'll be back soon." He sounded sure of himself but… He had to try.

The worn granite rocks, twigs from the underbrush, and needles from the forest of trees, made the descent slow going. A couple of times he lost his footing and grabbed a manzanita bush to stop his fall. *Hell.* The idea was to reach the car in one piece not nose dive and lay dead next to the disabled vehicle.

He fell the last few feet and landed on his hands and knees, out of breath, but glad to be on flat ground. His wound throbbed and he considered resting. No time. The men driving the SUV, if they were any good, would return to complete their job of taking any pertinent info left in the car.

With the tools stored in the trunk, he unscrewed the license plates and stored them in his backpack, found on the floor near the jump seat. He discovered Emma's bag and hooked it over his shoulder. From the open suitcase, he shoved what they might need into his backpack. He tore the labels from clothes that wouldn't fit in the pack and stuffed the scraps of fabric in his pocket, then removed the nametag on the overnight bag.

The ascent was harder than he anticipated. With one careful step at a time, he pulled his aching body up the rocky terrain. His muscles burned with exhaustion as he climbed. Locate the correct foot and hand hold and all would be fine.

Damn. His old injury started to bleed. He could feel a trickle of blood run down his abdomen. *Emma's waiting. Push your ass up the damned hill.*

He saw her sitting near the two-lane road, looking down at him, relief in her expression. She smiled, but they didn't speak.

Later, he plopped down next to her. She leaned against him and sobbed. He put his arm around her and held her close. Finally, he said, "We better get on the road and find a ride." He helped her stand and cringed when he saw scratches on her hands and arms probably received while scrambling up the bank.

A stocky man, dressed in a black and red checked shirt and wearing a blue baseball cap, walked briskly toward them. "Hey, buddy, I stopped my rig as soon as I could. I thought you and the little lady were goners. Where's your sports car?"

"In the drink."

The trucker peered over the bank. "I'll be damned. Too bad. It's a sweet ride." He rubbed his jaw. "I got a first aid kit if you need it." He pointed to Webb's abdomen. "You're hurt."

"I'm good, looks worse than it is. Maybe a band-aid, and a lift into the nearest town?"

"You're on." He extended his hand. "Jeb."

Webb shook it. "Mitch and this my wife Dee. We're much obliged."

Emma did a double take at the strange names, but Webb smiled when she had the good sense to keep quiet.

The big rig driver found his first aid kit and opened it. "Take what you need."

Webb looked in Jeb's assortment of supplies. "You've got a drug store in here." He laughed.

"On the road alone, I learned the hard way to keep all sorts of shit for emergencies. Find anything you can use?"

"Yep. Thanks."

Emma took what she needed, then cleaned Webb's wound with an antiseptic swap and placed gauze on the injury and held it in place with medical tape.

"Okay people, let's haul ass. I got a schedule to keep."

Webb used trucker's cell phone to leave a message for his brother, a few words notifying him he wouldn't make the next meeting.

As the big rig moved forward, a small brown dog crawled into Emma's lap.

"That's my dog, Jones. He's a mutt like me." Jeb introduced the animal. "I found him dirty and flea bitten dumped on the side of the road a few years ago. He's been with me ever since."

"Hi, Jones." Emma scratched his ear and the dog wagged his tail.

"He don't take to everyone. You should be flattered." Jeb chuckled.

"I am. I love dogs."

"Guess he can tell. You can't fool a stray. They can spot a phony a mile away."

Emma looked guilty for lying to the trucker, but Jeb didn't appear to notice.

Webb admired the man's rig and they fell into easy conversation about trucks and sports cars.

With the little dog sleeping in her lap, Emma closed her eyes.

An hour later, Jeb dropped them on the outskirts of a small town with an address of a woman who let rooms.

***

"What do you want?" A forty something woman peered out the front door of a nondescript fifty's rancher, much like the other homes on the narrow street.

"Heard you rent rooms by the night." Webb smiled.

With the door wide open, she pushed her dyed blond hair from her eyes and tightened the belt of her worn bathrobe. "I got a son in rehab, a dog on tranquilizers, and if a job offer doesn't come soon, I'll be on Prozac. So yeah, fifty bucks cash a night and one set of clean sheets for as long as you stay." She squinted and gaped at them. "I won't stand for anything illegal."

"Hey, lady." Webb put his hands up. "We need a room until we can make arrangements to have our car fixed. My wife and I were in a car accident and the trucker Jeb gave us a ride into town."

"He's a good man."

Webb handed her a hundred-dollar bill.

She started to leave but stopped. "Go around to the back. It's unlocked. The bedroom is right off the kitchen. I'll meet you there with the sheets and blankets."

"Thank you," Emma's words died half spoken as the door slammed in her face.

"A real character." Webb adjusted the backpack and walked toward the rear yard.

"Hope the bed is soft. I might sleep for a week. Hey, wait up." Emma ran after him.

The small aqua bedroom had a headless double bed against the far wall next to a marred wooden nightstand. With pleasure, she noticed a coffee maker with tea bags and a jar of instant coffee on a nearby stand. Two beige mugs waited to be filled. The analogue TV with a cable box sat on top of a chest of drawers and a television cable dangled to the green carpeted floor.

Emma found a small door expecting a closet, but with delight, discovered a tiny bathroom including a metal shower with a white plastic curtain. "Webb, a bathroom. Dibs on the shower. You can use it after me."

Back in the bedroom, she flopped on the unmade bed. "Not bad. Of course, a pile of hay would feel good after this day."

Regret shone in Webb's eyes. "Better take care of those cuts. Jeb gave us some extra band-aids. We need antibiotic cream. Maybe we can pick some up tomorrow."

Someone knocked on the door.

On guard, Webb demanded to know who it was.

"I got your sheets."

He slowly opened the door.

The landlady, now in gray Capri pants and an aqua cotton shirt the same color of the room, stood holding the white bedding and towels. "There's a comforter and pillows in the closet," she offered. "If you're hungry Joe's Hash House is reasonable. It's about a quarter mile down the main road. Don't be fooled by the name. The owner is Ernie and he's a damn good cook. He retired from a Sacto restaurant about five years ago and bought Joe out. Tell him Peggy sent you and he'll give you a good deal." Without waiting for a reply, she closed the door.

"Hungry?" Webb asked.

"Not yet. Maybe later. I want to know what's going on. Why would someone run us off the road on purpose and how did they find us? This morning I watched the SUV take a different freeway turn off.

Then in the middle of nowhere, they reappear behind us."

"Did the car drive close to us the first time you saw them?"

"They rode the Healey's bumper for a while. I thought they might hit us. In the fast lane, I believed they wanted to pass. I moved into the slow lane and was surprised when they did the same. They stayed behind our car for some time. Afterward, they drove by and disappeared."

"No need to follow any longer. I'll bet my eye teeth, they placed a magnetized GPS tracker on the bumper. The driver got close enough to allow the passenger shoot it over with an air gun."

"Are you kidding me?"

Has anything happened today to make me want to joke with you?"

She grimaced at his fierce expression. "No."

"I might have checked the car if you mentioned the SUV when it happened."

"Webb, I destroyed your car and we might be dead because I didn't tell you. Why don't you say so?"

"What's the point? It's over." He paused. "Move. I'll make the bed."

"Maybe if you shared what's going on instead of hiding stuff from me..." The accident was her fault. With a groan, she swung her feet to the carpet. With no chair in the room, she sat on the floor.

She glared at him as he handled the job with the precision of a military man. Perfect corners and she guessed a quarter might bounce off the tight blanket. Had he done military service? Sad how little knowledge she had about her husband.

"Webb, what did you find in the house we visited today?"

***

"Turn the car around. Smith wants proof the asshole, Lancaster, is taken care of," the SUV passenger demanded.

"I haven't eaten breakfast," the driver complained. "Let's buy some food first. He's not going anywhere if he's dead."

"Do what you're told, shithead or I'll dump you out on your ass and you can walk back to the city."

"Hey, what's your problem?" Swearing under his breath, the driver maneuvered a three-point turn and drove back the miles just traveled.

The passenger stared out the side window as the SUV drove up the country road. "How the hell are we going to locate the spot where the Austin Healey went off the road? The vegetation all looks the same. One crappy tree is like the next one."

"That's because you're a city boy. There are all kinds of different trees, Sugar Pine, and the huge Ponderosa. Man, you should see them reach for the sky."

"Don't call me a boy. Shut the fuck up and find the damned car."

You shut up, fucker. He didn't have to take this kind of shit. He slowed the SUV as a familiar turn in the road came into view.

On the shoulder of the road, he turned off the engine, got out, and glanced downward at the Austin Healey. The car, dented and scraped, sat at the edge of the river. "A hell of a long way down. No one could survive the fall."

"Get your ass to the car and make sure they're dead."

"I might break my neck."

"Move it." The passenger patted his left arm near the shoulder holster of his thirty-eight revolver. The guy used to be a police officer and was probably still comfortable using his gun.

"If you're good, this pistol is all you need," the officer had told him when they'd met this morning. Now, the man continued, "I took down more bad guys than I can count with this baby." He'd waved it at him. "When I shoot, they stay down. Saved the city a crap load of money by keeping criminals out of the court system." He paused. "Hurry up and check out the car."

With trepidation, the driver crawled down the slope. He stumbled to the ground, falling face down on the rocks. He grunted and glanced at his scraped hands, wiped them on his jeans, and proceeded to the car. The dented wreck was empty except for scattered clothes and an open suitcase. He saw blood on the driver's seat but no bodies. He took a photo of the car with his smart phone and searched for anything useful to help him locate Lancaster.

"What did you find?" the passenger yelled down to him.

"Nothing. They either went down the river or walked away," he yelled back.

"Anything in the car we can use?"

"Nada," he shouted up the hill to the older man.

"Shit." Standing at the edge of the bank, the guy pulled his gun and put a couple of bullets into the Healey.

"What the hell? Man, you might have killed me."

The passenger laughed. "If I wanted you dead, you'd be a stiff floating in the river by now."

"You're crazy!" He scrambled up the embankment and stood breathing hard. *Damn, Smith's hooked me up with a nut job.* "Where to now?"

"Drive to the nearest town."

***

Wrapped in a towel with another one around her head, Emma returned from taking a shower. Webb was on the bed leaning against the wall, a mug of coffee in his hand.

"Where's the backpack?" She ignored his grin as he scanned her, but tightened the towel.

"In the closet."

She grabbed the pack from the floor of the closet and searched for something to wear. He'd taken not only her clothes but her makeup bag, comb, toothbrush and paste. With everything she needed in her arms, she returned to the bathroom.

Fifteen minutes later, she sat next to him, dressed in a T-shirt and jeans. "Okay, what did you find at the house?"

"Let me look at those scratches on your arm."

"They're all right."

He gently took hold of her right arm and frowned. "This cut's deep. You need a band-aid and on this one too."

His touch sent a wave of longing spiraling in her. She yanked free of his grip. "Don't. I'll take care of it—later." She moved away from him and went to the coffee maker, poured a mug of the strong liquid, and dropped a spoon of powdered creamer into the steaming coffee.

The sun was setting as she stared out of the window of the small house in the middle of nowhere. "I'm sick of you avoiding my questions."

She stood at the end of the double bed and glared at him. "Either you answer now or I'm out of here. I'll take a bus or hitch hike if that's what it takes, but I'm done with your BS."

"Emmy, you're right." An expression of annoyance spread across his tense features. "Let's talk. Sit down. I won't touch you."

They sat on the bed, but didn't speak. Tension in the room increased, until she wasn't able to stand it. Finally, she blurted out, "Thanks for bringing my purse and clothes."

Silence.

"Webb." She hesitated. "I shouldn't talk to you the way I did. I'm sorry."

"It's been a tough day."

"I didn't need to take it out on you."

"Don't worry about it."

"Can I ask what happens next, Webb?"

The room darkened with the setting sun and she considered turning on a light. As if he understood, he reached for the lamp on the nightstand.

"As I've told you, the Rapid Advance Task Force is part of a larger organization, Force Fifteen. It has many links with similar goals, but the groups are autonomous. I work for a team made up of individuals and a leader. Think of it as a wagon wheel. Each of us is a spoke and the leader's the hub holding everything together. We report to the boss and info's passed along to the higher ups. There are many circles. I've met our team but no one in the other groups who compose the force.

"You don't all function as a unit?"

"We often have parts of the same operation, but if a person doesn't know the total mission everyone is safer. For example, if I'm caught, I can only give up what I understand. Compartmentalizing keeps the mission secure." He got up and started to refill his mug, stopped and shook his head.

She couldn't help noticing his bloodied shirt and remembered the day she found him in their mountain home. "You'd been tortured, when I found you at the cabin."

"They didn't get what they wanted."

"Who hurt you?"

He shrugged. "Doesn't matter now. This mission is what's important. At the mansion this afternoon, I didn't see a list, only a note with another place to go."

"We're supposed to go there?"

"Yeah."

"Why?"

"Think of it as a test. If I can be trusted to follow their directions, maybe at the end of this I'll secure the promised list."

"Of what? Why is it so important?"

"It's not my job to understand or even read the document. I'm a transporter, nothing more."

He would minimize his job. But she'd seen the important people he mingled and communicated with. A mere carrier wouldn't have those contacts.

He lowered himself to the bed and closed his eyes.

So busy thinking about her situation, for the first time, she realized the pressure he endured because he needed to complete his assignment and protect her at the same time. If she left, his stress would lessen. "You don't need me. Can I go back to the city, return home?"

"Sure. Go ahead if you want to end up like Karen."

She shivered and recalled her friend in the real estate office beaten and crying for help before she died. "Webb, you're cruel and I don't like your sarcasm."

"I'm making a point. This is not a kid's game. These men play for keeps."

She glared at him. "I'm aware of that. Tell me something I don't know."

"Hey, Emmy, I wish I had the answers." He paused. "If we're lucky, the next location will be the last. I'll grab the note and we can all go home." He reached for the TV control on the bed stand and the screen lit up. "Let's check the local news."

"No more talk? Nothing more to tell me?"

He shrugged.

"Don't do that thing with your shoulders. Whenever you don't want to deal with me you brush me off with a shrug.

Despite the tense conversation, he smiled. "I didn't realize."

"Webb, I'm scared. How is this going to end?"

With a surprised look, he started to lift his shoulders but stopped. "If I have my way, at the next location we'll find the list. Afterward, you can go back to the city. I'll put you in a safe house until the team discovers who is tracking us."

"What will you do?"

Chapter 10

Emma startled and sat up in bed. For a second, she didn't recognize the room with its aqua walls and flowered comforter.

The only sound in the room was her rapid breath. She gasped as yesterday's car accident played in her mind. Her body ached and the deeper scratches on her arms had reddened.

"Webb. Webb, where are you?" Out of bed she checked the bathroom.

Gone. Why be surprised? He'd walked out before, but last time she was at home not in a rundown town in the middle of nowhere. Did he take her money too? She stumbled out of bed and stubbed her toe. "Shit." Ignoring her throbbing foot, she hopped to the closet and opened the door.

Her purse sat in the closet on the floor next to the backpack. She rummaged in her old leather bag until she found her new red leather wallet. With a sigh, she grabbed it and checked inside. The money remained. More importantly, so did her credit card. Why did she always jump to the wrong conclusion? Webb might disappear, but he would never rob her.

So much for him taking her to a safe house. *What now?* Yesterday, Webb paid for two nights. Maybe she should stay tonight and think about what to do next.

"Thanks, Peggy." Webb said as he entered the room. "Emma, you ready to leave? What's wrong? You're pale as a ghost."

A shudder ran through her. There it was again, her fear of abandonment.

"Emmy."

"Give me a minute."

Webb opened the bedroom door to the hall and carried in a vacuum. "Borrowed this from the landlady. I'll clean while you do whatever you need to finish. Tell me when you're good to go."

He lifted the plastic bag from the bathroom trash can.

"What are you doing?"

"We'll take it with us and toss the somewhere else. No point in leaving our DNA all over the room. I'll vacuum and empty it in the bag too."

You're kidding. She swallowed and stopped before she spoke.

"I've got a car. Peggy sold me the car her son used. He's in rehab and needs the money." Webb tossed the car keys to her. "Go wait in the sedan and I'll wipe the room down and meet you outside." When she caught the keys he said, "It's the ninety-two silver Acura."

"What do you mean by wiping the room?"

He emptied the vacuum into the plastic sack and started to wipe the doorknob. "Our fingerprints are everywhere." He tied the bag. "This won't remove everything, but it will slow them down."

"You think the men who ran us off the road will come here."

"Yeah. If they are any good."

"You're scaring me."

"I don't mean to. Let's get the hell out of here and find the next location."

Webb revved the engine of the silver auto. "Buckle up." He backed out of the landlady's driveway as Emma clicked the seat belt in place.

"While you slept, I filled the gas tank and picked up antibiotic cream, bandages, and a few burner phones." With a hard-left turn, Webb steered the vehicle toward town.

"What do you mean burner phones?"

"They're prepaid cell phones and can't be traced. We use all of the available minutes and throw them in the trash."

"I want one."

"I'll hold them and if you need to make a call…"

After everything they'd been through, he didn't have faith in her good judgement not to call and tell someone where they were located. "You don't trust me."

He glanced at her then to the road. Chilled by his grim expression, she stopped talking.

To her surprise, he drove into the rural town and parked behind the Hash House restaurant on the insignificant main street. They entered and sat at a booth near the back of the room next to the exit. She ordered a cheese and mushroom omelet breakfast. Webb bought scrambled egg, pancakes and also ordered lunch "to go" for them as well.

After the waitress brought their food, Webb took out a paper map from his jacket pocket and set it on the table. "With no GPS, we are going old school. I found this at the gas station, a map of California." He poured syrup on the pancakes and took a bite. "I'm going to need you to act as my navigator. It should take about seven and half hours to drive to the next place."

"All right." She recalled the times she and Webb had gone to rallies with the Austin Healey. In the den of the house where she lived, she still displayed the trophies won at those assemblies. She should remove them because they reminded her of the past with Webb. Somehow, she didn't want to.

"Did you hear me?"

"I'm sorry, Webb. What did you say?"

"Stay focused. I'm depending on you."

She glared at him. He relied on her? What about the vow she believed when, years ago, he said, "I do"?

"The place is in the San Bernardino Mountains near Lake Arrowhead. We should arrive by evening if we don't stop, except for quick pit stops."

"I went to Lake Arrowhead once. My parents took me to Disneyland and we rented a car and drove to the lake. It was one of the last vacations I remember with my parents."

"Hmm."

By his response, he didn't care about her history. She took the hint, swallowed her eggs and asked for a second cup of coffee when the waitress came by to ask if she needed anything.

Without waiting for her to finish eating, he said, "I'll wait in the car. Don't take too long. The bill's paid. Here's the tip." He threw a ten-dollar bill on the table and left through the back door.

"Damn," she said under her breath. *Can't wait to spend the day locked in the car with a grump.*

The café was busy when she came out of the ladies' room. The sound of the cook's bell, to let the servers understand meals were ready, blended with the voices of the patrons. A giggling toddler ran into her as she worked her way toward the back door. She smiled at the teenage girl who followed him. "Sorry," the young woman said as she ran after the curly haired kid.

"No worries." Emma grinned. The child jogged to a table filled with what must be family members.

Normal life still existed—for some. What wouldn't she give to be one of those people?

***

"What the hell do you mean, you lost Lancaster?" Smith shouted into his smart phone, "You were on his tail." He stared out the window of his tenth story office in San Francisco, but the thick summer fog blocked his view.

The voice of the man on the phone whined on with explanations. The result was the same. Lancaster had disappeared.

"Tyler, find him," he interrupted. "Soon, damned soon." He disconnected and threw the phone. It sailed across the office just missing the Lalique decanter his wife had picked out for him. She'd be pissed if it shattered. Not to mention he'd be out a significant bit of cash.

He left the phone where it landed and tried to think what plausible reason, he could give his boss if

Lancaster wasn't found before his meeting in four days from now.

In two days, his private jet would be wings up from SFO heading for Reagan International Airport for his meeting with the man who had the ability to demand complete payment of his debt if he didn't deliver Lancaster as promised.

He'd worked hard through the years to give the impression he was in control and answered to no one. But that wasn't true for anyone. Even the president answered to congress and the people—eventually.

Earlier in his life, that truth prevented him from making a run for the U.S. Senate, though important men urged him to do so. Still, he stayed close to the Washington power brokers and at the same time remained independent of them.

He breathed deeply and poured three fingers of scotch into a crystal tumbler. He gulped down the drink and dispensed another. Lancaster jeopardized all his years of hard work. He started to reach for the decanter but stopped. It wouldn't help his situation if he got drunk.

His working-class parents had warned him not to "put on the dog." He must learn to be happy with his lot and live within his means. Maybe he should have listened to them. They had a platitude for every situation. What would his late parents say if they understood the mess he was in these days. What cliché would they chose?

He picked up his phone and put it in his jacket pocket. *Shit.* The most he could do at this point was wait for the men he'd hired to do their job.

"Baby, the gorgeous dress I ordered for the gala is almost ready. I just got the text."

His young wife waltzed into his office unannounced.

Even in his black mood, he couldn't keep his eyes off her ample breasts displayed in a beige sweater with beige slacks clinging to her tight ass.

"You should be proud of me, baby. I stayed in your hundred-k budget for my ballgown." She pecked him on his cheek and then quickly moved out of his arm.

A hundred thousand dollars for a dress she'll wear for one night and toss out. He suppressed a groan.

She must have noticed his frown because she added, "And that includes the shoes and bag too." Dancing to imaginary music, she glided across the room. "I can't believe I'm going to meet the president, maybe dance with him. Me, from Detroit. Thank goodness I was born beautiful or I might still be nowhere. I am beautiful, don't you think?"

"You know it."

"Make love to me. Here on the antique Persian rug."

"Are you crazy? Do you have any idea what I paid for the carpet?'

Her luscious lips pouted. He used to love seeing her full mouth tease him. Today, she annoyed him. Still, the image of her nude on the carpet...

She loosened his silk tie and unbuttoned his tailor-made shirt. "Come on, you can't deny me. I've been a good girl." She took his hand and put it on her breast and rubbed her hips against him.

As his breathing quickened, she said, "Baby, I'm all yours. Take me."

Hell. He grabbed her blonde hair and forced her to the rug.

***

In the late afternoon sun, the small Southern California burg bustled with vehicles sporting camping gear. A rural mountain town, there still appeared to be a rush hour. On the main street, vehicles spewed emissions from the idling cars fouling the clear, high-altitude breeze.

Yet, Emma admired the charming village architecture and hoped they might stay in one of the picturesque hotels. After being in the Acura all day, she imagined stretching her legs with a walk near the lake and having a leisurely dinner before tumbling into a feather bed—alone?

Webb drove through the town without stopping.

"Aren't we going to take a break? Maybe buy some dinner?"

"This isn't a vacation. I have an agenda to keep."

"Webb, we need to eat." She'd been patient during the long seven-hour drive and had even taken a turn at the wheel so he could catnap. Now she required real food after a day of high calorie, low nutrition snacks.

"Later." With one hand on the wheel, he tossed a small bag of chips at her, bought at the last gas station.

With a reflex action she caught them and threw them back at him. The bag bounced off his broad shoulder and fell to the floor. He yanked the steering wheel hard. The sedan slid to the side of the two-lane road, skidding to a stop. He glared at her and for a second, she feared what he might do.

"Emmy, you always did have a good arm." He grinned and reached for her hand, giving it a gentle squeeze.

His smile sent relief spiraling down her spine. "I shouldn't have thrown the potato chips back at you. I'm so hungry, but I can't face anymore junk food."

"Sometimes I get too focused. I forget the basics. You're good for me." He cleared his throat and coughed as if he'd admitted a secret.

Without looking at her, he made a U turn and headed back to town. "Pick a restaurant, and if it isn't too busy, we will find a table," he said as they entered the main street.

All the eateries appeared to be local establishments, so she chose one by its outside ambiance and was pleased to find the place occupied but with tables available. She looked at a spot near the front window with a view of the street. He nixed that idea and took one in the back of the room, no view but it was near an exit.

"Always good to be close to a backdoor if we want a quick and discreet way to leave."

She'd believed the men who'd run them off the road in Northern California couldn't follow. She and Webb were safe in densely populated Southern California. So why did he take the extra precaution? Though the evening was warm, she felt a sudden chill. "What do you know that I don't?"

"Nothing." He started to shrug but stopped and smiled. "Don't worry. Relax, Emmy. It's my job to stay alert."

They settled into a booth and faced each other.

"We'll eat and retrieve the list and be on our way to the safe house." He opened the menu. "Steak or pizza. It's a tough decision." He grinned again, but the smile only went to his lips. Watchful, his eyes narrowed in the dim light of the room.

The aroma of grilled food and the sound of patrons' laughter again reminded her not all the world had gone mad—only hers.

He chose steak and baked potato with grilled vegetables and ordered the shrimp salad and homemade sourdough bread she desired.

Savoring the meal, she ate in silence.

He glanced at her. "This ordeal will be over soon. We should be at the residence, where the list is stored, in about twenty minutes and then on the road heading home." He reached across the table and held her hand for a second.

Heat ran up her arm and an odd sensation fluttered within her. Under these strained circumstances, she wouldn't think about what it meant.

"I'll use a burner phone to contact my brother and he'll make sure the list goes to the right person." He pushed his brown hair from his forehead and she became aware of the tension in his eyes.

"Webb, you must be exhausted."

An expression of astonishment met her gaze. Didn't he realize she cared at least enough to be concerned for his physical well-being?

"I'm fine, Emmy. We can stop somewhere on Highway Five and spend the night. Can you manage a few more hours in the car?"

"Yeah, I'm good." She paused. "Thanks for buying dinner."

"I hate to admit it, but I'm glad we stopped to eat."

As they walked to the car, she resisted the urge to take his arm and lean her head on his shoulder. How would he react and what the heck was she thinking? In less than a day he'd be out of her life forever.

Emma leaned back in the seat of the Acura and gazed at Webb. He stared at the road and pressed on the accelerator, taking the turns at the maximum speed the country lane would allow.

She didn't speak. Somehow, everything that needed to be said had been expressed during dinner. If not forgiveness, at least an understanding with him had been reached. Soon her life could enter the recovery phase.

***

Hours later, the densely treed area made it difficult to see the houses on the narrow lane. Mail boxes and driveways marked the road to indicate a home.

Webb slowed the car. "Watch for the sign with painted chickens and eggs, 'Lander's Farm.'"

"You're serious."

"Yep. Didn't you know raising chickens for their colorful eggs is all the rage among the upper middle class these days?"

"Guess I missed that." She laughed.

A quarter mile down the road, she saw the sign. "Webb, on the left."

He turned left and dodged the pot holes and ruts on the private road. The land opened up to show a huge wooden structure with floor to ceiling windows covering the length of the home, most likely allowing a view of the surrounding forest.

"Wow. It's beautiful. Who'd think a house like this would show up in the forest? It could have been designed by Frank Lloyd Wright. I'd be able to sell this in a second, probably with multiple offers." She undid her seat belt. "I've read celebrities always want getaway properties, out of sight of the paparazzi."

"Emmy, it's good to hear you talk shop, but stay in the car. I'll be as quick as possible, and check it out."

"No way. I'm not passing up the opportunity to look at a house like this one."

"Okay, but don't touch anything. No need to leave our fingerprints as a calling card." He pulled on thin plastic gloves.

She wandered around the modern glass and chrome home, dazzled by the panoramic vista from each room. On the deck, the sun was setting and the stars would soon appear on the horizon. If only they had time to enjoy watching it.

"Go to the car. There's nothing here. I'm going to check the out-buildings." Webb's gruff voice startled her.

He rushed her out the front door. "Lock the Acura. I'll be back." He tossed her the keys.

***

Webb surveyed the other buildings on the property. Which would be the more likely place to hide the list, shed or barn?

He started with the smallest building. A lock hung on the door but had not been fully engaged. He pushed the door open and entered. Lawn furniture, grass mower and garden utensils, nothing more. *Shit.*

It might be dark before he finished his search.

How long would Emma wait in the car?

The stainless-steel lock closing the double doors of the red building came free with the help of the screwdriver he discovered in the gardening shed.

His back crawled as he peered into the dimly lit building. Too many dangers might lurk in the dark. He searched for but discovered no light switch.

Shadows prevented his complete scan of the place. Still, he sensed it was empty, cleaned out. In the dimness, it appeared to be laid out in the same fashion as other building of this type, with horse stalls, hayloft, and an open area. As he expected, the outbuilding seemed to be devoid of animals or tack.

Where the hell would the list be? He moved through the room heading toward the cupboards in the corner. When he opened one, a huge rat jumped out and skittered across the floor near his feet. "Damn." He had faced knives, guns, even grenades in the hands of the enemy. Yet, it was strange the thought of a bite from a wild rodent sent a shiver through him. The critter might carry an exotic disease. How many more rats lay in wait?

With no flashlight and expecting to be bitten, he used his hand to wipe the shelves in the cupboard, hoping to find the list in paper or digital form.

Nothing. No files. No thumb drives.

About to leave, the sound of movement caught his attention. Another rodent?

"What the hell are you doing here? This is private property."

Webb spun around to face a large man pointing a shotgun.

Chapter 11

"Who are you?" Webb demanded, staring at the man holding the shotgun.

"I asked you first." The stocky, gray-haired man smiled, deepening the lines around his blue eyes. He moved the gun toward Webb's chest and a sardonic expression showed he believed he had the upper hand.

Webb didn't blink and matched the man's countenance. "Put the gun down and we can talk."

Silence.

The stranger's eyes narrowed, but his hands continued to hold the weapon steady.

"Webb, where are you?" Emma yelled as she entered the barn.

The gunman glanced at her, and Webb grabbed the shotgun's barrel pointing it toward the ceiling as a bullet shot into a beam. He twisted the stock from the man and struck him in the jaw with it.

Emma screamed and the stranger slumped to the floor.

"Get back to the car," he shouted at her, but kept his eyes on the aggressor as the guy rolled to a sitting position. "Don't move."

"What's your problem, buddy? You had no call to hit me." He rubbed his chin. "You're trespassing, not me."

For the first time Webb noticed the man spoke with an accent, English obviously not his first language. Was it Baltic, Russian? "Do what I tell you. I'm holding the gun now." Where was Emmy? Had she run to their vehicle?

"Please, mister. We want to retrieve something and then we'll be gone," Emma pleaded.

"Damn, Em, go to the car."

"The list," the man said.

"What do know?" Webb stepped closer.

"Miranda," the dude whispered. "Miranda."

Stunned, Webb answered, "James, three."

"I'm the list you're searching for."

"The hell you are."

"I gave you the password. What more do you want?"

"The paper list or thumb drive."

"We have a problem." The man stood and brushed off his pants. "Everything you want is in my head. You can put down the shotgun. I'm no threat. On the contrary, without me you and the country are in jeopardy. Ivan Popov." He extended his right hand.

Webb ignored it.

"Okay, don't shake my hand and keep the weapon if you feel safer."

"Give me the information and we'll be off."

"I'm coming too."

"Those aren't my orders."

"Call your boss. Life changes. Who knows that reality better than I? Like it or not, you're stuck with me."

Webb made the call and learned the ex-FSB agent had turned double agent after his oldest daughter was jailed and later died in prison after she, among others, protested against the treatment of the Russian press and the murder of a politician running for office. With another daughter in possible danger, he retired and quietly left the country, taking his secrets with him for protection. Now years later, who would think he'd have relevant info? Well somehow, he did.

Webb broke the burner cell phone with the gunstock. Later, he would toss the phone pieces out of the window over a couple of miles of freeway.

"Okay, we're out of here," Webb said.

They walked to the small car and he stored the shotgun in the trunk.

"Ivan, sit in the back of the Acura," he demanded.

"In this piss ass little car. I'm too big." Ivan paused. "Miss, you ride there."

Webb looked at her and shrugged.

"It's okay. I don't mind. He can take the passenger seat." She crawled into the backseat.

"Everybody settled? Strap in, we're on the way to San Francisco."

"Not until we stop in the San Fernando Valley. A burger drive-in on Ventura Boulevard."

"You're kidding."

"I, Ivan Popov do not kid. You want the list or not?"

Shit. Webb revved the engine and drove out of the driveway.

Dangerous Web

***

Thousands of lights from the San Fernando Valley sparkled like a giant mirrored disco ball, sending shards of light reflecting in every direction. From a distance the amazing view was not marred by traffic noise or congestion from the population of about one million, seven hundred thousand souls.

"My home for the last few years. Beautiful."

Emma watched Mr. Ivan Popov and wondered who this man was and if they should trust him.

"I love this place, the noise, the crowds and the over indulgence of the people," Ivan said as he stared out of the window from the passenger's seat. "You can't be too rich or too thin here. I'd add more. You can't spend too much or be too garish. Indulging one's whim is encouraged." He laughed. "All the capitalism that was forbidden in my old life is good here."

"Ivan, you talk too much," Webb said, irritation showing in his voice.

"Exactly what my first wife said." The man chuckled. "Of course, it's why I took a second spouse." He sat forward and took a deep breath. "Oh, the smell of a second stage smog alert. The aroma of free enterprise. Got to love it." He sucked in another quick breath. "Turn onto Ventura Boulevard and go west. You'll see the long line of cars waiting to enter the drive thru." He paused. "My little girl works there. She's nineteen and lives with a roommate. I must say good bye and warn her to be careful. If I just disappear, she might go to the police for help finding me. I'll tell her I'm going out of town on business. Afterwards, I'll go wherever you want."

Webb grunted, but his expression softened. "You wouldn't have to leave her if you gave me the information tonight."

"No, not the plan, Mr. Lancaster."

Later, Ivan munched on one the three cheese burgers he'd ordered to go from the burger place, then drank part of the extra-large chocolate milk shake. "Nothing like it." He spoke with his mouth full. "I've had burgers all over the world. These are the best."

"Ivan, shut up and eat," Webb demanded.

"Whatever you say." He turned to the back and winked at her and smiled.

For the first time Emma realized his talk masked his stress. It was hard to believe this jovial character was involved in espionage and was a retired Russian agent.

Ivan finished the first burger and wiped his mouth with a napkin. "Mr. Lancaster, transport me to your boss and when I am sure he can be trusted, I will give the list to him. Until that time, see I stay alive or the names will die with me."

Webb's knuckles whitened as he tightened his grip on the steering wheel, nine pm and almost dark, still the weekend traffic clogged the boulevard. They drove east toward the 405 freeway and north out of the valley heading to the Grapevine on the I-5 interstate to the San Joaquin Valley.

The calm torrid air hovered over the valley, trapped by the smog. The nineteen ninety-two Acura hadn't let them down on the long trip south, but now heading north the car slowed. Perhaps the heat and dirty atmosphere had affected the old auto.

Hot, Emma sorely missed the lack of air conditioning in the sedan and searched for something to use as a fan. With nothing useful available to her, she gave up and did her best to ignore the stifling breeze coming through the open windows.

"Why can't we take a plane?" Emma stretched and leaned forward. "We would be at SFO in a little more than two hours after we boarded the jet."

"That's the first place someone would look for us. They'll watch local transportation hubs, bus stations, airstrips, etc. And airports have more cameras taking photos of the crowds than anywhere I can think of. Not to mention we'd need to show our ID."

"I didn't think. I should have realized we're hiding." She shuddered, remembering when the black SUV found them.

She leaned back and settled in for a long, hot ride, and admired Webb's skill as he maneuvered through the dense congestion, apparently an everyday occurrence on the multi-lane Ventura Freeway.

The drone of Ivan's voice continued as he gave a monologue on the virtues of living in Southern California with the shopping, concerts, and schools. He delighted in swimming in the ocean all year round. Was this an act, the jolly man without a care? Or was this tradecraft of an experienced foreign agent with the ability to be whatever person he thought the people around him appreciated?

Webb responded only when absolutely necessary. Other times Popov murmured on without encouragement as the Acura wound its way up the Tejon Pass through the Tehachapi Mountains heading north.

She answered Ivan's questions and agreed with him concerning the Los Angeles basin and its tourist attractions, doing her best to cover the lack of response from Webb. Finally, she curled up on the jump seat and listened to Ivan carry on about the wonders experienced since arriving in So Cal. Finally, the hum of the engine appeared to lull him into silence.

About to close her eyes, she startled when Webb said, "We can take a pitstop in Gorman and I'll fill the tank. Don't be too long."

A few minutes later, he drove to a self-serve pump near a Mini Mart.

Emma ran into the bathroom at the back of the store to freshen up, relieved to find it was clean. Afterward, reluctant to return to the car, she strolled through the aisle of junk food, cheap sun glasses, and hats.

Webb grabbed her from behind and whispered, "Look at the blue pickup."

"God, you scared me, Webb."

"Do you see the one I mean?" He let her go.

"Yeah."

"Keep an eye on it. It's probably nothing, but it followed us all the way here. Now they're in the same gas station. I don't like coincidences."

"You're making my back crawl."

"Emmy, it may not be anything, but let's not take chances. At over four thousand feet up in a mountain pass, I wouldn't want to go off the road like we did in the Healey."

"Now you're frightening me."

"Just stay alert. Oh, and remember Ivan is an ex-Russian agent, not a friend no matter how much he pretends to be. He might not be on the up and up," Webb suggested. "We don't know his game, yet."

"All right. I'm cool". She held out her trembling hands. "A little shaky, but calm." She paused. "This weather's oppressive, but I think I'll buy a cup of coffee to stay awake and watch the truck."

The blue pickup had left the station by the time she returned to the car. Relieved, she was about to sit back and enjoy the rest of the trip, when Webb said, "The truck's back."

In the dark it was hard to keep track of the vehicle. Still, she did her best to be aware of the pickup's movements as it worked its way through the mountains, sticking with their sedan but not too close.

No one spoke and in the silence of the night she found it difficult to keep her eyes open, even after the cup of fresh coffee from the gas station.

"Your woman, Emma, she's a good person," Ivan spoke, his voice booming in the quiet night. "Like my daughter Tasha. Oh, they look nothing alike. Tasha is a bear of a girl—big, tall." He used his hands to make his point. "Not small and delicate as your wife. But they are blessed with the same sweetness—gentle hearts. They will be good mamas, no?"

She saw Webb tense. Knowing him, he most likely wanted to tell the Russian KGB/ FSB officer to put his thoughts where they wouldn't see the light of day.

When Webb didn't respond, the man turned to her. "Your man, he is moody, no?"

She'd be fine if Ivan didn't mention Webb or her again. However, he continued to talk unaware neither she or Webb wanted to hear what he had to say. She understood the one topic they were interested in would not be mentioned. The list.

The blue truck stayed with them.

***

The air cooled and the traffic thinned, except for the tractor trailer rigs populating the interstate. Conversation dwindled. Soon the quiet hum of the car's engine was the only sound.

Ivan, the big bear of a man, leaned against the passenger's side window. The double agent probably hadn't had much sleep in the last couple of days while he waited to be contacted in the mountains. The man started to snore, interrupting Webb's thoughts.

He glanced in the rearview mirror. Emmy appeared to be asleep.

After midnight was not Webb's favorite time of the night. It was too lonely, with no talking to fill the dead air. Easy to let his mind wander back to the past and all the mistakes he wished he could change. What good was twenty-twenty hindsight if his broken promises and regrets remained impossible to alter?

Emma did her best not let it show, but he saw fear change her demeanor. Damn, he'd never forgive himself for his selfish behavior years ago. If he had walked away without starting a conversation with her that day in the bookstore, she wouldn't be in danger now.

The truck dogging him still followed, though the vehicle kept back from the Acura's tail. He really didn't mind, because at least he understood where it was.

The two men in the pickup's cab sported beards and baseball caps, making identification difficult. White, twenty something, brown hair sticking out of the bottom of their caps, but nothing distinctive about them. They'd be of average height and weight. That's what he would choose if picking men for the job.

He increased the pressure on the gas pedal and the truck sped up as well. If the guys stayed with him, he planned to confront them at Buttonwillow.

Ivan snored louder. Where did he fit in? Did he know who was shadowing them and why?

Until Webb understood more about the Russian, it might be better to hold off confronting anyone.

Shit.

He drove by Buttonwillow and continued north on I-5. By four or five in the morning they'd be in the San Francisco Bay Area. In the East Bay, he'd lose the guys following them in the truck and be free to continue to their destination. By six am Emma would be placed in a safe house in Petaluma.

Later, he and Ivan would take a private plane from the Oakland Airport to Washington, D.C. in time to dump Ivan Popov in the lap of his boss. Mission complete.

He relaxed his shoulders, lightened his grip on the steering wheel and continued to drive.

On schedule, the sign for Petaluma appeared on the right and he took the exit to the west side of town heading for a small two-bed rancher on a large plot of land with few houses on the same street. They'd be in time for an early breakfast.

He'd used the house once before. The people were kind and dependable, so until the situation improved, Emma would be protected.

He pulled into the graveled driveway of the old single-story home and turned off the engine. "You two wait in the car until I make sure they're ready for us."

"Okay." Emma stretched and smiled at him.

Damn. He didn't want to leave her. *You have no choice.*

Warm for this time in the morning, with no fog, things were clearing physically as well as metaphorically.

"Hey, boy," Webb said to the German Shepard laying on the front porch. "Remember me?"

The dog didn't move. "You okay, boy?" He started to climb the stairs but stopped. "Emma, stay in the car until I tell you to come out."

She opened the car's door. "What's wrong?"

"Do what I say for once."

At that moment, he noticed a trail of blood running from the dog toward the stair where he stood. "What the hell?"

The dog was dead, shot and left where it fell. Why?

He ran to the back of the house and looked into the kitchen window. A suit jacket hung on kitchen chair and milk and sugar were on the table near a place setting. A carton of eggs sat on the counter, and a French press full of coffee was nearby.

He yanked open the unlocked door and gasped— gas. He held his breath then turned off the range. The coffee was still hot. The owners couldn't have been gone long. What would cause them to leave in such a hurry?

He searched the home and found no one. Where were the owners?

His lungs hurting from holding his breath, he grabbed the suit jacket, a broken laptop on the kitchen floor, and stumbled out of the cottage to the fresh air.

Coughing, he stood in the backyard. What were the possibilities the people were still alive? The real question, what to do with Emma now?

"What's going on?" She came up to him and stared.

"I should've known you wouldn't follow my directions and stay put." With her hand in his, he ran back to the car. "Take these things in the back. He tossed the jacket and laptop to her. We need to go before the police arrive."

Ivan put on his seat belt, but he didn't ask anything.

"Why would the police be called?" she asked.

Webb started the engine and backed out of the driveway without answering.

"Hey, I thought I was staying here—what's happening?"

Chapter 12

"It's not fair. I don't want to stay in San Francisco." Julie Smith stuck out her bottom lip.

Smith stared at his wife. Then he spit into the ashtray on his office desk, before picking up his Cuban cigar again. "Not my choice. Until my business is finished, we're here."

"Baby, no. What about the gala? My dress is waiting for me. You said I'd meet the president."

"Julie, go ahead and pout. Nothing will change. Leave and let me do my work. I'll see you in the condo tonight. Maybe I can wrap this up in time go back east." He slapped her on her ass. "Take your gorgeous rear out of my face."

"Gorgeous, really?" She wagged her butt at him and blew him a kiss.

"Tyler, put your eyes back in your head," he said to the young male standing nearby. "You can't afford her." *I can barely keep her.*

"Sorry, sir."

"Report. Got Lancaster?"

"Not yet. The team followed him back from LA, they lost him in the East Bay." Tyler glanced down at his feet as if waiting for Smith's tirade.

Silence.

"Good idea you had to check the places Lancaster used before," the young man continued. "We found him in Petaluma and before he arrived, we took out the people living in the hide out. The safe house is out of business. He and the Russian are on their own." He finally looked up from the floor. "They were tracked to a local park."

"You left them?"

"Someone's watching. We can grab them if you want."

"No. Not until we're sure who else is involved and we understand why Lancaster needs the Russian." Smith puffed on his stogie and blew the smoke in Tyler's face.

He coughed, but didn't turn from the stale air. "I'll find out."

"You got twenty-four hours, if you don't nab them and the list by tomorrow midday, kill them.

"Including the girl?"

"Yes."

"I don't like to execute women."

"Who gives a shit what you like? If you're not man enough to do the job, I'll buy someone who is. Your scruples be damned."

"Hey." Tyler put up his hands. "I've been loyal to you since I was a kid. Since my dad retired and I took over for him, you've had no complaints."

"Don't give me a history lesson."

"Mr. Smith, I'll do whatever you need. No worries."

"Remember, you have one day to find the list or make them go away for good." He blew one last blast of smoke toward Tyler. "Get out."

Smith smiled as the door slammed closed. *Good boy*. Still, it never hurt to throw a scare into his workers, even the loyal ones.

Smith rubbed his eyes. His wife's carnal desires and the anxiety brought on by his rising debt had caused sleep to elude him. Was there enough left on his line of credit to make another payment on the buildings he owned?

His secure phone buzzed. Russian oligarch, Oleg Volkov was the only one who had the number. Volkov meant wolf, an apt name for the carnivore on the phone. His boss, a charming foreign banker, appeared amiable as he temped a man with his wares and he controlled more money than any America industrialist or a medium sized country. Nonetheless, if the wolf didn't receive the promised list…

Oleg controlled the people under him with a carrot and a stick approach. Deliver and be rewarded with a huge monetary recompense. Disappoint and be killed without regret. Oleg might not pull the trigger or apply the poison, but the result still meant death. Smith had seen the man's work. "Hell," he spit out the expletive.

The secure phone buzzed once more. With some trepidation, he answered, "Smith."

"Do you have it?" his boss demanded.

***

Ivan ate his fast food, chicken and fries sitting under a tree near the wooden bridge on the Petaluma River. Webb skipped pebbles in the slow flowing water. How could the retired Russian agent devour food and Webb play a kid's game when everything had gone wrong? Emma wondered.

144

She glared at the pleasant vista and stared at the mallard ducks float in the water, evidently undisturbed by Webb's rock throwing. Unbidden, she remembered the first date with him. They'd fed the ducks at the pond by the Place of Fine Arts in San Francisco. She had cried for help as the Canadian geese surrounded her, the large birds snapping at the food she'd offered to the ducklings. He'd protected her and grinned, claiming to be her hero. Back then, her naive heart believed him—no longer.

A safe haven was supposed to be waiting at the ranch house, but something had sent Webb on the run, fear in his eyes. He'd driven too fast from the place of protection, only to sit at the river bank and do nothing.

He and Ivan might be flying back to Washington by now. Instead, something in the home changed their plans. Her stomach growled, but the idea of eating sent a wave of nausea pushing bile into her throat.

She jogged to where Webb stood. "You going to tell us what went wrong at the house?"

He shrugged.

"Damn it, Webb. I've lost my patience."

"Keep your voice down. I don't want you calling attention to us."

"If you need my cooperation, talk," she said through clenched teeth.

He put his arm around her and brought her close to him as if they might be on an outing without a care.

Stunned, she glanced up at him and he smiled. She almost grinned back. Crazy. He still affected her, because she wanted to lean into his masculine embrace and believe she had a champion. She pulled out of his arms and stepped away. "Don't try to charm me. I'm wise to your tricks. Give me straight answers or I walk to the nearest police station and spill my guts."

The expression on his grim face told her she'd never make it to the station.

"Someone knew the address to the safe house. He entered the home before us, possibly no more than few moments before we arrived. I got into the kitchen, the stove was on, and the coffee in the pot was still hot, but the people were missing. Enough looked out of place to tell me they didn't leave of their own volition."

"How can you be sure they didn't go shopping or somewhere?"

"Their German Shepherd is dead on the front porch—shot."

"Oh, God." She grabbed her mouth to stop from screaming. A chill ran through her even in the ninety-degree heat. Had Ivan heard what Webb said? She looked back at him, a stoic expression on his lined face.

Webb stood above the man. "Ivan, who did you tell?"

The Russian dropped the chicken drumstick he was eating. "It can't be Tasha. My daughter would never betray her papa."

"You told her where we were heading," Webb insisted.

Ivan stood, displaying his commanding height and weight. The napkin in his lap flew on the breeze to land in the river and drift with the current. His mouth grim, he appeared to ignore the question and track the serviette. "She is my baby. Something might have happened to her. Tasha is not a traitor."

146

The two men glared at each other, a standoff.

"Guys, come on," Emma begged. "stay calm." Perhaps to Tasha, Ivan betrayed Russia by leaving their native country. The young woman had grown up there, only to move to the San Fernando Valley in her teen years. By all accounts she fit in with the valley culture, but who understands the mind of a teenager?

Nobody moved. Emma began to sweat as fear shook her. If the two men fought, could there be a winner?

Webb handed Ivan a burner phone. "Call your kid. Put the phone on speaker and ask her who she told. This time don't tell where we are. Keep it in English," Webb demanded. "I'm listening."

Ivan grunted, but dialed.

What if his daughter didn't pick up? Maybe she'd been abducted. Would the Russian give up the list to the kidnappers to secure the girl's return? Would she blame him if he did?

"Hey, who is this?" a young woman answered.

"Tasha, it's Papa." Ivan sank into the grass and held his head. "Little one, you are all right?"

"Of course. Is something wrong?"

"Nyet. I wanted to make sure you didn't need anything."

"I'm a big girl. I can take care of myself."

"Da, da." He paused. "Has anyone asked about me?"

"No."

"If someone contacts you, tell them you don't know where I am. Only say I'm out of town on business."

"Yeah. Okay. I got to go back to work."

When the phone went dead, Emma felt Ivan's disappointment. Still, his daughter gave the impression of a carefree adolescent annoyed by the concern of an overprotective parent. All good for a teen of her age.

Webb threw another rock into the river, this time with a fierceness that scattered the mallards.

"We're okay. Whoever followed can't be aware of our location today. Right?" Emma looked to Webb for assurance.

"I think we can assume the ranch house was watched and we are being tailed."

"Here?"

"Keep your voice down."

"Someone is with us now?" she whispered.

"I think from now on, we'll assume so."

"Shit," she murmured, more quietly.

Webb closed the space between them and put his arm around her. "Emmy, I thought you'd be out of this. It was never my intention to involve you."

"I remember your intentions," she said bitterly.

"We need to plan," Ivan interrupted. "You two can fight later."

"Let's sit under the black oak tree. It's harder for anyone to obtain a clear line of sight." Webb let her go.

When they were settled, he dialed the burner cell.

"Har du det bra?" he asked.

"Ja," a male answered.

"Er det en god tid å snakke?" he continued.

"Nei. Pappa venter på å se deg. Møt ham på hytta. Du har to dager. Vær forsiktig."

"I'll be careful. Du også. Ha det." Webb disconnected.

In shock, Emma stared at her husband. "I didn't know you spoke a foreign language. Who was on the cell?"

"I'll tell you—someday."

"Yeah, right." Annoyed, she walked a few steps away from him.

"Ivan, there's two days to deliver the list to my boss. I don't like it, but we can't go to the office. Something's up."

"Where?" The man appeared unfazed by the change of plans. The guy pulled a clean napkin from the bag, grabbed another piece of chicken from the box, and munched on it. "You picked a place?" he said, his mouth full of food.

"You bet." Webb leaned against the tree trunk. "Tonight, after dark, we'll take a drive." He laid down and put his hands under his head and closed his eyes. "Relax. We're here for a while." He opened one eye. "And Ivan, don't think you can go out on your own. They'll grab you in a second. We are safer together. The men tracking us understand I'm wired to an organization ready to take them out."

Was he telling the truth? She'd lived with Webb and recognized the small inflection in his voice and the turn of his lips that expressed concern. What had he learned on the phone call? Did it cause him to worry?

The sun was still high when she leaned back and took a slow breath. *Chill out. You're stuck here.*

***

"Emma."

She blinked and saw Webb's handsome face.

"It's almost dark. We'll be leaving soon."

149

"I must have fallen asleep." She yawned and stretched.

Ivan slept, curled up on the grass, snoring.

"If you want to freshen up, there's a ladies' room on the other side of the park." Webb pointed to a small building where the lawn ended.

"Okay, I'll be right back."

"Be careful."

As she walked toward the bathroom, an older gentleman threw a ball for yellow Labrador puppy.

A woman pushed a toddler in a stroller while she spoke on a cell phone. "We're on the way home. I'll have dinner ready by the time you get there. Love you."

Emma, turned from them, feeling it was wrong to spy on a stranger's life.

Webb had mentioned two days to deliver. In forty-eight hours, her worries would be over.

In the bathroom, she splashed cold water on her face and combed her hair with her fingers. She stared into the mirror above the sink. "You look like shit," she muttered, just as a little kid came out of one of the stalls.

"Ah, not you kid. I was talking about me."

The little girl ran from the bathroom.

"Great. Now I'm scaring children," she mumbled as she washed her hands.

The park was completely dark when she exited the building. The wind blew fog in from the ocean and the area's streetlights had an eerie glow. She wanted to run but didn't see the car. Webb wouldn't leave without her. Would he? Did he suggest she freshen up to get her out of the way so he might escape, leaving her stranded?

Someone clutched her shoulder from behind. She gasped.

"Don't scream. It's me."

"Webb, you scared me. I thought…"

"I moved the car." He took her hand and led her across the street to a parking spot in front of a closed antique shop. Back at ten am, the sign in the window read.

Ivan sat in the passenger's seat of the old sedan, buckled up and ready to ride. She went into the backseat on the driver's side.

"Now Emma is here, we can buy food?"

"Is that all you do, eat?" Webb asked.

"I'm a growing boy." Ivan slapped his chest and laughed as if he'd made a funny joke. "I want sustenance."

Webb grunted, but Emma noticed the corners of his mouth turn up. "We'll find a place to grab something on the road."

"I observed a burger joint on the way into town."

"You can't wait?" Webb asked.

"I'm a big man. I need three cheese burgers, fries, and pop. Do you know how much a burger costs in Russia?"

"Too much."

"Da. I never bought three of them at once in my home country. Too many rubles."

"All right. Three hamburgers and afterward we drive nonstop until we arrive at the destination."

Unless someone waylays us. Emma glanced out of the window searching for—what? In the dark one vehicle looked pretty much the same as the next.

An hour down the road, only the hum of the engine broke the silence. She assumed, each of them was lost in their own thoughts, including her. What were the men thinking? Were they making plans for the eventuality of a confrontation with the guys who might be following? Maybe they were deciding how to keep Ivan and his secret list safe? She couldn't say.

She drifted into a daydream about the weekend she and Webb made love in Carmel. They had rented a home overlooking the beach. Back then, she'd admired the flash of the engagement ring on her finger. In two weeks, they'd be husband and wife. In the idyllic setting of perfect weather and blue surf, Webb had joined her in the swimming pool. He'd scattered kisses from her shoulders to her neck and finally to her waiting sun warmed lips. He slowly stripped off the bikini and caressed her until she begged him to enter her. In one swift movement he'd filled her.

Stop. It did no good to remember. She slowed her breathing and hoped no one detected her labored breaths. If she were honest, she still wanted Webb.

"I think we've picked up a tail." Webb interrupted her thoughts.

"How can you tell? I don't see anything unusual."

"Emma, this isn't my first rodeo." He pressed on the gas pedal and changed lanes, then continued into the fast lane. He suddenly pulled into the far-right and decrease the auto's speed. She saw a dark sedan do the same maneuver.

"Now the driver understands we're on to him. It will be up to him to make the next move." Webb continued to drive at a moderate speed.

"Is it okay he knows we've seen him?"

"Time will tell. If he plans to confront us, I want it to happen on the open highway, not on a secluded road with no Highway Patrol Officers to help."

"Okay."

As they drove out of the Bay Area the traffic eased, but the tension inside the vehicle remained high.

Ivan crumpled the wrapper from his last burger and dropped it to the floor of the vehicle. "Lukas, the world is an odd place. No?"

Webb glanced at the Russian. "What the hell are you talking about?"

Ivan called Webb, Lukas? Had the strain of the last couple of days sent him over the edge? She leaned forward to hear more.

"You want to play games, Lukas," Ivan grumbled.

Webb swerved the sedan to miss a stalled car in the lane. "I'm not playing, Ivan. What's your problem?"

"Me? I don't have a care in the world." He slurped the last drops of his drink, belched, and tossed the cup out of the passenger side window.

They drove in silence for a few miles, but Emma noticed Webb's tense shoulders and the way he occasionally glared at Ivan. He wouldn't hold his questions for the Russian much longer.

"Okay, Ivan, spill it."

"This is an idiom I do not recognize—this spilling."

"Talk."

"Da. You are like your papa." He paused. "Your daddy worked for MI6. Nobody told you?"

"The hell he did."

Webb nearly choked on Ivan's words. She thought he might stop the car and throw the guy out on the freeway.

"How did you know my father?"

"He and I investigated money laundering done by Russian oligarchs in London and New York."

"This is crazy talk. My father wasn't a spy."

"You really met Webb's biological dad?" Emma asked.

"Da. He came to my home land several times."

"What kind of work did he do over there?" she asked, wondering if Webb might tell her to butt out.

"He toiled with numbers, a forensic accountant." He looked at Webb. "Mr. Lukas Eriksen was proud of his first born, Lukas Ethan Eriksen. You are his name's sake."

"The hell. I don't understand what your game is, but…"

"No tricks. I thought you realized that is why they sent you to me. We are connected by an event. I understand I can trust you because of your papa."

"I might ask you to describe my dad, but I'm sure you've seen his photo." Webb growled. "Tell me something only the family would be privy to. Prove you met him."

"I journeyed to London twenty-four hours before the vehicle hit and killed him. On the terrible day, we walked to lunch and didn't perceive the auto coming at us from behind. The car jumped the curb." Ivan hesitated. "It knocked me over. I broke my leg, but the car ran him down and his secretary was slain as well. Your father's last words: 'Tell Bunny I'm sorry I won't grow old with her.'"

"Damn." Webb swallowed hard. "My mother's name is Barbara. Only the family knows he called her Bunny."

"It was no accident the vehicle murdered him," Ivan continued.

Webb appeared to slump over the wheel for a second, then recover. "I always wondered—about that day."

She gasped and wanted to comfort him, but what could she say?

"Father never talked about his job. I thought he must work for a big multinational corporation because of all the travel involved, but MI6? Still, working for the Secret Intelligence Service explains so many situations back in the day, the hushed conversations, the odd phone calls, the locked office in our home." Webb increased the speed of the sedan. "And Father's unexpected departures in the middle of the night…"

The miles rushed by in silence. She stared out of the rear window searching for the men following them.

A truck looked suspicious, no the SUV or was the minivan following them? It was impossible to tell in the darkness, might as well stop trying to figure it out.

Two hours later, after listening to Ivan moan and complain about needing a bathroom, Webb pulled into a rest stop and turned off the engine.

"I thought we weren't stopping until we reached our destination." Emma leaned forward in the car and touched Webb's shoulder.

He shook her hand away. "You and Ivan take a quick bathroom break. I'll stay with the car. Make it fast. So far, we're alone. I want to be gone before someone else comes here," he said gruffly.

***

Nerves. Webb's hands tingled. He should have kept driving. The last thing he wanted was to confront the men following them. At least not until he comprehended their objective. Were they sent to kill or did they intend to kidnap Ivan? Whatever the plan, with Emma in the car, he didn't want to deal with the guys. Maybe later after he delivered the list and Emma was safe, the traitors could be tracked.

Anger raged in him. He shook his arms to bring blood to his hands and flexed and relaxed his fists, the need to slug someone almost overwhelming.

His mother knew the truth, had to. Why didn't she tell him? As the oldest sibling, he had a right to understand his father's death. Would knowing have made a difference?

As Emma walked out of the bathroom, a nondescript car with dark windows drove into the rest stop and parked two spaces from their sedan. She paused as if she wondered what to do. He waved and she ran to him and jumped in the car and crawled to the back seat. "Where's Ivan?"

"Still in the men's room." He stared at the other vehicle. "Why don't they come out of the car?"

"Maybe they're not the people tracking us."

"Oh yeah, it's them. I feel it in my bones." He flexed his fists. He paused, checked the glove compartment, then retrieved the G17 pistol.

"You need a gun?"

"A precaution."

"Why are they waiting? They must realize another car might pull in the rest stop at any second. Don't they want to end this ASAP." She grabbed the back of the seat as if it was a safety line.

"Where the hell is Ivan?" Webb hit the dashboard with his fist. "Shit."

"What's wrong?" she asked her voice raising in volume.

"They're waiting for back up. That's why they don't get out." He started the engine.

"What about Ivan?"

"I'll try to draw them out before anyone else arrives. I'm going to pretend to check the map I see posted near the drinking fountain."

"It's too dangerous."

"Slide into the driver's seat after I leave and keep the engine running."

"Webb, no."

He exited the car and slammed the door, the pistol held at his side.

Chapter 13

Stay **safe, Webb.** Emma wanted to close her eyes or look away. Somehow, fear wouldn't allow her to turn from him. Appearing confident with the gun still at his side, he strode toward the map near the drinking fountain. He paused and took a sip of water, but she thought he glanced at the sedan that had parked a mere ten or twelve feet from their car.

She surveyed the vehicle, but in the dark with the shaded windows, she couldn't see any movement. Still, the occupants must be watching.

Damn, where was Ivan? The Russian might need Webb's help. Besides, they were in this situation because of him.

Emma looked down at her hands and tightened the grip on the steering wheel. She had to be ready to flee, but had never driven the stick shift on the old Japanese sedan. Was it the same as Webb's Austin Healey?

Seconds might count and Webb's life could depend on a quick getaway. What if she couldn't put the transmission in reverse? The pattern might be different from a British sports car. She stared at the shift knob, not the original, instead a shiny silver skull with red rhinestone eyes. Probably a young male's idea of cool, but it had no markings showing where each gear was located.

Apparently unaware of the threat, Ivan came out of the men's room still zipping his pants. A bullet hit him, spun him around and he fell to his knees.

Shocked, she screamed as Webb dropped behind a cement trashcan and returned fire.

Ivan crawled back toward the bathrooms leaving a trail of blood, visible even in the low light.

The barrage continued until several of Webb's bullets penetrated the front windshield on the passenger's side of the enemy's sedan. A man inside yelled. The car backed up and screeched out of the lot as Webb fired and punctured one of their tires.

In the driver's seat, Emma trembled as she turned off the engine in the Acura, grabbed the key from the ignition, and jumped out.

"Where's Ivan?" Webb yelled.

"In the men's room. Dear God, I think he was shot," she shouted and ran toward the bathrooms.

When she entered, Ivan was slumped against the wall, his eyes closed, and his breathing labored. She touched him and he grabbed her, twisting her arm until she screamed and dropped to the ground. "Ivan, you're hurting me. It's Emma."

He released her. "Pardon, little one. Go, before you are killed by those men. Perhaps for my sins, I am to die on the dirty floor of a washroom in the middle of nowhere in a country that does not welcome me, but you must live."

"Always pessimistic, hey, Ivan?" Webb said as he entered the bathroom. "Shut up and let me stop the bleeding and we'll take your sorry ass to my boss as planned."

"Da," the Russian grimaced. "Always optimistic, you Americans. Will *you* never learn?"

Webb grinned and opened Ivan's shirt. Emma saw the torn skin from the bullet.

"Damned if you didn't get lucky," Webb declared. "The bone isn't broken."

Ivan laughed, but she didn't like the abnormal sound.

Without saying anything, she gathered paper towels and toilet paper from both the bathrooms. Webb pressed much of it onto the injury, then put pressure on Ivan's shoulder wound. Though she had no prior medical experience, it appeared to slow the bleeding.

"Emmy, keep the pressure on the wound."

"Okay." Reluctantly, she took over when Webb removed his hand.

"Press harder. We need compression until the blood coagulates."

Webb handed her more towels. "Don't remove the old paper, just put these on top."

As she did, blood oozed into them. She swallowed the bile that rose from her stomach to the back of her throat.

Webb took off his shirt, removed his white T-shirt and wrapped the cotton cloth as a bandage to hold the paper towels in place. "Come old man. Let's go back to the car."

"Who says I'm an old man? I can fight two of you."

"Exactly what I wanted to hear—old man." Webb smiled.

Emma noted the effort it took to lift Ivan to a standing position.

Without being asked, she ran to Ivan's other side and put his arm around her shoulder. Though Ivan was more than a foot taller, she managed to keep him steady as he took an uncertain step.

The journey to the car seemed farther than Ivan might manage. He grunted with every movement and Webb was breathing hard carrying much of the big man's weight.

A minivan with a woman and two children parked beside their car. The kids rushed out and ran toward the bathrooms. The woman must have seen the bullet casings and Ivan covered with blood, because she yelled at the kids to come back. Her voice was shrill in the night air.

"Mom, I have to go," the youngest complained.

"Get in the damn car!"

Emma wanted to tell the mother it was all right, but…

The van drove out of sight.

In the car, Webb said, "Do what you can for him, Emmy. I'm leaving before someone else arrives."

He reloaded the G17, stored it in the glove box, and drove out of the pitstop at top speed. Did he think the people that had followed them had called for backup and were due at any moment or was it the police he worried about?

Ivan grumbled and sat up straighter in the passenger seat.

"Sit still, old man. Don't make the bleeding any worse than it is. Em, put pressure on his shoulder."

"He needs a doctor, a hospital."

"Nyet. No hospitals." He coughed. "Go to our destination."

"Ivan you're bleeding. It needs to be stopped." She pressed on his shoulder to slow the blood and to underscore her words.

He grunted but patted her hand. "Don't worry about me, little one."

"I just…"

"Da, I appreciate…"

About a mile down the road, a farmhouse came into view. In the backyard, clothing and sheets hung on a rope clothesline. Webb brought the car to a sudden halt. "I'll be right back. We can use that laundry." He left the car door open and ran toward the yard.

The early morning air wafted into the sedan. *Going to be a scorcher today.* She hoped only the weather would be uncomfortable.

The sheets and clothes were still damp when Webb tossed them into the back seat. "Maybe Ivan can wear one of the shirts." He started the engine. "I grabbed the big cotton bag too. Put his bloody shirt and the soaked paper in there. We'll throw them out later." He handed her a Swiss Army knife. "Tear the sheets into strips. We can use them for bandages—put on your seat belt."

Ivan had to be in pain, but he didn't make a sound. So, she did what she could to help him, then pulled on her seat belt and stifled a yawn as exhaustion overtook her. Yet, it felt wrong to sleep while Ivan was suffering.

"Webb, do you think the car is trailing us?"

"I doubt it. I'm sure they've called for backup and there'll be a new group on our tail now. I'd watch for a drone."

"Oh great. You sure made me feel better."

"You don't have to be sarcastic, Em. I'm giving you the lowdown."

"Got ya." She searched the sky.

In silence, they drove toward the destination only Webb knew.

Ivan continued to worry her. In the short time they'd been with him, the man always chatted, a stream of random details, complaints and requests. Today, he said nothing—not a good sign.

Yellow fields, black oaks and occasional gray granite outcroppings sped by and the day grew warmer in the Sierra foothills. Pickup trucks carrying hay drove in the opposite direction. On the way to a nearby farm? However, no vehicle appeared interested in them—at least none she could determine.

Webb white-knuckled his hold on the steering wheel and pressed on the gas pedal. Was the deadline to deliver the secret list on his mind? She leaned back and tightened her seat belt expecting a fast ride.

"Em, wake up."

"What? Where are we? I guess I fell asleep."

"You slept for a couple of hours. We're in some small burg." Webb took a quick breath. "I need you to buy food and a few medical supplies for Ivan. There's a small grocery down the street. I'll go to the gas station across the way and fill up. Meet us there."

"Okay." She yawned and ran her fingers through her hair. *I must be a sight.* Outside the car, she adjusted her shirt.

To her surprise, Webb came to her side and took her hand. "I'm truly sorry you're stuck in the middle of this mess." She stared into his deep blue eyes. "I wish—" he said, paused and pulled her to him, but instead of kissing her as she expected, he caressed her cheek, then let her go. "We'd better move."

Disappointed? Overwhelmed? She didn't want to deal with her emotions.

He crossed the street, his head held high. How much sleep had he lost the last couple of days? Pressure to finish his assignment had to weigh on him and now she was in the mix, a responsibility he didn't need or want. Again, the possibility of leaving him came into focus. No. She might help with Ivan's care and allow Webb the time required to concentrate on reaching their destination—alive.

The "mom and pop" grocery store was right out of a nineteen fifties movie, wooden plank floor and fluorescent signs selling beer and cola. Neatly stocked aisles of food and paper goods led to a freezer and refrigerator with ice cream and other milk products. An elderly gray-haired woman sat at the checkout counter, watching an old model TV. A women's talk show blared.

Thank goodness the store had a public lady's room. Emma did her best to freshen up, then found the food items Webb requested, plus bottled water, painkillers, coffee, deodorant, toothpaste and lipstick among other items. At the counter she added three bags of chips and several candy bars. Might as well have a sugar fix, after all, they might want the energy.

"Excuse me. Are those single use cell phones?" She tried to catch the clerk's attention. "Are they for sale?"

"Yep. We can't keep them on the selves these days. You'd be surprised how many people want them."

"I'd like two of them. One for my husband and for me—if they aren't too expensive."

She didn't' have enough cash and considered using the credit card Webb had given her at the hotel in the wine country. Instead, she paid with her bank card and hoped it was all right to do it that way.

Later, at the gas station, Webb took the bags from her. "We're changing cars. Let's get the hell out of here. Gather your things and come with me. Ivan's already in the other car. I need you to drive it."

"Where did you find a car?"

"I'll explain later." He put the bags in the back seat of the 1990's four door silver Volvo wagon. "Meet me five miles from here. Make a right where the barbwire fence starts. Afterward, keep going until you see me." He tossed an ignition key to her.

With a reflex reaction, she caught the key chain and at the same time squelched questions that demanded answers. Did he buy a used vehicle, or was she being asked to drive a stolen car?

The vintage wagon performed well as they drove down the road devoid of other traffic. She turned right and drove the graveled lane wondering if she'd taken a wrong turn. At the end of the path, Webb appeared standing next to the Acura parked in a blacktop parking lot.

"This is a desolate place," she shouted out of the window.

"You sure all your stuff is out of the car?"

"Yeah, but I left the bloody clothes and paper towels in the back seat."

"It's okay. Leave them."

"Webb, I smell gas."

He tossed the license plates from the Acura into the back of the wagon. "I soaked the inside of the car. I'm going to set it on fire."

"OMG. Are you crazy?"

"Look, I can't clean out all our DNA and fingerprints from the car. The people after us aren't going to give up. They're looking for this car and any information we leave. After a fire its's pretty damned hard to retrieve much information. Drive down the lane a bit and I'll meet you."

"Be careful."

"Go."

He started the engine, opened the car's window, stood back, and tossed a lit box of matches into the front seat, then ran.

He jumped in the wagon and shouted, "Drive."

They just entered the two-lane road heading toward town when she heard the explosion.

***

Smith paced in the penthouse waiting room of a New York high rise. As a show of respect, he'd arrived early to the appointment with Mr. Volkov. It wasn't reciprocated. Already an hour late, the oligarch continued to make him wait.

On the walls, German, French, and American modern art mingled with Egyptian antiquities, likely smuggled into the country illegally. Still, they were displayed openly. A dare to the U.S. government or a sense of entitlement?

A young, cheeky bastard, Oleg Volkov could buy and sell him a million times over. Hell, if he wanted to, the man might buy a country and declare himself king. Maybe that's what he had in mind for the United States, Smith thought. Could be a clandestine takeover of the U.S. government, and the shithead was tied to the Kremlin. Oleg might strut around New York, but one misstep and the guy would find his ass back in Moscow.

"Mr. Volkov will see you now," a female voice came over a loud speaker.

Ten minutes later, the meeting was over. Anger and self-loathing swirled in Smith's gut. Would he do the assigned task or lose the financial security and power it had taken a decade to secure? He should have questioned Volkov about his motives. Too late now.

Why had Smith been given the task? *Stop.* He understood. No one else could easily acquire an invitation to the president's closed event, then be willing to harm President Nielsen, the vice president, and the chief of staff.

Bound to Oleg, a charming, despicable man with no moral compass and only revenge to influence him, Smith might be looking at an image of his younger self. Back in the day, he'd have done anything to be near powerful people.

Smith was obliged to complete the mission. However, if he looked at the truth, he wanted do the appalling deed because he sought the influence it would afford him. When the Chief of Staff, Harold Lancaster, died, chaos would rule the administration until an authoritative man took control. Russian sleeper agents waited to put the strong arm of authority on the U.S. government and muzzle those who might speak up for democracy. The president and vice president weren't the only target. The destruction of the Republic of the United States was the mark.

Smith touched the small plastic box in his jacket pocket. It encased a poison pen. One poke with the tip and Chief of Staff, Lancaster, would die, then the VP and President Robert Nielsen would follow.

He dialed his operatives. The list of Russian agents, the Task Force searched for, must be in Smith's hands before the presidential gala, and Ethan Lancaster aka Webb Craig had to be dead by then too.

***

In the living room of his New York penthouse, Oleg Volkov paced. He needed a bath after being in the same room as Smith, the slimy conspirator. Too bad he had to use such men.

He stripped off his polo shirt and tossed it onto the leather divan and took a deep breath. A tall man, he flashed on the comparison of his height and that of the current Russian leader. The little man was growing old but still held centralized power and disputed any idea of sharing authority even in the smallest degree. At thirty-six, Oleg would wait. Father time always won in the end.

In the prime of life, he remembered his years in the GRU, military intelligence. Now as a banker, opportunities to serve the leader were many and luckily, they also gave him the opportunity to retaliate for his father's death. Afterward, when the right occasion arose, he'd be in place to move up in the Kremlin.

He flexed his biceps and pushed out his chest before doing a series of one-handed pushups. Service in the army trained him to remain ready, physically and mentally, for any situation. Better cut back on the cigars and booze.

Ethan Lancaster aka Webb Craig was always on his mind. Smith and Tyler had best do their jobs or he'd kill the guy.

***

"Pull over, Emma."

"We just got out of town. I thought…"

"I don't like Ivan's look. I've got to take the bullet out of his shoulder before we go any further. And we all need rest before we go on."

"True, but…" She guided the wagon to a stop on the side of the road. "Do you have an idea where we can stay?"

"Maybe there's a campground nearby."

"Could be. Call me crazy, but in a flyer at the grocery store, I saw a cabin for rent."

"You're irrational, leave our name and credit card info to be tracked. Emma what are you thinking?"

"You don't understand. I borrowed the store's phone and called the number and asked about the cabin. It's vacant and available. I told them we wanted to view the property." She hesitated. "Dear God, I can't believe I'm about to say this." She held her hand over her mouth and closed her eyes.

"What's the problem?"

"I was told, by the listing agent, we might meet in three days to see the place. The cabin is closed now. We'd have two days if I broke in. We could rest and care for Ivan."

"Damn. I never thought you having a career in real estate would help us."

"I memorized the directions."

"Then, go."

Fifteen minutes later, the huge two-story log cabin, set on a knoll, reached toward the blue cloudless sky. Large windows faced the front of the building. A lockbox hung on the wrought iron door handle.

"I won't disturb the front door," she said. "It's my experience people tend to spend time and money securing the front of their homes, but do little to protect the back. Give me a couple of minutes to check."

"Do it, Em."

A wall of glass glistened at the back of the house and beckoned a person to examine the panoramic landscape. She stumbled over the word cabin. Hardly. It was a grand open beam structure with magnificent views of the spreading river valley below. The surrounding decks and lower patio allowed a choice of verandas for lounging and enjoying nature without road noise or neighbors.

What if someone else drove by to look at the cabin? Would they notice Ivan groaning in the passenger seat of the wagon, blood seeping through the ill-fitting shirt, stolen from the clothesline?

If they did, the police could be called. A chill ran down her back. Webb's idea of finding a campground was becoming more appealing, or sleeping in the car—not so bad.

Hurry and find a way into the place. She checked a small window on the side of the building. Someone had left the window in the laundry room unlocked. "Yes."

She ran back to the front of the house. "Webb, I crawled in a window. Come around to the rear. I opened the slider on the deck."

He helped Ivan, while she carried their supplies. "Go through the living room and take the first room on the right."

In the living room, furnished with what appeared to be handmade log furniture and plush woven carpeting, Emma stared up at the grandeur of the cathedral ceiling. A brick and stone fireplace ascended to the height of the room. *Whoa.*

She turned to close the slider and was stunned by the peaceful mountain view, a counterpoint to the hectic life she'd lived the past few days.

"I need your help," Webb yelled from the bedroom.

"I'm coming."

***

Emma leaned back in the chaise lounge built for two. She snuggled in the soft green cushions. Webb had placed the lounger on the back sundeck and returned to the house. She stared at the rolling hills and a meandering river in the valley. Gorgeous, but the images of today's chaos overrode the serenity. So much blood, too much pain.

Suddenly aware of a headache, she rubbed her brow. A long soak in a tub might help. Too much energy needed to even take a bath. Her strength had disappeared earlier in the afternoon. Still, she'd continued on willpower, but now that too had vanished.

"Mind if I join you?"

She shaded her eyes from the sun and looked up. "Of course not, Webb." She scooted over.

He leaned back on the lounge chair, his hands behind his head and his long legs stretched out in front of him. "Nice view."

"How can you look at the scenery after today's, shootings, explosions, blood?"

He took her hand. "Emmy, calm down. We made it. We're okay."

"You saved Ivan's life, Webb, by taking out the bullet and stopping the bleeding."

"Well, I hope I did no harm." He released her hand and glanced toward the vista. "Now, if there's no infection…"

The sky began to turn from azure blue to a salmon orange and a slight breeze caressed the black oaks dotting the countryside.

"Webb, remember the last time we watched the sunset?"

"Seems like a million years ago." He ran his hand through his hair.

"Let me look at your hand."

"A bullet grazed it at the rest stop. Nothing to worry about."

She sat up in alarm. "Oh God, you might have been killed."

"Hey, there you go, thinking the worst. I'm fine. Enjoy the evening."

"I should clean and bandage…"

"Later. Come here."

She rested her head on his chest, closed her eyes, and took strength from his steady breathing. Could she relax, at least for tonight? "Webb, you feel good."

He kissed the top of her head but didn't speak. Even so, leaning against him, she felt his heart quicken its beat.

Finally, he said, "This place reminds me of the cabin in the Scottish Highlands where my family spent a summer. Oh, the landscape is not the same, but the impression with the river… I bet the fishing is good here." He held her tighter. "We took the vacation a few weeks before Father was killed—after he died, I promised I'd make him proud."

"Your father would be."

He shrugged. "Doesn't matter now."

She wanted to argue and say it did make a difference. Instead, she kept her thoughts to herself. He'd never shared his emotions and talked about his past, his real history. She wouldn't spoil it with a debate.

"Growing up, I never had a long vacation. My mom and I might take a weekend at the beach or a day shopping or go to a movie. Those outings qualified as a vacation. Mom worked in retail and to make ends meet, as a single mother, she took as much overtime she could get. Still, there wasn't enough money for a long holiday."

"No father in your life?"

"Not that I can remember, always just the two of us." Odd Webb was curious about her family now. Before they married, he'd shown no interest. Of course, back in the day, loving each other seemed more important. Or maybe as an American Task Force member, he had investigated much of her history.

"Did you ever go fishing, Emmy?"

"Me?" She laughed. "No. Mom worked at the makeup counter of a department store and spent a great deal of time doing her nails and putting on her face. I can't imagine her in hip waders hooking a fish. Let alone cleaning it."

"I wish—never mind." He took a slow breath and continued to hold her as the sky grew darker, but the summer heat remained.

In his arms, she drifted off to sleep.

Perhaps it was the sound of silence that woke Emma, no traffic, no barking dogs. She rubbed her eyes and stared at the unknown room decorated in oak furniture. In a four-poster bed, still dressed in her street clothes, she blinked to clear the sleep from her eyes.

A satin down comforter was tangled around her feet. She sat up. The last thing she remembered was being on the lounge chair in Webb's arms.

A realization slowly filtered into her waking brain. While she was asleep, Webb must have carried her into the bedroom. She scanned the room. No sign of him. Then she noticed the indentation on the pillow next to hers. Had he sleep next to her last night?

Someone knocked on the bedroom door and Webb entered carrying a mug.

"Good, you're awake." He handed her the mug of coffee.

"Thanks." She avoided touching his hand, grabbed the cup, and took a careful sip of the hot liquid. "How's Ivan doing?"

Webb sat on other side of the bed and shrugged. "As well as can be expected. No infection that I can see. Still, I don't know how he'll do when we start to travel."

"When are we leaving?"

"Finish your coffee and get ready. We can talk at breakfast." He leaned toward her, scanning her, stopping to gaze at her face.

"What? Webb?"

"Nothing. I'll see you downstairs in the kitchen."

Before she could respond, he was gone. If only she was able to decipher his expression. Something was on his mind and it concerned her.

Chapter 14

Webb poured a second cup of coffee and sat at the island in the kitchen. It was too much stimulant on an empty stomach, still, he took a gulp and glanced out of the window to the rural setting. The morning stillness jarred him. He wanted the sound of the city to flood his mind and drown out his thoughts of Emma. The sudden yearning to return to her bed sent heat to lash him, and triggered an internal rebuke. She was off limits. Even if she welcomed him, which was doubtful, making love to her would only complicate an already increasingly difficult situation.

He'd watched as she slept last night. The wish to caress her and take her to him had clawed at him. The remembrance of what they'd shared during their short marriage had heightened his awareness.

Taking advantage of her desire to restart their failed relationship would only jeopardize what little trust she appeared to still have in him. He finished the last drop of coffee and refilled the mug for a third time. It might serve him right if acid burned his gut. Maybe that's what he required to remind him she was out of bounds. His job was to keep her safe while he delivered the list and Ivan to his boss. Emma's return to a life without him, his penance for the lies and the betrayal.

The third mug of coffee sat untouched on the island while he went to shower and dress for the long day ahead. Later, outfitted in blue jeans and a navy T-shirt, he checked on Ivan. Still sleeping, the poor guy needed it.

Webb's stomach growled. What had Emma picked out at the store for their supplies? He'd been grateful to find the coffee. In the fridge he discovered eggs, cheese, milk and bread. He tossed six eggs into a pot of water to be cooked as soon as everyone was awake, then he sat at the island again. He stared at the cold mug of black coffee but shook his head.

With the "pay as you go" phone Emma had bought him, he dialed his boss for the third time.

Still, no response.

A grinding dread forced acid into his empty stomach. The private and secure number had never gone unanswered—until now. A premonition sent a shiver through him. *Something's wrong. Dammed wrong.*

Procedure demanded he check with his boss before delivering Ivan and the list to his superiors. But now… "Shit." If he couldn't connect with the person in charge, there was no guarantee the meet would take place. If not, what would he do with the Russian and his information? If someone already infiltrated the Task Force, what then?

Better not to let Ivan know there appeared to be a glitch in the works. The guy had been shot and depended on the whole team to protect him now. If Ivan believed they couldn't, he might bolt and disappear with the vital data. Or worst yet, he might run, be captured by the enemy, and be compelled to release the secret list to the enemy. After all, the guy changed allegiances once before. Who could say he wouldn't do it again, given the right motivation, like the life of his only living daughter?

To get a good phone signal, Webb went out to the back deck where he and Emma had spent the evening together. What would become of her if he couldn't protect her? *Don't.*

The team headquarters' phone continued to ring without an answer. *Damn.* He didn't want to involve Jon, but…He dialed his younger brother's private number.

"God dag." He recognized Jon's stressed voice in the message recorded in Norwegian. An innocuous message, he hoped he'd never hear, told him more than he wanted to handle. The team was in danger. Did it mean no back up? With a deep breath, he dialed a different number, to be used only in an extreme emergency. This time, if no one answered, all might be lost.

"Ya."

"Thank God. What the hell is going on, Jon?

"Bro, the Task Force is closing."

"I don't believe it."

"The whole team is to stand down."

"I'm in the middle of an operation."

"Those are the orders. I'll help if I can, but you're basically on your own. Bro, someone's at the door. What the hell? Get out of my home."

"Jon, who's with you? Are you all right?"

His brother screamed and the phone went dead.

He called back. No answer.

"Damn it." He ran his hands through his hair as alarm rippled in him. Who broke into his brother's place? The need to help gnawed at him. He called the police, saying he was a neighbor who heard a disturbance at Jon's residence. That was the best he could do.

Emma came to stand next to him. "What's wrong?"

"Let's eat." He led her back to the house. "We can talk after breakfast."

When Ivan and Emma sat around the dining table, Webb pushed any thought of his brother from his mind and laid out their new reality. "The Task Force team is shutting down. We have to rethink how to proceed."

"What does that mean? I thought all you had to do was deliver the list and then I would go home." Emma glared at him. "Are you telling me that's no longer true?"

"It's not about you or me. It never has been."

"I—never mind."

"I know, little one." Ivan patted her hand. "Ethan, what is your plan?"

Webb stood from the table and looked out at the view. What would be the best approach? Convey the latest info? Carry on as if nothing had changed, with the hope that his boss would do the same? He felt Ivan and Emma eyes staring at him and rubbed the back of his neck to relieve the tension.

Take charge. He needed to reassure them he was in control of the situation and not to worry. Truth be told he wanted to wash his hands of the whole deal, walk away, and find Jon.

He and his brother had given too much of their lives to the Rapid Advance Task Force. *Shit.* To stop Jon's work, his wife and little son had been slaughtered by the enemy and yet his brother carried on, determined his family had not died in vain. The thought of Jon dying too... Webb couldn't think that way, not if he was going to complete this task.

Though he didn't fully comprehend the reasons for this current assignment—yet, much depended on completing the mission. The attacks on Emma and Ivan, then the rotten smell of the team being shut down at this juncture, made him think the list must be extremely important. It had to reach people at the top of the U.S. government ASAP. His concerns and those of the others at the table were irrelevant.

He poured a glass of water. "We carry on. This assignment has to succeed whether my team is together or not." He paused. "Ivan, can you travel?"

"Da, but..." He touched the side of his substantial nose. "Something is putrid. You noticed it too. A problem is in the works."

"Yeah, but Ivan, you're a military man. You follow orders. You and me, we do our job. If we're on our own, so be it." His mouth went suddenly dry, he gulped the water, and slammed the glass too hard on the table. "Ivan, it is time for you to tell us what's on the list. If you are killed, the information still needs to be delivered." He paused and stared at the man. "We need to trust each other."

"What about your wife? Once she hears the information, she can't unhear it. She is in for life."

Dangerous Web

The oath Webb had taken when he joined the Rapid Advance team played in his mind and the words of his boss echoed in his brain. *A time will come when you will disappoint your family and friends. They may call you a liar or be hurt by your silence. If you can't take it, leave now. When you sign the oath of secrecy, there is no going back.*

"I don't want her involved. Still, after what's happened, even if she doesn't have the list who would believe her? She's in danger either way."

"Hey you two, don't talk about me as if I'm not in the room. By the way, Webb you're right. I am in trouble and it's your fault." She glared at him again. "If you hadn't talked to me that day in San Francisco, none of this would be happening. Instead, you lied to me and now..." She covered her face and swallowed a sob.

He tensed but didn't speak. What could he say? He had one rule concerning women, don't get involved. He broke it when he met Emma.

She sniffed. "I'm sorry, Ivan. I don't want to give the impression I won't help you and Webb." She wiped a tear from her eye. "Whatever it takes, I'm in. Let's get this done."

"You sure?" Webb caught her hand and held it. "Emmy, I might find a place for you to stay until this is over."

"And if I'm discovered and you're not around, am I dead? Besides, you might need me."

Silence.

Ivan grunted and favored his left side. In obvious pain, he left the room.

"What the hell?" Webb said under his breath. "So much for trust."

"Now what?" Emma leaned closer to him. "Can you do without the list and maybe find out why your team is shutting down?"

"This whole damned mess is because of the data on the list and the consequences it will trigger. Regardless of the changes in the advance team, we need the info soon." He hesitated. "I—let me think."

***

Emma knocked on Ivan's bedroom door. "Can I come in and talk for a second?"

"Da."

She entered and found him shirtless and trying to remove the bandages from his shoulder wound.

"Let me wash my hands, then I'll help you." She returned from the bathroom, with antibiotic cream and took off his dressings. The injury looked better than she'd imagined, red but coagulated, no fresh bleeding. She applied antibiotic cream to the dressing, placed the non-stick gauze on the wound, and secured it with medical tape. "Can I bring you something for pain? I'm sorry, but I only have over the counter painkillers. Might help a little."

"There's water in the glass on the bed stand. Also, search in my bag and find my Hawaiian shirt, if you don't mind."

She brought the garish pink, chartreuse, and black shirt to him.

"I'm not wearing it. Help me with the California shirt you bought at the store yesterday."

She tugged on the 3x large shirt over his barrel chest, careful to avoid touching his injury, and helped him stand.

She suppressed a smile when she saw him in the white T-shirt that declared "Surf's up" in blue letters. She couldn't imagine the huge Russian on a surfboard.

He yanked on the shirt. "This is good for the hot weather."

"It looks fine. Uh, Ivan, you're a nice man. I trust you." She paused, hoping for a positive response at least in his expression. When he didn't respond, she continued, "I'm only a real estate agent, but I believe we have to stick together and help Webb, uh, Ethan, finish this assignment."

"Bring the Hawaiian shirt with you, Emma."

So much for her powers of persuasion. She sighed and followed him back to the dining table where Webb still sat.

The table was cleared of the breakfast dishes. "We can leave whenever you all are ready. I—that's the most hideous Hawaiian shirt I've ever seen."

"Da. I bought it because of this." Ivan sat in a chair at the table.

Emma took a place across from him.

"Is someone going to explain what the hell the hideous shirt has to do with our situation?" Webb's impatience vibrated in his deep voice. "Take it off the table."

"Nyet."

Webb's body froze, but his hand formed a fist.

She reached for his hand.

"This is part of the list." Ivan held the fabric to him.

"You're kidding, right?" She couldn't believe what he said.

"I'm not a prankster. I thought you understood this by now."

"I…spit it out, Ivan." Webb relaxed his fist.

"Oh, Webb, the spitting again. I chose this to be ugly to cause little interest. I could put it on and take the information with me and if I am searched, they uncover nothing, only a man with a poor taste in fashion."

"Well, I'll be." Emma gasped.

"Explain," Webb interrupted.

"These are palm fronds, yes?"

He stared at the fabric. "Yeah, Ivan, so?"

"From a distance, this is true. Still, with a closer observation, there are numbers, oh not every frond, but if you comprehend where to search…"

Emma glanced at Webb, waiting for his reply.

"Numbers for what? Bank accounts?" He sat back in the chair again, an expression of disbelief on his handsome face.

"Sleepers."

"The hell." Webb's voice rose in volume.

"Da."

"Here in the States?"

"Da. In the federal government and elsewhere."

"What's a sleeper?" Emma leaned forward.

"A foreign agent living incognito in the States, but in place and ready to be called up to complete a pre-planned assignment."

"You mean a Russian living in the United States?"

"Yes, behaving like a citizen. Maybe is a citizen but in either case, the person is in a trusted position to

184

betray the country when given a signal." Webb paused. "Tell us more, Ivan."

"These fronds contain numbers when held under the ultraviolet light. With the digits and the key, we can obtain names and job titles."

"No shit."

Ivan nodded. "No shit."

"You have what you need?"

"Nyet. Next we go claim the key."

"To open what? A safety deposit box?"

"Emmy, it's not a real key." Webb rubbed his chin. "It could be a book or even a thumb drive, but either way, it links the numbers and the people involved." He stared at Ivan. "Where is it?"

"I will take you there."

"Okay, good. Let's put this cabin in shape and leave."

Emma finished the laundry and replaced the linen in the closet. Webb was wiping down the fridge as she entered the kitchen.

"I think everything in the rest of the house is ready. The bathroom is clean. Hopefully, the realtor renting the place will never guess we stayed here." She glanced around the room, then sat at the table. "Looks good in here. Where's Ivan?"

"Out back on the deck, resting. He pretends he's fine, but I don't think he is as well as he wants us believe."

"Hm—did he tell *you* where the key is?"

"Yeah." He closed the refrigerator and stretched.

"Webb, your hand is bleeding. Don't pull away. You should have taken care of this yesterday. It's becoming infected."

"Only a…"

"A scratch, I know." She smiled. *Men.* "Take a minute. Give me a chance to help. Come in the bathroom."

"Em."

"Webb."

She led the way and, with a groan, he followed.

He grimaced as the warm water flowed over his torn skin.

"Sorry. I'm hurting you, but dirt is still in the wound." She held his hand under the water again.

Stoic, but with a fierce expression spreading across his face, he didn't move.

"Better." She turned off the water and patted the wound with sterile gauze and held his open palm to her cheek. "Thank God you weren't killed."

She looked up and his expression softened, but he said, "Finish. We don't have all day."

After she applied the antibiotic cream and a bandage, he left the room without another word.

I'm such a fool. Did she expect him to stop everything and take her in his arms and kiss her?

Then she remembered he hadn't even told her where the key was located.

***

Tyler unfolded his legs from the cab of the pickup truck and jumped out. Smith had given him twenty-four hours to find the list and kill the men and the girl. He slammed the driver's side door closed. He yanked a phone from his pocket, and glanced at the screen. Yep, this is the right place. Rural, with a small population, maybe that's why Emma Craig had chosen the town as a hiding place. Using her bank card, while undercover, demonstrated she was an amateur, rather than a trained operative. It gave him the opportunity to track her, thanks to Smith's ability to acquire her bank records. His boss had ordered him to kill her. Still, the plan didn't sit any better with him now than it had the first time the man demanded it. But...

In a town with a population under five hundred, there'd be a good chance Emma would be noticed and remembered, making his job easier. He'd try the grocery store and talk to the local folk.

In the store, the conversation settled on the burned car outside of town. No one appeared to have any idea who owned the wreck, but the auto appeared to be a complete loss. No bodies had been found.

He listened hoping for any information related to Ms. Craig. Nada. With a soda and a pack of gum in his hand, he talked to the old woman at the cash register.

"I remember the girl you mean." The lady rang up his sale and gave him his change. "A pretty little thing. I couldn't help noticing her violet eyes and lovely smile. She bought a bunch of first aid stuff and a couple of "pay as you go" cell phones."

"You don't say?"

"Yeah, kind of unusual in these parts. I sell mostly bread, milk and beer, food stuff. Thought I'd be stuck with those damned phones. I told her we sell them all the time." She laughed. "Can I get you anything else?"

"Uh, no thanks, I'm good." He hesitated. "She didn't happen to tell you where she was heading?"

The store clerk startled. "Well, I... not in so many words, but she spent time reading the flyer over there on the wall and called to find out if the cabin was available."

He thanked her and went to read the poster. "Bingo."

After topping up the gas tank of the truck, he drove toward the cabin with the hope he might shoot her quickly and leave. His stomach churned at the thought of killing a "pretty little thing with a lovely smile" as the old lady described Emma Craig.

For the amount of money he'd receive, taking out men was no problem. A chill struck him in the middle of a heat wave. Would he be able to assassinate his first woman, someone who, as far as he understood, had done nothing except be in the wrong place?

He parked the truck and grabbed the high-powered rifle hanging on the gun rack in the back window of the vehicle. He walked the private road and up onto the tree covered ridge overlooking the impressive log cabin. Prone on the ground, he adjusted the scope and scanned the house.

The place looked quiet. Too quiet.

***

Emma peeked out of the backdoor to the deck of the cabin. "Ivan, Webb's gone to town to gas up the car."

Ivan rolled to a sitting position and yawned.

She walked outside to join him. "When he returns, we can go. Are you ready?"

"Da." He stood, favoring his injured shoulder.

"Remember your Hawaiian shirt."

As he reached for it, something struck him in his chest. He dropped to his knees and blood seeped onto his white "surf's up" shirt.

She screamed.

A look of disbelief spread across his face. "Go back, little one." He coughed.

"I'll help you."

"Emma, go!" Another bullet slammed into him. He slumped to the ground and didn't move.

"Ivan!" She dropped to the deck behind the lounge chair, reaching for the Hawaiian shirt as she did. The Russian's blood ran in a stream on the deck near where she lay. Ivan had to be dead. A man couldn't lose so much blood and survive.

No. No. I don't want to believe.

She breathed deeply to calm her racing heart. Fearing the next bullet would be for her, she clutched his shirt and crawled toward the back of the house.

Thank God, she hadn't closed the door. She threw herself through the opening and slammed the backdoor closed, locking it.

Trembling, she fell to the tile floor. A scream clawed at her throat and blinding tears streamed down her face. With a shaky hand, she tried to wipe them away. *Get yourself under control or you'll die too.*

Instead of following to her own advice, she covered her face and rocked back and forth sobbing.

Are you ready to die and let the killer have the link to the key? "Hell no."

She ran to Ivan's bedroom, rummaged through his pack, and found a handgun. Shells were in the chamber. He wouldn't bother to carry an empty gun when he was in danger. Her hand trembled so hard she thought the weapon might discharge when she picked up the revolver.

Holding the barrel pointing down toward the carpet, she glanced out of one the living room windows. If she saw someone approaching, did she have the guts to fire? What if a neighbor came to find out what the shots were about? She might kill an innocent man. "Dear God, I don't want to do this."

What about Webb? When he drove up the driveway, he'd be a sitting target for the killer. She wouldn't let that happen.

She squinted and glanced out of another living room window facing the hill where the shots came from. All was fine as far as she could tell.

What should she do next? Damn, she was a real estate agent, how the hell did she know? No police. She understood that much.

To protect Ivan from being sunburned, she wanted to take a blanket and cover him. What was she thinking? "I've lost it—he's dead." Shuddering, she leaned against the wall, gripping his firearm with both hands.

Before a projectile hit, would she be aware of the bullet and hear it coming to kill her?

Don't cry. Damn you, don't cry.

The back doorknob tuned. When the door didn't open, someone pounded on it.

"Get back. I have a gun," she yelled. "I will shoot you."

Chapter 15

"Emmy, stand back."

With one swift kick from Webb, the cabin's back door flew open and he faced a handgun aimed at his chest.

"Whoa, point that somewhere else."

"Damn. I could have shot you. I didn't believe..." Emma relaxed her grip on the pistol and brought it to her side. "You said to stand back, but I was afraid— afraid it was the shooter."

He took the gun from her shaking hands and set it on a table, then held her in his arms. "It's okay. The sniper's gone. When he realized I had a weapon, the guy headed for his truck and hightailed it out of here."

"Thank God." She continued to tremble as she clung to him.

"Em, where's Ivan?"

"We were on the deck and he—he. Dear God, Ivan's dead." She gulped down a sob. "Someone shot him."

She cried softly against his shoulder.

"Hush, Emmy." Anger surged, but he hid his emotions because it wouldn't help for her to understand he was upset too. He embraced her until she stopped whimpering. "We need to go." Against his desire, he grudgingly released her. "Grab your gear and make sure you don't forget anything."

"We can't leave Ivan out there—alone." She stared to weep again.

He had to calm her before she lost it completely. "Don't worry. I'll take care of him."

If Ivan was dead, it changed everything. He crouched low and made his way to the Russian's body. The man was bathed in blood. Still, he checked Ivan's carotid artery, then shook his head. The assassin had done his job too well.

Anger raged in his veins, and his heart raced. He needed to control his emotions. Everything depended on his cool calculations, if he was to stop the enemy from working against the U.S. He had to carry on and finish the job for the country and for Ivan. His death should mean something.

Could he do that and still protect Emma?

They spent time in the cabin and surrounding deck erasing anything that might identify them. One fingerprint or strand of hair might be enough to send the police on their trail. Of course, he couldn't be positive all evidence had been removed. Still, it was worth a try to keep the local law at bay for a time. When they identified Ivan, the FBI would be brought in on the case and the locals would be taken out of the loop. Meanwhile, he planned to grab the key and be on his way. He prayed the boss would be at their designated meeting place.

After the sun set, he and Emma made their way to the car and drove, without headlights, to the main road. He'd done what he could to protect Ivan's body until the officials arrived. He tried rid himself of the notion he should've done more for the man. The Russian comprehended the risks in the job and made the decision to continue in his chosen career. The realization didn't lessen Webb angry reaction over Ivan's death.

Few cars were on the road at what must be a late hour for the farmers in the small community. As the Volvo rolled down the two-lane highway, he decided to turn right and head toward civilization. With some relief, he realized the nearest big town would provide some anonymity.

Emma didn't speak. Instead, she clung to the ugly shirt that once belonged to Ivan, cradling it as if it somehow kept the man alive.

Finally, she said, "I can't believe Ivan's gone. He was such a big presence. The car feels empty without him." She paused. "I've never felt this way before, but I'd shoot the killer if he were in my sights—dear God, what about Ivan's daughter?"

Webb didn't have a suitable answer, so, he didn't respond.

The miles rolled by and neither spoke again.

Guilt for bringing Emma into this dangerous mission, shook him. Three years ago, he should have ignored her appeal and walked by her. E*nough.*

"I don't often say this to anyone, but I'm sorry, Emmy. I truly am. You're involved in this mess because of me."

"What do we do next?" she asked, ignoring his apology. "We have the shirt with the numbers, but now where do we go?"

He switched on the headlights and increased the car's speed. "When we reach a decent-sized town, I'll stop at a hardware store and buy an Ultra Violet black light so we can read the numbers." He concentrated on taking a sharp turn in the road. "Somewhere on the shirt is a zip code. When we have it, we'll know where to find the key."

"Afterwards?"

"Ivan told me where to locate the key, once I find the building. Not only that, I have a prearranged meeting with my boss to turn over the information. When that's done, I'll receive new orders or be apprised of the situation on the disbanding of the Rapid Advance team. You can go to a secure site. I'll be in touch to explain when the mission is completed and you can go back to your home." He stumbled on the word "your," about to say "our" home. Had Emmy noticed?

"What if the Task Force is already shut down and your boss doesn't show up?"

"They'll be there."

"How can you be sure? Maybe we're doing this for nothing."

"Whether the Advance Team is terminated or not, we'll meet because we both love the country."

"You're sure?"

"Yeah."

"Where is it?"

"Safer if you don't know."

"How would I keep the meet if something happens to you?"

"It won't." For Emma's sake, he tried to sound confident. Truth be told, he didn't understand what he was up against or if the old team existed anymore. And his brother Jon, was he alive or dead like Ivan?

He couldn't deal with the thought, not if he wanted to function. Compartmentalize, he had to keep each part of his life separate and in their own niche, clean and neat. Could he do it? He'd always lived that way, no reason to change at this point. He forced his mind back to the task at hand.

When the night air cooled, he rolled down the window and let the breeze fill the interior of the car. Emma appeared to sleep. At least, her eyes remained closed, but she still gripped Ivan's shirt.

At six in the morning, he parked the vehicle in the lot of a hardware store. After he bought the black light, he'd drive on to find the key. He rubbed his tired eyes and decided to catch an hour of sleep while he waited for the place to open.

***

"How long have I been sleeping?" Emma sat up and looked around the area. "We're in Marin County."

"Yeah, according to the zip code on Ivan's shirt, what we are looking for it here. The mission to be exact." Webb continued on the freeway. "We'll be in the main part of San Rafael soon." A bedroom city for San Francisco, he grumbled as commute traffic slowed their progress.

"It's devastating Ivan isn't here." Emma covered her mouth and her throat tightened as she recalled the dynamic Russian with a quick smile and rapid wit. "Without him the key would have been lost." She blinked away a tear. "Let's get this over with. I want to know what the hell the key is all about."

Living on coffee all night, Webb appeared alert and ready for whatever the day might bring, but her brain wouldn't focus. Two deaths, her friend Karen, and now Ivan, it was too much. She struggled to hold on and remain calm.

How did Webb carry on with this assignment? She'd seen him in pain from his wounds and noticed the shock in his expression when Ivan died, but he kept going. No situation appeared to deter him. Was he devoid of emotion? If true, how had she ever loved him? "Nothing bothers you, does it?"

"Emma, what are you getting at?"

"Show some reaction. Let me see you're as upset as I am. Karen's dead. Ivan's dead. You're untouched by it."

His powerful hands squeezed the steering wheel and his mouth formed a grim line. "What do you want from me?"

"I..."

"Would you prefer I swear and pound my fists at the injustice of it all? Maybe you want me to cry, fall apart and say I can't deal. What good would that do? How would it defend anyone?" He glanced at her and his eyes narrowed.

"I want to understand that you care."

"Care!" He took a deep breath. "What the hell do you think? I'm defending the country, guarding you, and trying not to wonder if my younger brother is dead like Ivan. Yeah, I have feelings, but showing them helps how? You tell me."

"The brother I met in at the hotel, the guy with the piercing blue eyes?"

"Jon," he said, his deep voice raw.

"I didn't realize—I'm sorry."

"I need another cup of coffee." He drove until he saw a coffee shop, got out and slammed the car door.

Embarrassed, she covered her face. Why hadn't she realized he was stressed too? Lost in her own situation, she hadn't given a thought about what Webb might be going through. She wanted to apologize again. Still, it might be better if she didn't say anything—unless he asked a question.

When he returned, he handed her a paper bag. "Eat, you're going to need food." She set it on the seat and didn't bother to check inside. Her stomach would never hold anything down.

"According to Ivan, the key is in a mission called Mission San Rafael Arcángel.

"But where? Some missions have several buildings?"

"He told me enough to locate the key... Damn." He slammed on the brakes as the traffic came to a sudden halt in front of them.

***

In Washington, D.C., Smith answered the phone in his office before his secretary picked it up. "Talk."

"Lancaster and the woman are on the hunt for info. It won't be long now."

"What about the Russian?"

"Dead," Tyler asserted. "I put a tracer on the Volvo. They changed the license plates, but so far they haven't discovered they're being tracked."

"Grab the key. Kill if you have to. At this point, Lancaster's Task Force is finished, so he's on his own."

"And the girl?"

"Do whatever you want with her, but make sure there are no witnesses, no links back to D.C."

"President Nielsen isn't in the White House. He's at Camp David, right?" Tyler asked.

"What's it to you? You planning to visit the man?" Smith asked sarcastically. "Do what's ordered and don't try to go above your paygrade. I'll be in San Francisco waiting to hear from you—don't disappoint me." If Tyler didn't deliver, he'd be obsolete. The search for the key would continue with other men.

Smith glanced at the designer bags sitting next to the office door. The limo would collect him and drive to the airport for the red eye flight back to the west coast. *Damn.* Julie would cry when he left her. His wife cared nothing about his business and demanded a good amount of his time. If she understood they wouldn't attend the gala, she'd throw a temper tantrum and withhold her sexual favors from him. When he'd first married her, the outbursts and pouting turned him on. Too old now, and overburdened with his own concerns, he didn't enjoy her sexual games. Still, needing to be serviced by a man, before long, she might search for a "boy toy." He shrugged, apathetic to the idea.

If all went as planned, she might dress up and flaunt her beauty in front of another president. Later, when things cooled down, after the disaster about to befall the United States. Of course, the top man at the White House would not be the current president.

Once the key was found and put in his hands and the sleeper agents were safe from exposure, the attack on the electrical grid would go as scheduled.

Smith flicked on the TV. President Nielsen smiled on the evening news. Damned near sixty, the man didn't look a day over fifty. Dressed in a jogging outfit and appearing healthier than any male of his age should, he had stopped his morning run to answer reporter's questions. Hostile or softball ones, he maintained his smile. Soon, the president waved and jogged away, two young secret service officers running with him.

"President Nielsen is taking a few days off at Camp David," a reported stated.

Smith didn't understand when the video was taken, but according of his information, the man was now in California. If not, he wouldn't be packed and ready to fly on a midnight flight to San Francisco.

He shut off the television. President Nielsen might look like a movie star, but he wouldn't be reelected. Not after the electrical networks went dark and the stock markets and banks went down, not to mention airports, and traffic signals. Canada's East coast might also be affected, causing a rift between good neighbors.

Afterwards, the president would be run out of Washington, D.C., lucky if he kept his skin, let alone his pension. Smith grinned. As part of the administration, the vice president would be run out too, but the leader of the House of Representatives would have the "go ahead" to calm the situation. An asset of Russia, Leader Johnson would take control without the rest of the legislature understanding his connection to the Kremlin. Johnson would become the President of the United States as per the U.S. Constitution.

Smith contemplated which department he wanted to run when the House Leader became president.

Commerce? State Department? No Home Land Security. He laughed.

***

The small community of San Rafael, population of about fifty-nine thousand, bustled as many of the inhabitants rushed toward the freeway going south. Avoiding the traffic congestion in the main part of town, Webb drove past the mission, his target, and parked a block away from the church.

"Emma, let's go. I need you to be the lookout while I hunt for the key."

She exited the car and followed him. St. Raphael Church with its bell tower and archangel over the main door, sat surrounded by palm trees and a modest rebuilt mission stood off to the side of the main chapel.

"Which building?" She ran to catch up with Webb.

He entered the Saint Raphael Church and walked down the aisle. She stopped to admire the beautiful white chapel with the beige and gold altar and wondered if she should try to cover her head as her mother's friend use to do, when she entered the Catholic church near their home.

Webb called for her to join him. She scanned the room. Observing no other person, she walked down the aisle. "I don't feel right about this. It gives the impression we're stealing."

"Keep your eyes on the door while I check under the pew."

"Webb, wait. What if someone comes in?" Too late he had already disappeared under the bench.

What if the priest appeared? Should she ignore him or maybe ask him to pray for her? Either way, the

Father must not find out Webb might take something from the chapel. Not only to defend the information, but to protect the Padre. He shouldn't be entangled in the intrigue.

Her hands tingled as she stood facing the entry.

"Are you waiting for someone?"

"No. I..." Emma blinked and brought her eyes into focus on an older woman dressed in black, her gray hair pulled into a tight bun.

"My dear, if you are here to pray, the altar is in the other direction. Turn around."

"Yes, ma'am. I..." Emma fidgeted and ran her hand through her tangled hair.

Apparently satisfied with her instructions, the woman walked away as Webb popped up from under the pew and shouted. "Nothing here, Em. Must be..."

"Young man, you are in the house of God. Lower your voice. And what are doing, rolling around on the floor in the Lord's church?"

"Sorry. I lost something over there—I think." He pointed to the seats lined up on the other side of the room.

"Pointing is rude." Shaking her head in what appeared to be disgust, the old woman continued to move toward the altar. Stopping at the pew in front, she genuflected, made the sign of the cross and sat, then bowed her head in prayer.

"Let's get what we came for and leave before anyone else comes," Webb whispered and proceeded to the third bench from the back. Again, he disappeared under the seat and Emma waited, her heart beating faster as time passed.

"Can't loosen the damn thing. I don't want to tear…"

She leaned down to check. His hands appeared too big to reach into the small space where something was taped. "Webb, let me."

"I think…yeah it's coming free," she murmured as a small manila envelope fell into her hands. In her excitement, she sat up and hit her head on the seat bottom and swallowed a curse.

"Em, you all right?"

"Yeah. I can't believe we found it." An outburst of giggles hit her. She tried, but couldn't stop them. *Dear God, I'm becoming hysterical.*

Webb ushered her from the church as she burst into laughter.

"Emmy, calm down."

"I thought the whole thing might be a hoax." She gasped for air. "I…"

"Keep your voice down. Back to the car."

"Ouch."

"What is it? Let me look." He touched the top of her head. "The skin isn't broken, but you're growing a bump here." He gently pressed on the spot.

"Oh."

He took her hand. "I'll stop somewhere and buy ice for you."

"I'm fine. I want to see what's in the envelop."

She expected Webb to open it in the car, instead he said, "Buckle up." The Volvo wagon sped away from the curb. "Be on the lookout for anyone following us."

"Okay—nothing as far as I can tell." She carefully lifted the flap of the envelope.

"You understand we should x-ray and test it for poison before you open the thing."

"I…"

"Never mind. I'm trusting Ivan would've warned us if he thought that would be a problem."

"Dear God, Webb, you sacred me." She held her hand to her rapidly beating heart, then. poured the contents into her lap, a thumb drive and a typed message. "I can't read the note. The language is foreign. Damn, I'd hoped I'd find out what's going on."

"Might be Cyrillic script. Russian, the alphabet contains thirty-three characters, if my limited knowledge is correct. Derived from Ancient Greek."

Webb signaled his intent to turn and drove in the opposite direction.

"You can translate it?"

"Afraid not."

Emma glanced up from the document when the car stopped. "We're back at the church."

"Wait here. I'm going check with the priest and find out if he has the name of someone who reads Russian. I'd rather not involve him, but we need help."

Chapter 15

The Italian priest gave Webb a letter of introduction to Miss Natale O'Donnell, French and Russian language teacher at the local high school.

After two rings of the doorbell, O'Donnell answered the door of her small bungalow on a cul-de-sac near the high school. Webb stepped back when a large boned woman, of undecipherable age, with flashing blue eyes, flaming red hair, yanked open the front door. Two black miniature poodles rushed out, sniffed his hands and barked.

"Chiens, back. Asseyez-vous" They continued to bounce on their back legs, ignoring the command to sit. "Useless mongrels," she said with affection.

"Miss O'Donnell?" he asked making sure the dogs couldn't nibble on his fingertips.

"Yes."

He gave her the note from the Padre. After she read it, she nodded. "Come in."

They entered the immaculate living room decorated in pale blue with the predominant furniture being two red upholstered dog beds sitting near a white brick fireplace.

"Aller se coucher." She smiled as the poodles retired to their beds. "Ice tea anyone?"

"Yes, thank you," Emma spoke for the first time.

Natalie ushered them to a wooden, whitewashed table in the dining area and served tea in tall frosted glasses, then added a plate of biscuits de citron. She explained Father Bianchi had met her when he was a Chaplin in the army and she worked at Landstuhl Regional Medical Center in Germany, many years earlier.

"Thanks for seeing us on short notice. We were in a bit of a fix and turned to Father for help." Emma sat at the table.

"No problem. We, the dogs and I have little to do until school starts in a few weeks." She munched on a biscuit and swallowed. "Anyway, show me the note."

"Before we do, could I borrow your computer? I have a jump drive I need to check." He sat at the head of the table and slid the note toward Natale.

"Of course."

The lap top was booted when she gave it to him. He plugged the drive into the USB port of the old machine.

Emma took a gulp of tea, sighed, and ate a cookie.

In silence, Miss O'Donnell studied the letter.

Webb tried to concentrate on the computer monitor, but kept glancing at Emma staring out of the window, her skin pale and her mouth grim. Exhaustion, or did she now realize the seriousness of their situation and the likelihood of the mission's failure?

To her credit, she didn't complain. Somehow, that caused him more guilt. He needed to shelter her and build a haven where only they could go. The reality was he might not live to see this assignment completed. Whether he survived or not, he'd be damned sure Emma was safe in the end. Easy to say, but could he ensure her existence if he wasn't there? *Stop.* None of his speculation helped their situation.

He opened a file on the jump drive. NERC, The North American Electric Reliability Corporation electrical grid map formed on the page. The mission of the NERC was to secure the reliability of the North American power system.

They oversaw eight regional geographical grids in Canada, Untied States and the Baja California area of Mexico. The Eastern Interconnection reached from Central Canada eastward to the Atlantic coast and south to Florida, then west to the edge of the Rocky Mountains. He ran his finger over the shape of the Eastern grid on the screen. That would cover the seat of the U.S. government and the seat of commerce.

The western connection stretched from the west side of Canada to Baja California and eastward to the Great Plains. The Alaskan gird was self-explanatory.

He ran his hand over the stubble on his jaw as he scanned the map. Eastern and Western and Alaskan networks were marked with a check. Meaning what? It appeared Texas, Mexico and Quebec were unmarked.

The map detailed how each area was connected with a specific geographical region in the US and Canada and Baja. "What the hell?" he said under his breath. If the women heard him, neither reacted.

Why would the connections be important? Unless. He didn't want to think the unthinkable. Still, given the circumstances, was there a choice? What if the three the largest electrical grids in North America shut down at the same time, say on a busy Monday morning? There'd be no traffic controls, no gas pumps, no operating banks. Would air traffic control towers be able to carry on? What about if the grids quit on a Tuesday in November during a major election? Imagine all the afore mentioned disruptions and the voting machines going down at the same time. The blood withdrew from his extremities as he considered the possible consequences. Would NORAD, North American Aerospace Defense Command, crash too?

What to do next if he wanted to stop the plans that might be underway? Where to turn now the Rapid Advance Task Force was shut down, cutting off the links to people in the U.S. government? He had no rank, no top-secret clearance to help him reach the right people in the administration.

He might be wrong, totally off the mark. Should he cry wolf to anyone without real evidence, only a map and an idea of danger?

Emma touched his hand. "Webb, are you all right? You look so fierce."

"Just tired." He gave a reassuring smile. No reason to worry her any further until he had proof.

"After driving for hours, you must be beyond exhausted. I could take the wheel when we leave."

"Yeah," he said noncommittally.

The teacher didn't look up from the letter she was deciphering, but he thought she was listening to their conversation.

Finally, Miss O'Donnell said, "This is the translation." She handed him a hand-written page and the original note. "I've given you my cell phone too, if you need anything else translated, please call first."

She stood. It was a clear signal she had completed her job. It was now time for them to leave her home. Her dogs woke and barked as if to support the idea their welcome was at an end.

He resisted the urge to read her memo. Still, he glanced at the strong cursive writing.

"Thank you, Miss O'Donnell." He folded the papers and walked to the door with Emma at his side.

Out on the cul de sac, he paused. "I don't want to go directly to the car. I'll circle around the block where we parked and make sure no one is watching."

"The man who shot Ivan ran from the cabin and didn't follow us. How would anyone else find us?"

"I don't know, but it never hurts to be careful. That's why we didn't park near Miss O'Donnell's house. She's not involved in this and I want to keep it that way."

Emma's eyes widened and he thought she might say something, but instead, she nodded in agreement.

"I'll be back with the car. Stay here." He hesitated. "If I don't return in an hour take the first bus you see. Doesn't matter where it's going. I want you out of here."

"I won't leave you."

"Emmy, please do what I ask." Before he could think better of it, he hugged her. "I need to be sure you're safe." She tensed at first, then clung to him trembling, her breathing rapid.

His body heated as his need for her grew. "If I don't come back, go to the hotel we saw off Highway 101 north of the city and…"

"Just come back."

"I will." He handed her the jump drive and the letters. "Give these to me when I return."

"Okay." Fear flashed in her eyes. "Be damn sure you come back."

***

Webb rubbed his chin as he walking causally toward the parking space where he left the car. A local resident might not hurry or be too interested in the homes or the vehicles, so he didn't search the area as he headed toward the auto.

Late summer, the sun remained high in the blue. From a distance, the sedan appeared unmolested. Across the street, a middle-aged man swept his sidewalk and didn't glance in his direction. Only a guy doing clean up duties. Right?

Webb squashed the inclination to rush to the car and drive to Emma before she became more anxious. That wouldn't happen until he secured the sedan and could be sure not to lead anyone to her. He had disregarded the anxiety in her expression when he left, but it gnawed at him. How much more could she handle? He shook away the question. *Focus on the job.* If all went as he hoped, the meeting with his boss would take place as planned. Afterward, what?

With a grunt, he dropped to his knees as a blow struck the back of head. He rolled away as a second strike landed but missed its mark. He grabbed the attacker and they stumbled onto a nearby lawn. As they exchanged blows, his fist slammed into the guy's solar plexus. The man slumped and Webb sent a final disabling hit. He rolled the guy over and the man stared wide eyed and opened mouth as if to speak. A bullet struck the stranger between the eyes.

Another bullet whizzed by Webb's ear. He scrambled out of the path of the next shot. Apparently, the gunman used a silencer making it harder for Webb to understand the slug's trajectory. He clambered behind the sedan as another bullet collided with the vehicle. His head aching, he squinted into the sun. If he knew where the shots came from, he might understand if the attack had ended or had only begun.

When he chanced a look, the man sweeping the walkway had vanished. Did he shoot or was he in his home to calling the police? He shouldn't wait to find out, but wished for the opportunity to go through the dead man's pockets. Still, if the jerk was a professional, his pockets would be empty.

Webb unlocked sedan's door. With his head down, he jumped into the driver's seat of the old auto and put the key in the ignition and turned it. Nothing. *Hell.* "Start! Turn over."

A bullet cracked the windshield.

***

How much time had gone by? Emma glanced at the sky as if it could tell her when to leave. Webb said to wait an hour, but she didn't have a way to tell the time. How would she understand when the sixty minutes were up? Damn, she was lost without her cell phone.

She folded the letters and put them in her purse and shoved the flash drive in her pants pocket. It might be safer to keep them separate.

A bus stopped, but she shook her head. The driver shrugged and drove from the curb. How late did the buses run and where did they go? She might end up in San Francisco. If so, she wouldn't dare contact a friend or an associate. Not if she wanted them to continue to live. A memory of her wounded friend, Karen, flared in her mind. Emma shivered in the summer heat.

Sitting in the glass covered bus stop, she held her head in her hands and closed her eyes. Webb might be upset with her, but she wanted to run to the car and find him. With a sigh, she remained seated. She'd follow his instructions.

The sun was setting when she took a bus heading north and found a seat next to a gray-haired woman who moved her packages to let her sit down. Unable to carry on a coherent conversation, Emma smiled but didn't speak and much to her relief, neither did the older woman.

Later, as directed, she registered at the hotel Webb had mentioned and waited in the room, barley noticing the clean but bland décor in tan and beige. She dropped onto the bed, but with her rapid heartbeat and staccato breathing, sleep seemed impossible.

Finally, she walked to the window and stared at the parking lot. *Webb, where are you?*

After a shower, she called room service, then turned on the TV, and watched a cable news report about the president and his wife staying at Camp David. Webb told her the president now resided in the Sonoma Hotel and Spa, three thousand miles from Camp David.

The club sandwiches she ordered sat on the round table near the window. Trying to remain positive, she purchased one for Webb too. Instead of eating, she poured a cup of coffee from the carafe brought by the waiter and drank a sip before adding cream to the strong brew.

If Webb didn't return, she must keep the meeting with his boss. With the decision made, she took a bite of a French fry. It caught in her dry throat. He would come back to her. She wiped moisture from her eyes.

Careful not to get food on the papers, she opened the translation. As a citizen with no government clearance or special right to comprehend the information in the letter, she hesitated. It might be a mistake to read the note. It couldn't make her safer, on the contrary... *If only Webb was available...* "He's not," she whispered into the quiet room. *Since he can't finish the assignment, I have to.* Could she? With no experience in law or espionage, was she fooling herself? If the enemy took out Webb, what chance would she have?

With a deep breath, she began to read.

What did she expect? A road map to a crime or the address of foreign agents? Was that her hope? Disappointed, she folded the translation. Numbers linked names. Russian names and American names all related—how? Joe Smith is Misha Abramov, Joe Jones is Misha Kuzmin, Joe Wilson is Misha Rarin for the men and whether Smith, Jones or Wilson, all the women's first names were Tanya. The females' Russian last names mimicked the men's surnames. All this might be important to Webb, but to her, nothing. Still, better memorize as much as possible, even if she didn't comprehend the importance of it.

Certain she could list the people she took time to eat half of the club sandwich waiting on the table.

To stop the beginning of a headache, she rubbed her forehead, opened the letter again and read the rest of the translation. She had to remember it wasn't her job to decipher or stop whatever might happen, only to remember as much of this as possible, numbers, dates, grids, etc. Well, to be honest, not her role to do anything, but if Webb didn't, couldn't...

He appeared to be right about some of the networks being marked and the numbers on them seemed to link the American names with the grids. Were they the Russians working in the United States undercover? Sleepers?

She recalled Webb's explanation of a sleeper. A Russian or other foreign national opponent put in place in the United States, to work and live as any citizen, maybe for years. They wait for instructions from the Russian FSB or others in the government to act against the country they resided in. A prearranged act of treachery.

She rubbed her eyes and read on, "The various electric utility grids are tied together in normal cooperating conditions at an average of 60Hz." What the hell did that mean? She sold houses for a living the most she understood about electricity was to pay the bill when it arrived and to turn off the lights when she left her home or office.

This whole situation remained way out of her pay grade. She put the paperwork away and slumped into a tan club chair. She needed an aspirin and some sleep. But more than anything, she required Webb.

Please stay safe. I want you. Not for the assignment, but because I love you. She sighed, her petty emotions held no importance to him or to the success of his mission.

***

In the rearview mirror, Webb saw the man who'd killed Ivan. The guy stood staring, revolver in one hand, cell phone in the other. Why didn't he continue shooting? Was it because he wanted to know where his prey was heading?

Webb turned the ignition key, and the old car coughed but didn't start. *Hell.* He tried again and the vintage engine sprang to life. With quick movements, he maneuvered the auto down the hill driving toward town. There had to be a tracer on the sedan. Time to dump the vehicle before the man caught up with him again. The last time he glanced in the mirror, the killer was running to his car, no doubt to tract the vehicle's progress.

After he was out of the man's sight, Webb made a U-turn and drove away from town toward the water in the direction of China Camp. With little traffic on the road at most times, there was none tonight.

A sharp curve in the road would to do the job. The old car had been seen, so he had to get rid of it and believed the tracer wouldn't work under water. He parked near a turn in the road.

For the first time he sensed the burn of the broken skin on his right arm. When the killer shot, a bullet must have grazed him, but with adrenaline pumping in his veins, he didn't realize it until now.

Ignoring the pain, he took out their belongings from the trunk and set them on the shoulder of the road, out of the way of his planned route. With the engine running and the car door open, he entered and put the auto's transmission in drive, pressed on the gas, and jumped out, rolling to the ground with a thud as the sedan plunged off the high bank into the bay water below. He ran to see the vehicle slowly disappear into the dark water.

With a grunt, he picked up the bags and started his long walk back to the city. The mist thickened the atmosphere, and the wind picked up. He shivered with the incoming fog and recalled summer nights in the San Francisco Bay Area could sometimes be as cold as a winter's day.

Shifting the cases to the left hand, he did his best to ignore the worsening pain in his right arm. The drive had seemed to be a quick ride to the high bank road, walking not so much. As the fog darkened the night, he forced his tired body to move faster, even though his muscles complained and his right arm ached in response to the bullet wound.

Was Emmy okay? He wondered if she'd followed his directions. Did she wait at the hotel, safe and secure? *If anything happens to her it will be your fault.* Could he want to carry on without her?

At a gas station he called for a cab to take him to the hotel. The cabby looked reluctant to drive a man in Webb's condition. He must look a sight with his dirty and torn clothes, and his arm bloody. The wad of cash Webb offered for the short ride apparently removed the man's concerns. The guy opened the back door and placed the suit-cases in with him. As the cab whizzed through the night, he leaned back and ignored the sense of foreboding causing his breathing to quicken.

The lobby of the upper middle-class hotel was empty of guests. A uniformed bellman leaned against the far wall, appearing to nap.

Good, not many eyes to track his movements.

The desk clerk recoiled when he stared at his disheveled appearance. No doubt wondering if he should call security. "A bit of an accident, I'm afraid," Webb said in the Queen's English and forced a practiced smile meant to disarm the average person. "I believe my wife has already checked in, Mrs. Emma Craig."

"Of course, Mr. Craig" The clerk's shoulders relaxed. "She told us to expect you."

The man looked about ready to ring for the bellman when Webb said, "I can manage my bags."

"If you prefer, sir." He hesitated, "Do you need a doctor?"

"Thank you, but I'm fine." He made his way to the elevator, and punched the button for the third floor.

In room 308, he set the bags in the closet. The television was on in the plush, well-appointed room. A waft of floral shampoo floated in the air, but Emma was nowhere to be seen.

***

Smith grabbed his carry-on bag and exited the private jet with a nod to the pilot who stood at attention. He stifled a yawn as fatigue seeped into his body. He hated sleeping on airplanes and hadn't manage more than an hour or two on the flight from Washington D.C. to San Francisco.

A limo waited and a suite at the Sonoma Hotel and Spa would give him first class accommodations, thanks to the Speaker of the House of Representatives,

216

even though Speaker Johnson would not be there. Arrangements had been made to have Johnson hard at work in D. C. when chaos struck the U.S.

In the hopes of staving off gridlock in congress, the president, vice president and the head of the senate gathered for a brainstorming session.

Speaker Johnson, from the other party, didn't receive an invitation. Possibility not the best plan as he was the person left in place to become president, in the unlikely event the others were unable to serve.

During the blackout, all staying in the Sonoma hotel would be blamed for the mishandling of the national crisis. A public relations campaign was in the works to make sure the three were held responsible for allowing an attack on the nation's electrical grids. "President Nielsen, the VP, and the Senate Leaders play golf in luxury while the people suffer the worse attack in the country's history," the headlines would read.

He wasn't worried about the military brass being concerned. According to the U.S. Constitution, the Speaker of the House, Johnson would take his rightful place as head of the government, when the others were discredited and forced to resign. The defense department and military would support the rules of ascension to the presidency. Speaker Johnson was in place for a neat, bloodless coup with no one the wiser.

The Sonoma hotel, where Smith had registered, possessed its own electrical backup system, allowing the president and the VIPs to manage in comfort during the early days of the coup. Smith would be able to report the details to his Russian handler, Oleg Volkov.

The average person would be unaware the government had changed. A beautiful plan, appearing to keep the status quo, when in reality nothing would be the same.

***

Before entering the sports bar, in a less than desirable neighborhood in San Francisco, Emma stopped. A chill ran down her back as she took a slow breath. Webb was depending on her. Could she do this?

When she entered, a cheer rose from the men in the room for a homerun, playing out on the huge flat screen. She followed the Giants, but after everything, baseball was the last thing on her mind.

She sat in a back booth with the reserved sign on the table, leaned back against the tufted seat, and tried to appear nonchalant. A young man, wearing a jersey from a local baseball team, stared hopefully but turned away when she shook her head. Somehow, she understood he was not the right guy, too early and no password.

The prearranged meeting should start in fifteen minutes. If only she carried a secure cell phone to text and make sure the meeting was still on. What if no one showed up? What if…

A tall, slim waitress in a body-hugging T-shirt displaying her up-lifted breasts leaned over the table. "What you drinking?"

"Uh. A diet cola."

The young woman spun on her heel and left her to wonder who, in the crowd of mostly men, would contact her with the correct password. She knew it by heart. Didn't she? The code had been on Ivan's shirt for any who understood. She had memorized it, never thinking she'd be here tonight without her husband.

Dear God, she missed him, needed him. And he believed in her enough to trust she'd follow through with his assignment if he couldn't. If not, he wouldn't have given the directions and needed information to carry on if necessary. Now gone without a trace, he might be dead. *No.* Suddenly her cold hands began to tremble. *Don't let him down. Don't forget the details. Don't make a mistake.*

The patrons cheered again, when, on TV, a ballplayer slid onto home plate. The cola was served, and she swallowed a gulp. How long should she wait before the realization no one was coming to meet her sunk in? What then?

The jump drive in her pocket felt warm when she touched it to be sure it was still there. Russian and American names and numbers swirled in her brain. She struggled to remain calm, keep her nerve, and not let fear overtake her good judgement. *Don't leave. Not yet. Hold on.*

The eighth inning was wrapping up and the score was tied. If no contact, the best time to leave was the end of the game with the rest of the people, less noticeable in a crowd.

"818 387 55621," a middle-aged woman said as she slid into the booth and faced her, then adjusted a baseball cap shading her eyes. Her hair was tucked in the hat, making it hard to see, though her voice sounded familiar, Emma didn't recognize her.

Emma gave the needed response to the password and the woman's expression turned grim. "Where's Ethan Lancaster?"

"I don't know." She hesitated, surprised by Webb being referred to by his other name. "He was to meet me at the hotel, but didn't arrive. I hope…" She stifled the emotion crawling up her throat. "I understand the Rapid Advance Task Force has been shut down and you know Ivan is dead."

"Yes, on both accounts. This mission must continue regardless of the current situation." The woman flicked a wayward strand of hair from her eye and smiled.

"I know you. Oh, my God, you're the first lady." She covered her mouth to stop from using the woman's name. "I thought I was meeting Webb's, I mean Ethan's boss."

"You are."

"But…"

"I'm his boss. I can explain later. Now we need to deal with the current information. I need Ethan's help. Do you have a car?"

"I'm afraid not. I…"

"But there is a safe place to stay?"

"Yeah." *For now.*

"Let's get the hell out of here. Use the back door."

Emma followed the middle-aged woman, dressed in a baggy sweatshirt, jeans, and runners, as she briskly walked toward the exit, moving with ease in and out of the crowds now on their feet shouting at the television.

At first glance, no one would guess this person could be the perfectly coiffed and gowned wife of the president of the United States, the same lady who spent her days giving speeches about the importance of funding the national museums and reading to preschool children.

Emma checked to be sure the jump drive was still in her pocket, then ran to catch up with the older woman.

"Lady, the transit bus is a couple of blocks from here. It goes to Marin. We should make the last one for the night." Emma glanced to see if anyone followed. *So far, so good.*

A guy wearing black jeans, a leather jacket and sun glasses, joined them at the bus stop, a guitar case strapped over his shoulder. Ordinarily, she might not have noticed him, but tonight...

With relief, she got on the bus to Marin with President Robert Nielsen's wife, leaving the guitar carrying musician watching as the bus left the curb.

The vehicle had two other passengers. One talked to the driver and the other appeared to sleep. They found seats at the back, away from the other riders. Emma let out a sigh. Soon, they'd be safe in the hotel. And Webb, could she depend on him to be waiting?

"If you don't mind my saying so, you're different. I mean from the lady I see on TV."

"She's not real, only a figment of the public relations engineers who worked for my husband's campaign." She pushed her cap up from her face and Emma saw the clear blue eyes she'd noticed on the flat screen when she watched a speech given by the president's wife.

"After losing his first spouse in childbirth years earlier, Robert wanted to marry again. We were dating under the table you might say. We did our best to keep a low profile. Still, the press got hold of the story and found out I worked as an undercover police officer in New York City." She paused as if remembering the past. "By the time the presidential PR people finished with me, I became a nice lady who worked in New York City Hall, one of the thousands of office workers who toil for the city. The story played better in the polls. Before long, I didn't recognize myself."

Was there a touch of laughter in the woman's voice? Emma turned from the bus window and glanced at the nondescript appearance of a middle-aged white woman, brown hair, blue eyes. "I had no idea."

"You weren't supposed to. Could be what made me a good undercover cop. I appear to be many people. No one looks at me, let alone suspects me of anything, unless I'm made up as the first lady." She adjusted her position in the seat, stared at the driver and glanced back at Emma. "After the news broke that I was engaged to the president, his election committee got hold of me and cleaned me up." She grinned. "New hair style, better clothes. They wanted to change my New York borough accent, but I balked. I was proud, and as it turned out, the way I spoke helped the president carry the state in the election." She paused again. "Don't get me wrong. I love my husband. Unlike some presidents before him, he's honorable, trustworthy, and kind. And nobody loves this country more than he does."

"I'm sure." Emma faltered. "Uh, I admit I didn't vote last year. I meant to, but life was so confused and…"

The lady shrugged as if the excuse wasn't new to her. She patted Emma's hand. "You're helping now. That's what counts."

Heading north, they rode across the Golden Gate Bridge in silence. The summer fog obscured the magnificent view with only enough lights apparent to give an impression of the dazzling city of San Francisco.

The woman broke into her thoughts. "You know the president is Robert Nielsen, but I prefer, Kate to First Lady Kathryn Nielsen."

"Okay. I'm Emma Craig, Ethan's wife."

"Ah." The woman stopped appearing to evaluating the information.

"On the news you're always called Kathryn, never Kate," Emma said.

"My husband's PR man's idea, I never liked it. Too high end for me and the McCarthy household. McCarthy's my maiden name. Katie, Kate or hey you." She laughed. "With eight kids in the family I've learned to answer to anything."

"I wish I had a large family."

"No brothers or sisters?"

"Only me and my mom."

"Well, I'd say a big family has pros and cons. Of course, I wouldn't trade any of my siblings for the world—though they can each be a pain in the ass."

She laughed easily under what must be strained circumstances. Maybe her quick wit helped soften her husband's more serious demeanor. Still, Emma sensed this woman had a core of steel. She was a trained undercover police officer after all.

At the bus depot in San Rafael, they took a cab to the hotel and Emma found the back entrance.

"We're on the third floor," She punched in the code to unlocked backdoor, given to her by the front desk clerk. The latch didn't release. She was about to try again, when a man rushed toward them from the shadows.

Chapter 16

"Don't scream. Webb whispered. "Emma, it's me."

"Dear God, I thought you were dead."

She grabbed him and held on as if he was her life raft. For a split second, he embraced her. *Dammit, he wanted to tighten his hug and never let her go.* No time for dreams. They weren't coming true. He pulled away and dialed in the code to the hotel's back entrance, then stopped.

"Kate!" he said, amazed to see the first lady.

"Ethan."

"Go." He pushed both women through the opening and slammed the door shut. "Let's get to the room. ASAP."

They headed toward the service elevator. He gave the "be quiet" signal, his finger to his lips. No one spoke on the ride to the third floor. There must be cameras and might be microphones as well in the elevator.

Emma stared at him until the doors opened again.

They entered the carpeted hallway and followed the arrows toward room 308. He relaxed when he found the hall empty of other guests.

"Ethan, you look like shit," Kate offered as her way of a hello when they entered the hotel room.

"I bet I do." He smiled and glanced at her sports team sweatshirt. "Guess I'll check and see if our team won. Nice ballcap too."

The Kate grinned, and flicked the rim of the hat as if to say "up yours."

He laughed out loud and she joined him, but given the circumstances, he saw Emma only managed a frown. She wouldn't understand the banter of buddies working on dangerous assignments and their need to keep it light as long as possible. He cringed at the thought of losing a game with real consequences for the whole nation. He considered what might happen if Russian sleeper agents, in living in the U.S., were free to subvert the current government undetected.

Kate glanced up from reading the translated letter. "Webb, you're bleeding on the carpet. What happened to your arm?"

Emma gasped.

"A scrape. I'm going to clean up. Got a band-aid?"

"You know I never travel without a first aid kit." Kate reached into her bag and tossed it to him. "I'll order pots of coffee and food. Looks like a long night."

He caught Em's worried expression. "I'm fine. Really." She wanted more, an explanation about the incident. He wouldn't go there. No point in upsetting her further with the news he'd been grazed by a bullet. Thankful he'd carried the suit-cases from the car and had stowed them in the closet, he grabbed what he needed and went to clean up.

Later, he returned dressed in blue jeans with a long sleeve navy T-shirt. Sitting at the table he ate a burger and fries delivered by room service while he was in the bathroom, then started on a second burger, ignoring the salad he should be eating. He hadn't touched anything green in days.

"When was the last time you had a meal?" The first lady refilled his cup.

"I don't remember." He washed a bite down with black coffee. "Kate, heard anything from my brother, Jon?"

Emma sat near him at the table and leaned forward.

"He's in ICU at a local hospital." Kate sighed. "A hit and run, but it looks like he took a beating too. I don't have a recent status report from the doctors yet." She hesitated. "Since the Task Force shut down, it's hard to obtain quality info. And if I, the president's wife, was found to be interested...I don't want to call attention to Jon and alert whoever tried to kill him, he's still alive."

"Webb, I'm so sorry." Emma reached for his hand and he let her.

"First my father and now my brother in a hit and run *accident*. Not bloody likely." He wanted to strike out at the unknown perpetrator. He'd lost one family member and Ivan had said it was a planned hit. Now his brother? *Too much.* In ordinary circumstances, there'd be a police report and he would be by his kid brother's bedside. Would anything ever return to normal?

"He's registered under an assumed name and is receiving first-rate care. I'll make sure it continues.

Juan is discreetly on guard." Kate interrupted his thoughts. Her smiling demeanor had disappeared and the police officer training showed in her calm but stern voice.

"How many of the team are still working with us?"

"Not as many as I'd like." A frown wrinkled the first lady's usually smooth forehead. "But I needed to be sure I could trust those who asked to stay when the force was dismantled."

"You think someone worked against the team," Webb said more a statement than a question.

"I'm afraid you're right. So, I kept only the core group that was with us from the beginning, you, Jon, Lex, Marty, Juan, Charlie, Alejandro, and Joaquin, field ops, Gilbert our techie, Abby linguistics, Jen my aide."

Damn few team members from a group of two hundred and forty-five. "Good people." He paused. "I'm ready to work."

"I wish I could tell you to rest first, but…"

"No worries, Kate. I wouldn't sleep—I want those assholes."

***

While Kate and Webb huddled over a map of the electrical grids of the United States and Canada, Emma walked to the hotel room window and pulled back the curtain. In the late-night, mist meandered around the parked cars and gave a mysterious glow to the lights in the lot. Funny she'd never noticed it before. Maybe her perception had changed. Living in the Bay Area, heavy drizzle was a way of life, but now it appeared sinister, a cover for those who would do harm to the very fabric of society.

She rubbed her eyes and wished to forget everything and go back to a day before she met Webb and be the young woman with no worries. She had been ignorant of the people who fought to keep the country and the constitution free from attack. Nevertheless, now she was here in the room with the president's wife and Webb. She was useless to both of them. Under today's circumstances, a real estate agent was of no help. Without realizing, she moaned.

"You all right, Em?"

"Yeah, I'm good." Had she convinced him? No matter. It was the best she could manage. She forced a smile, but Webb had returned his attention to the map and the letter spread out on the table. The design of Ivan's Hawaiian shirt was being examined too.

"Are you sure Russians killed Ivan?" She closed the curtains and walked away from the cold glass. "I remember reading about an ex-Russian agent being poked with an umbrella and another had poison put in his tea at a restaurant. Do you remember in the UK, Russian agents put Novi—Novi something, I can't recall the name.

"Novichok," Webb competed the word.

"Yeah. They put it on the door handles of an ex-spy's home. He and his daughter almost died." She sat down at the table. "Attacks, but subtle. Harder to prove than a blast with a weapon like they used on Ivan." She swallowed hard at the memory of the scene at the house in the Sierra mountains. She put her hands under the table and hoped Webb and Kate didn't notice them trembling. The thought of Webb dying in the same manner as Ivan was too much.

"Surprising he used a firearm, if a Russian killed the ex-agent," Kate agreed.

"Why didn't he poison Ivan?"

"Well, Emma, maybe we prevented him from getting close enough." Webb stared at a map of the electrical grids.

"Oh God, I thought we were helping Ivan."

"There are five known nerve agents and they are generally colorless liquids, hard to detect, but they can kill in minutes and are dangerous to the person delivering the poison too," Kate said as if to change the subject. "The ingredients for Novichok are not on the banned list in the international chemical weapon treaties and it's much easier to deliver, with less risk to the courier," she added. "Developed to avoid the chemical the weapons treaty, the agent is absorbed through the skin."

"What is the world coming to?" Emma asked, not expecting an answer.

Webb stood, stretched, and looked at her. "Needless to say, the government has been working on an antidote to lessen and or block the effects. Still, I don't think they thought the real danger to Ivan and others would be so overt as a gun blast to his chest."

They sat in the silent room until Emma asked, "Why would they consider doing something to our electrical grids? That's so blatant."

"Maybe they're tired of waiting for results." He shrugged. "They've tried interfering with U.S. and European elections and worked to break the North American treaties and the EU, not to mention NATO, the North Atlantic Treaty Organization." Webb poured more coffee and gulped what must be cold liquid.

"And now they're in the country to do no good?" Em asked.

"To put it mildly." Webb finished his coffee.

"I need to give this information to the president. He was in a meeting with his staff when I left. They thought I went to bed alone, an occurrence that happens too many nights." Kate lamented, then picked up her bag. "No one will miss me at least for the moment." She paused. "Webb, while you showered, I texted my aide, Jen, to pick me up. She's the only one who has a clue I'm not at the Sonoma hotel." She retrieved two smart phones from her bag. "One for each of you. The rest of the team have phones as well and you're to contact them when needed. The cell phones are as secure as possible, but use them sparingly." She paused. "Webb, you understand what we have planned?"

"Yep."

"If there is a sleeper agent in the government and we don't stop him, I'm afraid the result will be disastrous." She paused as if in deep thought. "There are people in the FBI I can trust to find and stop the sleepers, because thanks to you and Ivan, we have identified how to track the infiltrators."

"Okay."

"Webb."

"Yeah, Kate."

"Before we take the sleepers, we have to find out who in the U.S. is directing them. If it is a person in the United States House, Senate or Executive, I need to know ASAP. They must be disabled before they give the orders to damage the grids." She hesitated. "Don't kill them. Bring them to me or I'll come to you to for the interrogation. As leader of the team, I'm depending on you to find the mole."

He tensed but said, "Got it."

"Emma, I understand you secured a house in the Sierra mountains for the three of you to stay. We are going to need a place here in the Bay Area. Somewhere central for the Rapid Response Task Force to gather."

"Oh?"

"My guess is we won't need it for more than two or three days, maybe a week." She paused. "Can you arrange it, covertly?"

A chill shook Emma as Kate and Webb stared waiting for an answer. "Sure. No worries." Did she sound confident? Hell, she hoped to be able to come through.

"Good." Kate smiled.

Webb walked the first lady to the door. "I'll see you to Jen's car."

"No need. I'll go out the back and it's better if we aren't seen together. I'll text your phone when I'm in Sonoma."

***

Emma kicked off her shoes, slumped into an easy chair and closed her eyes. Aware of Webb's movements in the hotel room, she didn't have the energy to find out what he was doing.

She must have fallen asleep because she woke up in bed. She had a vague recollection of him picking her up. Glancing downward, she was still dressed in street clothes.

The slit in the blackout drapes sent light moving across the comforter to focus on Webb sleeping next to her, on his back with one arm behind his head. Bare to the waist, shadows highlighted the plains of his muscled physique and subtle light danced on his pecks. Asleep, scarred and injured, he still exuded strength. He'd been through so much to help the country. He did his job without fanfare. There'd be no reward, no medals. Few men could summon the courage to do the same.

For two years, she'd hated him for leaving. Now she understood he'd tried to protect her from the cruel danger surrounding him. If only he had taken her into his confidence. She rubbed her temples to release the tension. During the last few days, he'd sounded gruff, but kindness had flashed in his expression. In the dimness of the room, she scanned him once more and desire was ignited.

She wanted to stop the longing for him, but couldn't. Joined by a bond of love, the union between them was unbreakable. She understood he'd tried to cut the connection, but at this moment it appeared that would never happen, at least not for her.

If things were different would he want her too? Should they share a night of lovemaking? There might not be another chance. *Stop*. She turned her back to him. *Get some sleep.*

For too long, she lay awake listening to his slow, steady breathing. Their relationship was finished, but the prospect of him being hurt or killed was devastating. Maybe they should make love one last time. She slipped out of her clothes, lay down again. She inhaled the aroma of hotel soap and man, then put her head on his chest near his heart.

"Emmy." His strong arms gently encircled her.

Her rapid heartbeat made normal breathing almost impossible. She snuggled nearer and relished the contact of his bare skin against hers.

"Take me, Webb."

The gentle flutter of his kiss against her lips surprised her. He sat up on one elbow and scanned her face. "You sure? I can't offer you forever."

"Yeah, one hundred percent."

She leaned back in his arms and let the world spin out of control as sparks overtook her. She held on, moved in unison with him, and called his name as he entered her fully.

***

***

The next morning, after a shower and shampoo, Emma dried her hair and pulled it into a chignon, applied mascara and a touch of lip gloss. A normal business woman stared back at her from the bathroom mirror. Too bad the scared female inside couldn't stop trembling. What if she couldn't find a safe house for the team?

Crawling back into bed with Webb's was more appealing than she wanted to admit. But he showed no special interest in her and no dread of the coming day. Instead, she sensed an eagerness to right the wrongs about to take place. Did she dare disappoint him? *Not going to happen.* She squared her shoulders and ignored the anxiety pulsing in her.

In the bedroom, she stepped into charcoal slacks, a pale pink shirt and a gray blazer. With a long day ahead, she chose black flats, wishing they were runners.

"About ready to go?" Webb asked. "You should eat first."

He pointed to the eggs and toast on the sideboard. His demeanor serious. What did she expect? It wasn't his idea to make love last night. Still, the passion had overwhelmed her and she'd been convinced he cared. Her face heated with embarrassment. *You fool.*

"I want to call my mother." She took in his European cut, gaberdine business suit, white dress shirt, open at the collar. The Italian leather shoes he wore were polished to a shine and completed his look. Damn. He appeared ready to take on the world of finance.

"I'm going to call my mom. She hasn't heard from me since Karen died."

He cringed at her boss's name.

"Go ahead." He turned back to his breakfast.

She sighed and dialed the borrowed phone.

"Hello."

"Mom, it's me."

"Emma, where were you? I called and called."

"I don't have my cell. I'm using a friend's phone." She imagined Mom's reaction if she understood the president's wife had given it to her.

"Why aren't you picking up your messages?"

"Sorry. I've been busy. I…"

"Too busy to talk to your own mother? I saw the TV report about Karen's office being robbed and afterward you disappeared. I panicked. I went to your work and to the house."

"Mom, I should've thought. I… Everything is okay. I'm just, uh—traveling in California, looking for new properties to represent." Guilt. She'd always told her mother the truth. They were a team. Now …What kind of person had she become?

"Emma, I thought we didn't keep secrets from each other."

"We don't. I'm alright and I know you're getting ready for work so I'm going to go, but I'll call in a few days, when I'm home."

"Emma don't hang…"

She disconnected the phone and promised to make it up to her mom when the nightmare was over.

"Ready now?" Webb stared. "Emma what's wrong?"

"Nothing." She sniffed. "I talked to my mother and I couldn't tell her anything and she's so anxious. I feel terrible."

"If you told her everything that's happened, would she believe you?"

Em shrugged.

"The less your mother knows, the safer she is."

"Is she in danger too?" her voice rose in alarm.

"I'm sure your mother's safe."

Emma reached up, pulled Webb to her and rested her head on his chest. "You're sure she'll be okay?"

"Yeah." He kissed her cheek as if she were a kid. "A car is waiting for you in the parking lot."

"How…" She was tempted to ask where he got the vehicle but wasn't sure she wanted the information. She understood Webb kept several license plates in his backpack and they might be quickly changed out. He had demonstrated that. Still, ignorance appeared to be the best policy under these circumstances. He'd explained Kate would do what she could, but calling on government vehicles or officials to help might jeopardize the mission. If a mole infiltrated the upper echelon of the government, the taskforce would ferret it out only if they remained undercover.

***

Emma drove to San Francisco and parked the compact auto near the Palmer Real Estate office. A place where she'd happily worked for two years. Okay, she'd struggled with her finances, but Karen had been a reliable friend and they'd understood each other, enjoyed each other's company. The office had been filled with laughter before…

"If you find a good friend hold on to them," Mom always said. "Real friendship is hard to come by." But because of Emma's connection to Webb, her best friend had died. She slumped against the glass front door and put her head in her hands. She wanted to deny the memory, wished to believe Karen still lived. *Dear God, help me come to grips with the truth, I caused her death.*

Fear rippled down her spine. Did she possess the strength to enter the scene of her friend's demise? Her hand shook as she turned the key to open the office door. "The danger is over," she whispered. Webb killed the assassin who'd attacked Karen. Still, the image of the murderer, prone on the floor, plagued her.

Earlier, the police had checked the building and discovered no reason to stop the business from opening again.

Webb is depending on you to find a safe place for the team to stay. To do it, she needed her boss' files. If Karen used a cloud it would be easy to access them remotely, but the woman preferred her filing system and an old desktop computer.

Rational thought told Emma nothing in the office would hurt her. With trepidation, she pushed forward and entered. An eerie silence filled the room. Dust covered the furniture, the smell of stale coffee permeated the air, and a negative vibration pervaded the room. She shivered. With steel determination, she yanked on the blinds and opened the window to let fresh air and sunlight fill the darkened space. What was it they said about sunlight? Slowly, the air returned to normal and so did her labored breathing.

Standing alone in the room, she hoped the phone would ring with Karen on the line. Her boss offering to meet her for lunch at their favorite Italian restaurant down the street. *Stop.*

She glanced at Karen's desk and whimpered. A name tag and coffee cup waited for her friend to arrive. So often her boss, a type "A" personality, had breezed through the front door with a grin on her face and a declaration it was going to be a wonderful day. Emma swallowed a sob. She should remove the items belonging to Karen, but it seemed too soon to cast out the remnants of her best friend's existence.

It's too much. I can't do this. She considered leaving. *No.* She sat at Karen's desk and booted the desktop computer, then jumped when the office phone rang. Automatically, she answered it and assured the caller the office would be open in a couple of weeks. *Think positive.* She scheduled an appointment to meet a new client in a few weeks. Karen worked hard to brand the name of Palmer Reality on the landscape. Emma wanted it to continue and would do whatever she could to carry on under the Palmer banner.

She froze. *Assuming you live that long.*

The office must be cleaned and all signs of the horrible event removed before the office reopened. The police investigation, included officers fingerprinting the place and traces of their work remained on the desks, doors and windows. For now, she refused to think about the storage room and back hallway, where the violence had taken place. Still, in order to print the addresses of the possible safe houses, she had to retrieve printer paper from the back room.

With a shiver, she flipped on the light switch in the storage room and tried to ignore the dry blood stains left on the floor. She stifled a gag, and grabbed a reem of paper. On the way out of the room, her foot kicked something and it slid in front of her, a flash drive. It must have fallen from Karen's jacket when she was attacked. She picked it up, ran back to the office, and tossed it into her bag.

She punched the keyboard of the old desktop, hitting it harder than necessary and opened a file with the addresses of the homes her boss managed. Many appeared to be owned by wealthy executives who either traveled worldwide and or had several properties and lived in them periodically.

Webb suggested the safe house be large enough to accommodate several of the Rapid Advance Team at the same time. A building on high ground with a clear view of the area, to observe anyone approaching. Not to mention, a back entrance not too hard to defend and a possible escape from the place, if required.

How long would they need it? *No idea.* Better select a home with the possibility of staying for some time and one not employing a live-in caretaker. She printed the addresses of several possibilities and opened the small safe holding the keys and codes to the alarm systems of the various properties she'd chosen and locked the safe again.

As she turned off the computer, the backdoor opened and slammed closed.

Gruff voices argued as they entered. The men must believe the office was empty. She tried, but couldn't understand what they were saying.

Unable to get to the front exit before they saw her, she grabbed her bag, crawled under the desk, and pulled Karen's large chair in front of her. Scrunching into a ball, she slowed her breathing.

What did they want? What would they do if found her?

Chapter 17

In an SUV swiped from a "long term" lot at the international airport, Webb parked at a busy shopping mall out of the security camera's range and changed the license plate. Afterward, he drove within the speed limit toward the hospital trauma center in San Francisco, hoping his brother, Jon, would be allowed visitors.

He exhaled. Concern for Emma gnawed at him. Last night, he'd weakened and made love to her. Damn. He should have been stronger. Vulnerable, scared, and out of her league, she needed reassurance. Why hadn't he found a way to help her without—without... He loved her, always would. He couldn't deny it any longer.

It didn't matter. The relationship was finished. What could he offer her now? "Nothing," he answered out loud as if to emphasize the truth. "Walk away and leave her with a chance for a relationship with another man." *One who might give her stability, safety, children, and a future.*

Two years ago, he'd disappeared to let her start a new life and intended they'd never meet again. Why had he returned to the cabin and an opportunity for an unplanned encounter? Needing a safe place to stay to recover from his wounds, he might have found somewhere else. Had he unconsciously wanted to meet Emma once more?

He grunted. No time for stupid contemplation. It altered nothing in either of their lives.

***

On the second floor of the medical center, Webb glanced at the miniscule camera on the wall across from his brother's room. The average person wouldn't notice it, but to the trained eye… Of course, he hoped another camera would be nearby.

When he opened the door, a petite brunette, dressed in workout clothes of maroon and pink, smiled. She obviously expected him, though they hadn't talked to each other for months.

"Hey, Marty, good you're here, long time no see. I expected Juan." He gave her a quick hug. Some might think she'd make a poor bodyguard, but on the contrary, the gymnast, black belt, and judo expert also carried a thirty-eight, a small pistol, but lethal in her hands.

"Thanks for coming."

"Juan is taking a lunchbreak. I do the night shift but—don't worry, Jon is covered twenty- four seven, Ethan, or is it Webb now?"

He shrugged. "I answer to both. Thank you, it means a lot you're here."

"All for one and one for all. Right?" She grinned.

"Yep."

"Jon's sleeping, but I know he wants to talk to you. I'll be outside in the hall if you need me." The door closed noiselessly behind her.

In the darkened room, his brother lay in the bed, pale and thinner than the last time Webb had seen him, an IV drip connected to his hand.

"Hey, Webb," he said, his voice stronger than expected.

"Jon." He wanted to hug his kid brother. He remembered their usual greeting. He'd grab his brother's arm and pull him into a hug and slap his back—not today. "You've got one hell of a shiner," he said lightly.

"You should see the other guy." Jon laughed, then grimaced. "Can you raise the bed, Webb? I need to change my position."

"Sure." Too many days had been spent in hospitals as a visitor and a patient. He found the button to lift the head of the bed without a problem. "How's that."

"Good."

"Want some water?"

"I'm fine."

"Jon, what the hell happened to you. Did you recognize the car?"

"Didn't have a chance. I was struck from behind. I hit the pavement, they kicked the shit out of me, and I don't remember anything else. I must have blacked out."

"Shit!" Webb walked to the window and glanced out. "It's too much like Dad's 'so called' accident."

"Webb listen," Jon ignored his statement. "I stayed at the Sonoma hotel with the president and our stepdad and others. Even the vice president is there." He tried to sit up in the bed.

"Take it easy, Bro."

"Funny the VP was at the hotel because it was agreed, for the safety of the nation, the president and vice president wouldn't travel together or be in the same place at the same time." Jon hesitated. "I'll take something to drink now."

He poured a glass of water from carafe on the bedside table. "Here."

Jon swallowed and grunted. "You're aware the Speaker of the House is from the other political party. The whole government's focus would change if both the president and the vice president were unable to serve."

Digesting his brother's words, Webb sat in a chair and ran his hand over his chin. "You're predicting something is about to happen but not at the electrical grids? Could the story of the grids going down be a red herring?" Webb spoke more to himself than to his brother.

Jon took another sip of water and leaned back in the bed.

"I find the idea hard to accept." He paused. "Jon, are you saying the grids are safe?"

"No way. What do think would happen if the electrical grids went down at the same time the current president, vice president, and White House employees were all slaughtered, leaving the Speaker of the House in control?"

"The hell you say."

"It's only a theory, Webb."

"A damn chilling one. I want the first lady and any spouses of the cabinet members out of harm's way. Jon, think the Secret Service will cooperate?"

"Unless I miss my guess, Kate will make it happen."

"Good."

His brother held his side and closed his eyes. "Webb, watch your back. I have the sense you're next on the list of people to be taken out of commission."

"Don't worry. Get well. I'm locating a safe house. There will be a place for you when you're ready."

"Thanks."

"No hurry. Take the time you need to recover."

Jon wouldn't let on, but Webb could easily determine that with cracked ribs, a broken leg and a concussion, the guy was in severe pain. The doctors moved him out of ICU, but now, according to the medical staff, they waited for possible internal bleeding.

"Catch some rest, bro. I'll stay in touch."

"Will do."

Webb stood outside the door of his brother's hospital room and leaned against the wall. Rage against the men who'd tried to kill his brother sent his hands into fist.

***

Squeezed into the tight space under Karen's desk at the Palmer real estate office, Emma held her breathe as one of the men walked toward her hiding place.

"You sure he dropped the flash drive in here?" A man sat on the corner of the desk.

She pressed her mouth closed, to prevent a gasp.

"Yeah," the other guy said. "I told him to leave it with me, but he didn't listen and went to grab the girl, whatever her name is."

"Craig, Emma Craig. We'll find her as soon as we locate the drive."

They want me! She'd believed the hunters wanted her husband and Ivan. She'd only been innocently caught in their web.

She trembled, listening to the sound of drawers opening and closing and furniture being moved.

"It won't be hidden. It must have fallen out of his jacket somewhere at the back of the office. Did you search the storage room?"

"I glanced in…"

"Check again. I'm going to scope out the hallway."

The man near her grunted and the desk moved as he stood.

As his footsteps moved away, she peeked out. The front door wasn't too far. Could she get out before they realized she was there? She grabbed her shoulder bag and slid out from her hiding place. Her leg muscles cramped after being in one position for so long. So, she hobbled to the glass door, and pulled it open.

"Hey!"

She glanced backward and recognized the guy who shot Ivan. Her heart pounded in her ears. Would he use a gun on her too? Tripping over the threshold, she dropped to her knees, scrambled to a standing position, and ran. Terrified, she sprinted to the Italian restaurant she and Karen used to frequent and ran into the open doorway.

Busy as usual, customers crowded in line and the aroma of pizza, and wine filled the air. She worked her way to the front of the queue of people waiting to be seated, then turned to find out if the killer had come into the eatery after her. Out of the large window, she saw the assassin had followed her but appeared to have lost her. He stood on the sidewalk scanning the street, his body tense and his expression grim.

She turned to the maître d', "Hi."

"Hi, Emma, are you and Karen going to need a table today?" He smiled.

"Uh, no, thanks. Can I use the back exit?"

The stocky, dark-haired host appeared confused for a moment. "Okay, sure. Why not?"

"Thank you." She rushed toward the kitchen, found her way around the sous-chef and other kitchen workers, then went out the back door.

In the alley, she snatched a deep breath as she tracked the narrow street. Which way to go? Was it safe to walk to the car? Could someone be watching?

Her once safe neighborhood was now dangerous. The sooner she left the better. She removed her jacket, unpinned her hair, let it fall free and hoped the change of appearance would be enough to fool the men hunting her.

Circling the block, she entered the street where the car was parked. Relief flooded her. No one appeared interested in the compact, of course, no way to be sure.

On the busy sidewalk, fear crawled down her spine as she forced an unhurried walk to the auto. *Run before they kill you.* Afraid any fast movement would attract attention, she continued her slow pace to the sedan.

***

By the time Emma pulled up to the front of the first possible safe house, she could barely breathe. Fear robbed her of oxygen. The need to hide the compact car from the men chasing her overrode all else. She punched in the code for the automatic garage door opener, and drummed her fingers on the steering wheel waiting for the door to open.

She glanced in the rear mirror as she drove into the three-car garage. The street appeared devoid of traffic, but she remained anxious until the door closed. The small compact was sandwiched between an Italian sports car and a German sedan.

She leaned back in the seat and forced her shoulders to relax for the first time since running from the office. Safe, she didn't want to leave her car. Silly, but her need to hide in place intensified as she remembered the duties that must be performed this afternoon. She'd never thought of herself as a coward, or a heroine either, an ordinary person, danger hadn't been a concern.

How did Webb wake up every morning with the understanding he might be killed doing his job? Ivan had been murdered. Webb put up with being shot at and his brother nearly died after a beating. Yet everyday her husband rushed to do his obligation, clear headed and eager to find the men who were interfering with the United States Government.

No matter how small her part, it would be completed.

In a few hours, Webb expected a report on a safe house. If this place didn't meet the agreed upon criteria, maybe the next or another one or… She opened the auto's door, careful not to touch the huge sedan parked next to her car and got out. She dialed in the code to stop the alarm system long enough to allow her to enter the building through the mud room.

In the expansive kitchen of white marble and stainless steel, Emma shivered, not from the cold because she'd checked the heat, a perfect seventy degrees. Fear there would be no safe haven caused her trembling.

The mansion, with its many bedrooms and rec, media and family rooms and eight bathrooms, would do.

She should have known it wouldn't be so easy to find what they needed in the first home. When she glanced out of the back window of the living room, there was no quick exit. No road. Instead, the small backyard led to a dead end and a sheer outcropping of serpentine rock. Should the team be overrun from the front, they would literally have their backs against the wall and nowhere to go.

With a groan, she returned to the garage but didn't have the nerve to drive the compact again. What if the men looking for her saw the car? San Francisco wasn't a huge city. Not like LA where one might live for years and never accidentally bump into a friend, but in the city...

There was no way she'd drive the rare Italian sports car. If something happened to it, she might sell everything she owned and even then, wouldn't have enough to replace the antique. The vintage black four door sedan looked more manageable.

"It's not a burglary," she said, though there was no one to hear. "I'm borrowing it. I'll bring it back." *Dear God, theft goes against everything I was taught.*

In a position of trust, she'd not once considered breaking her promise to take care and diligence with her customers property—until now. Today, she would steal a car. No matter how she wanted to frame the situation it was robbery. Okay, there might be extenuating excuses. It didn't matter.

Circumstance and the need to fulfill her promise to Webb and the first lady forced the decision. Thankful the key was in the ignition, she punched the code to open the garage door, and fired the German sedan's engine.

***

On Billy Goat Hill in the Glen Park area of San Francisco, Webb surveyed the city, looking out and down toward Noe Valley and the surrounds. He had to admit amazement at the beauty at this angle and surprise at the growth in the city, nary an empty lot available.

In need of quiet to clear his head and make plans, he'd taken BART to the Church Street station and walked up the hills of residential streets to reach the steep park. As per usual when he visited the place, it appeared empty, except for a young mother, her baby, and a border collie. The dog demanded the woman play with the tennis ball he carried in his mouth.

Upon Webb's arrival, she nodded and said, "Time for lunch kids," speaking to the baby and her dog, but her wary brown eyes were on him.

It was sad how afraid people in the country had become. Still, she didn't have a reason to trust him. Being so isolated, he agreed with her decision to run from a stranger who might do her or the baby harm.

He had liked watching a family enjoying the city park. Too bad she couldn't understand they were safe with him. Cross-legged, he took the lotus position and did his best to free his mind of the current assignment, Emma, the Russians, the Task Force.

A quiet mind would free his subconscious, and he might find a needed solution to their situation.

Emma.

Don't think of her. He ran his hand over his face. In other tough missions, relaxing his mind and focusing on the task was not a problem. The team depended on him to develop an action plan as he always did. His wife wasn't involved in the other jobs. Now she might get hurt and he'd be powerless to prevent that from happening. He admitted the truth. In his mind, Emma would always be his partner.

However, so concerned about her safety, she screwed up his ability to keep his attention on the assignment. He wanted to be with her, wanted to caress her, protect her. With a groan, he stood and watched as the fog came over Diamond Heights.

Plan or no, he had to touch base with the first lady.

His cell phone signaled a text.

"Anything?" Signed, "K."

"I'll text u." What could he say to Kate? I got zip, zero, nothing. The Russians are winning.

Emma, contact me. I can't think until I'm sure you're all right. He jogged down the trail heading toward civilization.

If something happened to her, he'd deserve the blame for sending her out alone.

Chapter 18

Several hours after viewing the first house, and several others, Emma began to think the list of homes should be increased if a safe place was going to be found. Her feet hurt and her stomach growled. No time to rest and eat if she planned to report to Webb soon.

She entered the sixth home, a three-story Victorian so sought after in San Francisco. This one sat on a large lot and had been completely remodeled without losing any of the original features. It now offered new a kitchen, state of the art heating, cooling, plumbing, and had been wired to meet any high-tech requirements.

The building appeared big enough and could be defended from the front and the back with a quick exit if required. A three-car garage sat on a lot next to the house. The mansion fit all their needs.

She wanted to call Webb. With all her heart, she desired to hear his voice and be sure he was safe—No. He had enough to deal with. She texted his number and left the address of the safe house and hoped the cell phones were as safe as the first lady thought. Next, Emma sent a message to Kate.

After the horrific event in the mountain cabin, she was pleased alarm system worked in the Victorian home. She memorized the code before leaving to visit a nearby grocery store. Her backpack adjusted, she jogged toward the shop spotted on the drive to the house.

An elderly female walked toward her, an obedient golden retriever at her heel. The dog wagged its tail.

"Hello." The woman stopped.

"Hi." Emma replied. "What's your dog's name?"

"Hugo."

"Hi, puppy."

"How did you know he's a young dog?" The older lady smiled. "Most are fooled because he's so big."

"I always wanted a golden. I studied them when I was a kid."

"New in the neighborhood?" the lady asked.

"How long have *you* lived in the area?" Emma countered, testing to see if she'd been followed by the old woman or if this person did reside in the area.

"Well, it must be thirty years now. The gray and blue house on the corner. Everyone calls me the neighborhood snoop." She laughed. "Well, I've been here so long I understand where all the people belong." She paused. "We don't often get strangers on our street. You're the first in a long time."

"Really?"

"Oh yes. Most people moved in years ago." She dropped the dog's leash and gave a silent command for the animal to sit.

Hugo nudged Emma's hand and she rubbed his ear. "I'm only staying for a short time. Visiting."

"Hope the Painted Lady isn't part of the online rental market. What's the name of the company?"

"No," Emma reassured her. "A few of us are in the city for a meeting and the owners are allowing us to stay in the home as they're not in town. Nothing rowdy, won't be any parties."

The neighbor grinned and relaxed. "Well, you picked a wonderful time of year. Though you'll be working, it's warm and not too much fog."

"Nice to hear. Well, I'm off to shop for dinner. Good talking with you."

"You too, dear."

Hugo wagged his tail.

The mansion was being watched, but thank goodness it was by a friendly neighbor and her retriever.

***

Near the dinner hour, Emma completed the homemade red sauce, and stood at the sink cleaning greens for the salad.

Men from the Rapid Advance Team slowly trickled into the home one at a time. Each with the correct password given to them. She found herself surrounded by men head and shoulders taller than she was. Whether in their twenties or thirties, each man appeared to be in amazing physical condition. To her surprise, Charlie was a female, tall, slim, and of undetermined age.

Juan, a charming man, a little shorter than the other men, with black hair and a dazzling smile, mentioned he had worked undercover as a kitchen worker. He offered to help her while the rest of the group set up a perimeter to protect the house.

She tried to force her mind away from any thought of Webb. Forty minutes after the others arrived, still no Webb. She'd promised not to worry about him but gave that up.

Images of Ivan, dead on the patio in the mountain cabin, accosted her. *Please don't let it happen to Webb.*

"Hey buddy, about time," someone shouted from the other room.

She spun around and sagged against the counter in relief as Webb entered the kitchen. If they'd been alone, she might have rushed into his arms, but...

Their eyes caught and held. Raw emotion flashed in his expression.

Frozen, she continued to stare to confirm he was there and all right.

"Hi," she said, her voice husky even to her ears.

He moved closer scanning her, but he said, "Hey, glad you all could make it."

Suddenly, the team surrounded him asking questions.

Still looking in her eyes, he squeezed her hand, then left the room with his team.

***

About to leave the New York penthouse on Park Avenue, Oleg Volkov stared out of the living room window to the darkening skyline. He loved this view, one of the reasons he bought the place, not to mention a fast way to launder some of his funds.

He took a drag on a Cuban cigar and let the smoke spiral out into the newly decorated room. His wife never let him have a stogie in the house, but she lived in Russia, so he might as well smoke too much and eat too much in the luxury of the multimillion-dollar home. He stretched and glanced at the start of a protruding stomach. The result of many decadent meals in U.S. capitalistic restaurants. Last week at his thirty sixth's birthday party, he'd considered exercising more often in the private gym located on the first floor of the condo. He grunted, took another puff on his cigar and stubbed it out. Tomorrow, the exercise regime would begin.

He waited to receive a text from the Kremlin confirming his plans, then he'd move toward a quick conclusion. No word from Smith yet. Weak, sniveling, and inefficient, the guy was becoming a liability. If he didn't hear from him today, he'd make an end run around the old man and go straight to Tyler to finish the job.

The concierge buzzed him. The realtor was there to check out the place and give him an idea of the value on the current market.

He waved his hand in the air to decrease the smell of smoke in the living room. черт! Shit! If she didn't like the odor of expensive cigars, the woman could take her tight rear end out of his place and find another penthouse to sell.

Most of his stocks and bonds had been turned into cash and now sat in a Cypriot bank. This sale would be the last. He hoped to unload the real estate before he left the country for good, but if not, the realtor would send the money to prearranged account.

He made a quick call to Tyler. The old man, Smith, was about to be history and his young wife, Julie, the delectable bitch, would become a widow.

With Smith dead, there'd be no link to him. Disrupting the electrical grids and thereby upsetting the American way of life was only the beginning of the quiet war against the United States.

With the current administration in the White House blamed for not protecting the grid, the Kremlin would be pleased. The election of Nielsen was without Russian interference, unlike the last time. Still, the new president would soon be implicated in destroying the electrical grids for money. Not true of course, but the fake trail would lead to Nielsen's doorstep and devastate his reputation and those of the people working for him.

The only possible glitch, Ethan Lancaster, aka Webb Craig. Years ago, Oleg's father worked as an undercover Russian agent in the UK. Webb's father had discovered the truth and had killed him when he tried to escape.

Take out the family, including the kids, unless you want the offspring looking for vengeance when they grow up. Oleg understood, because payback had been the driving force in his life since he was a teenager and his papa was murdered.

Soon, Webb and Jon would die. So would Emma in case she carried a child who'd seek revenge later. But before Webb expired, he must be made aware his family was next and he couldn't prevent it. Oleg smiled satisfied at the thought.

The maid had packed his bags and the rest of his belongings were being shipped back to Russia. He would fly to California, wreak havoc on his enemy and then on to Mexico and beyond. Only a matter of time before the plans... the doorbell rang, breaking into his thoughts. He shook his head. Time to welcome the real estate agent.

***

In the safe house, Emma startled when her bedroom door began to open. She pulled up the covers to her chin. "Who's there?"

She fumbled to find the bedside light. No luck. "Who is it?" Her heart beat erratically.

Chapter 19

"**Webb?**" She blinked at the dim light coming from the hallway.

"Sorry to wake you, Emma."

"I wasn't asleep." She took a deep breath to slow her rapidly beating heart.

"The bedrooms are full, so I'll bunk in here with you—if you don't mind."

"No problem." She sat up, thankful she wore a tank top and panties to bed.

He could sleep on the sofa in the family room and they both understood that truth.

After entering, he stripped off his windbreaker, kicked off his shoes, and stepped out of his jeans, leaving his boxers and a long-sleeved T-shirt.

"Webb, I…" She hesitated not wishing to add to his difficulties.

"What's up? Your voice sounds worried."

Did he know her so well? She thought he ignored her and her emotions most of the time, but…

"Might as well tell me, Emmy." He sat on the bed and leaned back against the padded headboard in a relaxed posture.

She wasn't fooled by his nonchalant behavior. His fierce expression gave him away. Even in the shadowed light, she could see it.

"Emma, you going to tell me what's wrong?"

"I'm fine. You have enough to do with the team. I'm good."

"I never mentioned how pleased everyone is with this house you found for us. One of the guys called it posh. We don't often hear that word in relation to the places we stay."

She understood him too. He wanted to set her at ease. Then he'd insist she give in and answer his question, just as he'd done during their marriage. "Thanks, Webb, but…"

"Come on." He ran his hands through his hair and stifled a yawn. "Let it out, so I can evaluate the situation. I don't have time to cajole you."

Unable to stifle the next yawn, he covered his mouth, then rubbed his eyes. "Look, give me a break. Any information you can add to what we've already found out might help us in our efforts."

"The office was a mistake, but I needed to find a house." She hesitated. "Karen handled the rentals. I went there to look at her files. I…"

"Are you crazy? Didn't you realize the place is being staked out in case you came back?" He flicked on the bedside lamp and paced the room.

"I shouldn't have told you."

"I thought you were safe and…"

"Karen didn't use a cloud. Webb, I thought you'd understand. You don't use them either. I had to access her records and find a rental home. I assumed you'd be pleased."

"I am, but not if you've put yourself in danger."

"You're the only one who's allowed to do that. Right, Webb?"

"Dammit. I'm trained to handle things." He sat down on the of the bed again. "You're not."

Only the creeks of the old mansion to broke the night's silence.

Finally, he said, "You going to spit it out, Emma?"

"I've never been so frightened." She described what happened in the real estate office. "When the man sat on the desk, I shook so hard I was sure he'd find me." She hesitated. "Even when Ivan died, no one seemed to be interested in me. These men said *I* had to die. Why? What did I do? I don't get it."

A shocked expression spread across his face. "It's not you."

His right hand fisted as his features turned grim. "You're no threat to the electrical grid operation. No threat to a foreign agent." He rubbed his stubbled chin. "Why kill you? Somehow, they've linked you with me, and that puts you in danger."

Appearing to be deep in thought, he gave no reassurance she'd be safe, no hugs or words of encouragement. As she stared at his narrowed eyes, she shivered.

"I guess this is payback to hurt me."

"Webb, I'd say it's going to hurt me more than you. Sometimes you're a cold bastard."

"Oh, damn, I didn't mean…"

"Yeah. Whatever. I'm not important. Who cares about a realtor?" She moved to the far side of the bed. "I'm going to sleep."

"Emmy, really, I didn't…"

"Go to sleep, Webb." Fat chance of her doing that with him lying next to her. Not to mention anger toward the unknown men who wanted to kill her, sending the realization she had no control over what was about to happen.

"I hope you believe me. I don't want anything bad to happen to you, Em." He turned off the light and leaned against a king size pillow. "I made a mistake marrying you. Now, I'm trying to protect you. Please promise you won't take any more chances."

"Webb, I want my life back. Do that and I'll never need to see you again." She turned her back to him. *Liar.* More than existence, she wanted his love and to live with him, have the normal life the marriage vows promised. The scream rose inside of her. Damn him for making her love him.

"Em, did you see the men?"

"One of them." She rolled on to her back, securing the covers tightly around her.

"And you didn't recognize him?"

She closed her eyes and forced her mind to view the images of the incident. "I—I can't be sure. He wore a dark hooded sweatshirt, the hood covering his hair. Still, I had the impression it was the same man who ran us off the road and killed Ivan." Though she tried not to, she trembled and stopped talking to prevent her voice from shaking.

"Emmy." He reached for her.

"Don't." She pulled away.

"Okay. I get the message."

Was that pain in his voice? What did he expect, a wifely hug or more?

"The thugs' orders must have changed. This time he wants you as well Ivan and me. Promise you'll stay here where it's safe." He took a slow breath. "Things are coming to a head. The FBI is on the hunt to locate the men mentioned in the translated letter. Until the sleepers and others involved are caught, we need to be hyperalert."

"But these men were in my office searching for something. They were pissed at the man who died there. The one you killed," her voice cracked. "The guy had something important and they needed it. A thing he shouldn't have had."

"They didn't say what it could be?" Webb rolled to his side facing her.

"Just that it had to be found or they'd be in deep shit." She faced him and felt the heat from his body so close to hers. Earlier, he had reached for her. She could to the same. His arm could hold her and take away the coldness coursing in her veins. If she'd offer herself, he might take her. But it would be sex, not love. He'd made it clear there was no affection between them, only a mission that must to be completed and his responsibility to keep her safe until it was over. She sighed.

"You okay?"

"Yeah. But how does finding the thing they lost have anything to do with us?"

"I don't have a clue."

***

Dawn's light came through the curtains in the French antique furnished bedroom. Exhausted, but unable to sleep, Emma sat up. Webb moved in his sleep, and she thought he might wake. Instead, he

263

changed his position, covered his closed eyes with his arm, and continued to snooze.

Not ready to face him again, she relaxed. Every time they talked it ended in a disagreement and she was reminded how little he cared for her. It shouldn't matter anymore, but...

She shook her head to dislodge the painful memories of their past together. If only she thought of him as an associate rather than a husband.

What *was* on the flash drive she'd found on the floor of the real estate office yesterday? She'd forgotten the drive until this morning. Now in the quiet of the bedroom, an idea came to her. What if the drive she'd picked up had something to do with the men chasing her, not Karen?

Where did she leave her purse? Downstairs? Rubbing her eyes, she glanced around the bedroom. She couldn't believe, she'd been so stupid as to leave the bag unattended, but...

She slid from under the covers and reached for her clothes. A shower would be nice. Maybe after she found the flash drive and opened the files. Her suitcase sat at the end of the bed and she pulled out fresh underwear, black leggings and a baby blue sweatshirt. She stood and slipped the shirt over her head.

"Where do you think you're going?" Webb's deep voice startled her.

"I thought you were asleep."

"No."

"I'm going to the kitchen. I didn't eat much last night." Why did she lie? She'd always been proud of telling the truth. It'd be easy to mention the flash drive. If it was important, she shouldn't have treated the thing so carelessly and she didn't want to remind him she'd gone to the office, when he'd told her to stay away.

"You can eat later. I want to show you a few defensive moves. I don't want you left vulnerable like you were yesterday."

"But I…"

"There's a gym in the basement. I'll see you there in five minutes. Don't eat until after we workout." He walked into the connected bathroom and slammed the door.

Her first reaction was to say, no way. Still, she was beginning to understand when he worried about her it came out as anger. Why couldn't he say what he felt? Stupid question. Did men ever express their feelings?

She sat on an upholstered bench at the end of the bed and put on her runners. Damn, he was right. She needed a few moves to defend against the men who wanted to kill her. No point in wondering why they wanted to hurt her. They did.

Ignoring her growling stomach, she walked out of the room and headed toward the gym.

Chapter 20

Webb showered in two minutes, towel dried and yanked on his jogging sweats. He shouldn't be so rough on Emma. He stepped into his cross-trainers. If he were honest, he did it to keep from feeling too close to her. No one else bothered him like she did.

He could be strong against the toughest and nastiest people, but her kindness undid him. Her caring behavior and concern for others... *Shit.* He needed to focus on helping her stay alive.

When she had a few defensive moves, he'd be relieved of the nagging guilt for involving her in this mess. Afterward, he and the team would follow the strategies to stop the men planning to destroy the western grid. The FBI would handle the eastern grid.

The gym in the old house was surprisingly well equipped with state-of-the-art equipment.

"Chilly in here." Emma turned and stared at him.

"Exercise will fix that." He kicked off his shoes.

She did the same. "Wow, look at all the stuff. It must have cost a fortune."

Webb, shrugged. "We won't bother with the exercise equipment. All we need are the mats. Sit down for a minute."

She sat cross-legged on the thick exercise mat.

"Okay. Let's start from the beginning. First, try not to put yourself in a dangerous place, like a dark street, a parking lot, or your office."

"Really." She glared at him. "I didn't need to worry until..."

"You met me," he finished her sentence. "Let's not go into who put you in jeopardy." There it was again, his pang of guilt. "Just concentrate on keeping yourself safe in any situation." He sat across from her. "Did you ever take defense classes?"

"No. I belonged to the swim team in high school and college and I studied gymnastics, but no contact sports."

He rubbed his chin and noticed how cute she looked, like a kid with big eyes. *Focus on the job.* "There are several rules for a women's safety. Pay attention to your surroundings. Look strangers in the eye. Never talk or text on your phone when you're walking. Rules you know. Right?" Without waiting for an answer, he continued, "Follow your intuition. Bet you never thought I'd tell you that. But it's true. If you think something is wrong or someone is following you, believe."

"Webb, you're right. I wouldn't expect you to think of a woman's intuition. Men always make fun of such things."

He ignored her statement. "Beware of any stranger who asks you something, directions or whatever. Bad guys play on a woman's good manners. If asked a question, females will stop and try to answer. If she's asked for help, she will do her best to aid someone. It overrides their own survival instincts and prevents them from seeing the person asking as an enemy."

Her expression told him she wanted to contradict him, but instead, she nodded.

"Keep your car's remote with you at all times, even at your bedside at night. Set off the alarm if you hear someone in the house."

Her eyes widened, but she didn't respond.

"When you're out, don't let strangers stand too close. Keep them farther than arm's length. A man's arm. If they do manage to move closer, your elbow is one of the strongest points of your body. Use it to protect yourself." He hesitated. "The last thing you want is to be knocked to the ground, but if you are, kick free. Might be a good idea to wear a sturdy boot."

"I don't think I own any. I…"

"The weakest points on a man's body are his eyes, throat, groin and knees," he continued. "Don't bother hitting the chest or stomach. If you're grabbed, strike out for the eyes, most men will protect their groin, expecting a woman to go there."

He swallowed hard at the thought of Emma being manhandled by a thug again. "Carry keys in between your finger when you're out. If attacked, go for the eyes with them."

Emma whined. "I don't want to…I can't think about this."

"You have to." He turned from her, not wanting to see the shock and fear in her expression. "Let's practice."

Without waiting for her to agree, he helped her stand.

She leaned against him and he let her. He considered kissing her to reassure her everything would be okay. He didn't.

"Webb, I understand you're trying to help me, but I don't believe I can do what you want me to." She trembled and her breath quickened. "Violence is against everything I've ever—I grew up learning to help people."

"Even those who want to kill you?"

She pulled out of his embrace and stared at him. "Okay. You made your point. What do you want me to do?"

"Hit me."

She looked angry enough to do it. Instead, she glanced down at the floor. He was about to speak, when she slapped him hard in the face. Open handed, but it was still a solid wallop.

"Good one." He grinned. She would fight back. "Now if you had keys between your fingers…"

"I admit it felt good to hit you."

"Well, maybe I deserved a slap. Do it again." This time he grabbed her arm and twisted it gently behind her.

She gasped.

"Em, don't be surprised if they strike back. They won't be kind because you're a woman. Surprise is your best friend. The first move you make might be your greatest chance to get out of the situation."

With her arm still behind her, he took her to the ground. She kicked him harder than he expected and crawled away. "Good." He coughed. "Let's go again."

It was important she became used to the feel of someone trying to push her around. "If the opportunity arises, yank and twist the groin as hard as you can, then kick him in the knee if he's still standing. You want time to run away, nothing else. You don't need to win the battle, just jog to safety."

He grabbed her once more and she fought back. He took her to the floor again.

Later, after continuing to practice, they were both breathing hard. Still, she smiled at him. "Maybe I'm stronger than I thought."

"Yeah." He rubbed his face and grinned. A bruise might be forming, but she'd learned to fight back. Whether she was more powerful or not, he understood self-confidence was vital because a person's carriage depended on a sense of well-being. A tracker often selected the woman when she looked weak or lacked confidence. "Always look the man in the eye. That could put off an attack long enough to run away."

From the bag he brought with him, he took out two bottles of water and handed one to her.

She brushed hair out of her face and took a swig.

"Emmy, when you're in a parking lot, wait until you're close to your car to unlock it. A thug might target you in a lot." He took a gulp of water. "If a van is parked on the driver's side of your car, go in on the passenger's side. Or better yet, leave. Go where there are people, a shop or restaurant, and call for help."

"Right." She shivered. "Webb, I didn't want to do this, but…"

He thought she was about to say thanks, but she stopped short.

"Em, let's get out of here and find breakfast."

On the way out of the door, she turned and elbowed him hard. He fell to the floor and she ran up the stairs.

He laughed and rubbed his rib. Maybe she would remember the importance of surprise after all. His laughter was cut short.

God, he hoped she would survive this situation he'd put her in.

***

Emma's purse sat on the entry hall table, just where she always put her bag when she was at home. Stupid with a house full of strangers, no matter how trustworthy they might be. Maybe one of them looked inside. She grabbed her handbag and felt for the flash drive in a small zipper pocket. Curling her finger around the drive, she let out a sigh of relief.

"Come on, let's eat breakfast." Webb came up beside her and took her arm.

She started to say she didn't want to eat, but thought better of it. She'd declared her hunger earlier this morning. The flash drive would wait.

In the kitchen, the sideboard was laden with scrambled eggs, ham, toast, bagels and cream cheese. A bowl of colorful fruit and hot oatmeal sat there too. Two coffee pots and mugs had been placed on the table and the room filled with the aroma of Italian roast beans.

She grabbed a plate, and took ham, eggs, toast, and fresh cut fruit. At the table, she set her purse on the floor next to her chair and smiled at the woman sitting near her. "Quite a spread." She nodded toward the food.

"We take turns cooking, when we're on assignment. Lex does a mean breakfast. I'm Abby, by the way."

"Emma." Glad to find another woman among the male team members, she offered her hand to the twenty something female.

The woman shook it. "Hi."

Webb joined them, his plate piled high with everything except the oatmeal. "Hey, Abby."

"Hey." She smiled, before concentrating on eating her eggs.

Members of the team filled the room, talking to each other as if they were family.

So, Webb didn't need a marriage. He had the Task Force and they appeared to be enough for him, with no commitment to be home at night or divulge where he was going and when he might be back.

Emma finished the food on her plate, sat back and listened to the others converse as she sipped her coffee. After sitting long enough to not cause suspicion, she snatched her purse and headed for the den and the laptop she'd seen in the room.

If Webb noticed her departure, he didn't react—thank goodness.

In the small room, lined with white washed knotty pine walls and leather furniture, the computer sat on a mahogany desk. Had one of the team members used the laptop and left only to eat breakfast? How soon would they return?

She hurried to put the flash drive in the USB port, praying it hadn't been encrypted. If the files belonged to Karen, the records would be about real estate, but if someone else owned it...

The drive came on and several files were listed. Some documents appeared to be in the Cyrillic alphabet. This did not belong to Karen. Some were in

English. She opened an English one entitled Smith, Hubert.

At first, she didn't realize what she read. But it appeared to be a list of his debt owed to a Russian bank. Did Russian banks do business in the United States? And who was Hubert Smith? Did it matter? To pay his debt, he appeared to be doing some kind of work for the foreign bank.

She shrugged and clicked on a Cyrillic file. Clueless, nevertheless she looked at the meaningless words. Ivan Popov, the name written in English, jumped out at her. What did this report say about the man she saw killed in front of her eyes? She gulped back a sob and pushed down the images of Ivan dead on the deck of the house in the Sierra Nevada mountains. Chilled, she closed the report.

The next file had a readable name as well, but she didn't recognize male's surname.

"What do you have?"

She jumped at the sound of Webb's voice. Her cheeks heated. She should have told him about the flash drive. "I— this was on the floor of my office. I thought it belonged to Karen, but now I think this is what the men in the office tried to find. I didn't understand until now."

He leaned down and stared at the screen.

Webb, I found a file with Ivan's name. I can't read Russian, but I saw his name."

"Let's check."

She opened the file and stood so he could sit at the desk. "Do you read Russian?"

"I get by, but Abby is the one we need to check this out. She's our linguist."

"I found another name in a file, somebody named, Oleg Volkov.

"You're sure of the name?" he demanded.

"I—I think so." She stood back from him, surprised by his ferocity.

"Emmy, I didn't mean to be so intense. The man has a history with my family." His voice was softer, but his eyes remained fierce.

"Oh." She wanted to ask how but decided to wait.

He opened the file and sat staring at the screen.

"How does any of this help with the team?"

"I don't know if it does. Still, any new info is good and maybe we'll find something that will work for us." He stood. "If you don't mind, I'm going to let Abby glance at these. If there is anything helpful, she'll dig it out."

"Okay." She hesitated. "What does Volkov have to do with your family?" None of her business, still, she wanted to know.

"My father killed his father." His cold voice sent a shiver through her.

"Murdered him."

"The man was a spy sent to assassinate a diplomat in the UK, much the way Ivan was killed in the U.S. My dad stopped him. Later, father was run over by a hit and run driver."

"I remember. I'm so sorry," she whispered.

He ignored her statement, "Let's tell Abby about this flash drive."

***

The rest of the day, Webb and the team stayed in the family room, plotting the next move for each of them. She wanted to help, but what could she do? She had no special skills useful to them. Her best bet, stay out of the way.

After a shower and a change of clothes, she watched the cable news and half expected the reporters to mention the president in California. Nothing. According to the newscaster, the man still resided at Camp David taking a well-deserved vacation. Of course, she believed he and the first lady were in a resort in the Sonoma wine country. The vice president was with them and from her point of view, it was more a planning session than a holiday. Still, that was a need to know, seemed the public didn't need to.

The weather was hotter than usual. She listened to a debate on climate change and a discussion on the California fire season, but not a word about the electrical grids and their vulnerability.

She turned off the cable news and went online to check the real estate ads in the local area. If life ever went back to normal, she'd have to make a living again. Yet try as she might, she couldn't focus on anything but what was going on in the other room. Were they planning their move to protect the grids and arrest the men ready to attack the electrical system?

An image of Ivan's dead body flashed in her memory. But this time the form was Webb's.

There was a knock on the door and Emma glanced up to see the first lady enter the room, dressed casually but in high fashion. A pant suit of the finest imported wool in a dove gray, a red silk blouse underneath the tailored jacket, a string of pearls at her neck, she appeared to be a woman of importance.

"Kate." She stood to greet her and was surprised to receive a hug from the woman.

"Emma, how are you doing?"

"I'm fine, fine," she said too quickly.

If Kate understood her fib, she didn't let on. "We took a break in the planning session. I wanted to say "hi" before we start again.

"I didn't realize you were here. Do you want coffee or something?"

"I'm good."

An awkward silence filled the room as Emma strained to think of something to say. She'd believed Kate was her friend when they were at the hotel, but today the realization of the difference in their stations was clear. She swallowed hard.

"Sit down, Em. This isn't a formal visit. I want to tell you what's going to happen in the next little while. After what you've been through, you deserve some consideration."

"Thank you."

"By the way, the flash drive you found is proving to be a godsend. If everything is true, we have the name and address of the ring leader of the group involved in the plan to destroy the grids." Kate sat down next to her. "Along with the information from Ivan Popov, the plot to harm the nation is becoming clear."

"Can the team stop them?"

"We think so. Without this evidence, the attack on the country's electrical system could've been a total surprise."

"Oh God. What about the other names mentioned on the drive?"

"The Russian surnames will be a little easier to track down. The name of Smith is too common, but we'll start with those in federal government, congress and the administration and work our way outward. Abby's checking, be nice if you could give her a hand."

"I'd be happy to." She might be of some use after all, searching for info on Smith while Abby looked into the Russian names.

"You and Abby will remain at the house while the rest of the team leave to watch the western grid. If all goes as planned, the foreign agents will be taken fast with the public none the wiser. I'm keeping the president informed. This might be over sooner than later."

"I hope so." She wanted to ask about Webb and the danger to him. "Kate…"

"What is it?"

"Nothing."

"You're worried about Webb."

"Selfish of me, Kate, with so many more pressing issues. But I…" Her voice dwindled into silence.

"No need to explain to me. Every time the president goes out in public, whether he's to give a speech or visit a disaster area, I worry. He has Secret Service agents and they are the best, but I still pray he remains safe while he's out."

"Oh Kate."

"Don't worry. I knew what I was doing when I married the president. You didn't have the same option. You thought of Webb as a business man. Right or wrong, he let you."

"But this mission, will it be dangerous? I mean are they taking weapons?

"The team is always armed, Emma. However, the goal is to take out the infiltrators without incident. That's why catching them unawares is so important. One of our team is scouting the grid and identifying the culprits. Tomorrow the rest of the team will go to take out the Russians. Of course, this is on a need to know."

"Thank you for telling me."

"Emma, don't be fooled into thinking you know Webb. I'm not sure anyone does. Not even his brother." Kate paused. "No one is better at his job. Still, he's lived so long under the radar, I doubt *he* understands who he is. He's learned to be a chameleon, changing as necessary to do the assignment no matter what it is."

"You're saying he's a different personality to each person he interacts with. Nothing left of the man I thought I married?"

"I'm sorry to say so, but yeah. That's about the truth of it. Men like Webb, who live undercover, are invaluable to the U.S. government. They give us intel we couldn't find any other way, but understand, Em, after the years of lies, danger and killing, they lose their souls."

"No."

"Don't get me wrong. I care about him. And the country would be in trouble without him." She hesitated. "But he's not a guy a woman can depend on. His job comes before his personal life. Everything he does is a game. He's a phantom. The man you met is not real."

"I don't believe you."

"All he lives for is the assignment and the next and the next and... Let him go. Move on—save your own soul, Emma."

"He is my husband."

"The man you married doesn't exist. He didn't even give you his name. Did he?"

"No, but—I don't want to hear this."

"I'm telling you because I like you. You're young and deserve a better life. Find a teacher, a CPA, or a grocery clerk. It doesn't matter as long as he's honest and comes home every night."

"Am I interrupting?" A grey-haired woman stuck her head in the doorway.

"Jen, come in. Emma, this is my personal assistant and friend, Jenifer Jones."

"Sorry to bother you, Kate," Jen said. "We must leave if you're going to reach the donor cocktail party on time. People are waiting to offer money to the president's electoral campaign."

"I hate campaigning." Kate glanced at Emma and wrinkled her nose. "I'll be right there, Jen."

Appearing to understand it was her cue to depart, her assistant closed the door quietly behind her.

Kate reached for Emma's hand and squeezed it. "Your man lives in a dangerous web. You got caught in it while he was on a job in San Francisco. For your own good, think of yourself as collateral damage. Get out while you still can."

Before she could answer, Kate was gone.

Emma dropped to the sofa trembling.

Chapter 21

Dinner was over and the sun was about to set when Webb found Emma sitting alone on the back patio facing the dwindling light. The expected fog of San Francisco was held at bay by the summer winds from the valley.

"Warm tonight, unusual for this time of year."

She glanced at him but made no response. During supper, he'd sensed something had changed in their relationship. At the table, she'd avoided eye contact and sat far enough away to make it difficult for him to talk to her without everyone else hearing what he said.

"You okay, Emma?"

"Why wouldn't I be?"

Since his return, her life had become chaotic. She couldn't go home. Her best friend had been murdered before her eyes as was Ivan. It was all his fault. No wonder she wouldn't answer him. He rubbed his temple to slow a growing headache.

"Look, we need to talk." He sat next to her on the wicker loveseat and leaned in her direction. "Will you give me a chance?" He didn't want to think this might be his last opportunity to be with her. Even if he survived the mission, they had no future. How he felt about her didn't make a damned bit of difference.

Their partnership was over. He understood the reason. It was best for her.

"Emmy."

"Don't say that. You called me Emmy when we made love on our wedding night. I don't ever want hear you use it again."

She started to leave and he caught her arm. "Wait."

"What do you want from me, Webb, Ethan, whatever your name is? I've done everything I can to help. There's no more I can give you. Let me be."

"You're right..." He stopped before saying Emmy. "I'll leave you after the assignment is finished and it's safe for you to go home." He hesitated. "I want to clear up a few details between us before tomorrow. Will you listen?"

She yanked her arm from his grip, but sat down again.

"I regret misleading you about my situation when we married. Nothing I can do now," he muttered. "You want a fresh start and to go back to your maiden name. I get it. I'll sign divorce papers when you want them."

Her eyes flashed and a stunned expression spread across her face. At that moment, he was reminded of her beauty. No wonder she'd caught his attention years ago. He couldn't offer her a decent quality of life or keep the vows he freely gave. Until now, he never considered she'd been denied the truth when she declared "I do." back then.

"It's only fair to release you from your vow. I trapped you into this marriage."

281

One of the team peeked out of the backdoor. "Oh, I didn't know anyone was outside." The man quickly closed the door, leaving them alone once more.

"In case of my death, my estate, bank accounts, stocks and the other things I've accumulated, go to you," Webb continued.

"What are you saying?" she asked her voice alarmed.

"Everything will be yours."

"Is the assignment so dangerous? I thought Kate said there shouldn't be a problem."

"Em, I…"

"Webb, I don't want your money." She looked ready to run into the house, so, he touched her hand. "I believe you, but let me leave something to repair the damage I've caused in your life."

He took her face in his hand, surprised to find tears ready to fall from her beautiful eyes. "With the team's plan, things should go like clockwork," he said, weakly. He released her without the kiss he longed to steal from her pouting lips. "The arrangements for my assets is only a precaution."

Silence.

The sun dipped toward the horizon turning the sky a brilliant orange. Sitting with his wife enjoying the final light of the day seemed right. How foolish to think he might be allowed a future free of dread.

"You wouldn't fib about the hazards of the job?"

In the dimming light, her eyes beseeched him to tell the truth.

"This is a routine assignment, like any other." Good, his voice sounded more positive this time. No need for her to be informed of the reality. Tomorrow might be the last day on earth for someone on the team. He prayed he was wrong, but... "No fibs, Emma. Assignments can turn bad, but not this one, if all goes to plan."

"I'm holding you to your word, Webb. You better come back safe or I'm going to be so pissed at you." She sniffed and wiped a tear from her cheek.

"No worries." He slipped his arm around her shoulder and let her head rest on his chest. As the sun disappeared, he contemplated how dark his world would soon be without her.

***

Hubert Smith stretched and smiled as the waiter served him a cocktail at a poolside table of the Sonoma Hotel and Spa. Though in the evening, he breathed in the hot dry air, pleasant after the humidity of the east coast. He sipped a martini, his second. Later, he'd enjoy a late-night dinner in the dining room—might as well take advantage of someone else's dime.

Upon his arrival, the hotel had a room waiting for him. Though not in the same wing as the president and vice president, his room still met five-star requirements. Room service appeared to be outstanding and there looked to be no limit to the amount of food and drink available.

How easily he'd grown accustomed to the extravagance. If his God-fearing mother could see him now, she'd be sure he'd burn in hell for enjoying such luxury. All good men toiled at hard labor to remember they came from the earth, ashes to ashes, dust to dust.

Smith sat up and thought of the mission. A normal man might be apprehensive, not he. After completing the job, he'd be free of the debt strangling him and richer than he'd dreamed possible. Relaxed, he took another sip of his drink and waited for the text with orders from Oleg Volkov.

All he had to do was take out the current leaders. Until then, Smith would schmooze with them under the pretense of being a large campaign donor.

With a smile he nodded to the other guests sitting around the pool.

***

Late at night, Emma stared at the coffered ceiling of the bedroom. Webb wasn't coming to bed with her. Cold, she pulled up the comforter and touched the empty spot where he'd slept the night before. The need to curl up in his arms and feel his strength overwhelmed her good sense. Her desire surged.

Go to sleep.

Hours had passed since she and Webb talked on the patio. She ought to be pleased to settle their relationship. He offered a way out of her current mess and a road back to a single life. She should be thrilled to end this dangerous and chaotic existence. Of course, she wouldn't be the carefree person she used to be. Her world view now changed, gone was the cheerful young woman who believed the best in people. Today, the realization of evil in her midst plagued her.

Would Webb be preparing to leave with the team to take the grid into their hands and protect it from attack, preventing the electrical system from falling under foreign agent control? Kate had done her best to make the work sound easy. In the quiet of the night, Emma didn't buy Kate's story.

Her friend's statements about Webb played in her head: soulless, untrustworthy, undependable for a woman who wanted a reliable relationship, she'd be better off without him. Best to walk away while she could. Her head understood. Her heart wouldn't listen.

"Dear God, give me strength to do the right thing," she whispered into the darkness. "And please keep Webb and the team safe."

***

In the den the next morning the air was warm, but the atmosphere cold and tense with Emma unable to shake her foreboding. Abby assured her all seemed to be going as expected. The team had departed in the middle of the night to secure the electrical grid.

Still, Emma's mood continued to sour. She wanted to leave the house and do something proactive. What? She sighed and her heart pounded. Webb had told her to stay in the mansion after her close call yesterday in the real estate office. The men chasing her might force her to divulge the location of the safe house.

"Abby, how long do the assignments usually take?"

"Can't say." She glanced from her computer screen to respond to Emma. "Each job is different."

In her twenties, and dressed in jeans and a man's gray shirt hanging loosely on her bone thin frame, Abby pushed brown bangs from her hazel eyes, the rest of her hair cut close to the scalp in a military style. "I've learned to be patient."

"Yeah? Not my strong suit." She paced the room, then dropped into a club chair. Maybe she might do something useful. "Kate mentioned you were tracking the names in the flash drive I found. You speak Russian?"

"My expertise is linguistics," Abby answered. "By the way, the flash drive you found is a treasure trove of info on the Russian sleepers, their names, dates of birth and even their mobile phone number not to mention the connection to the GRU."

"I've heard of FSB, but I don't think I've come across the GRB."

"It's Russian military intelligence. Known for their department of cyber warfare."

"No! Are these people here in the United States?

"Yep, North America. Over three hundred people named so far."

Stunned, Emma stood looking out the window of the pleasant mansion in the peaceful city. What if they hadn't found the flash drive? She shuddered at the thought.

Abby returned her attention to the computer monitor.

"I don't mean to interrupt you, but thought I might help. Uh, I don't speak Russian, but Kate mentioned needing someone to check out the name of Smith, H J."

Abby grunted, but said, "Guess you could look up the names on social media. You good with that?"

"I'm okay."

The house phone rang, startling Emma. Though it jangled her already tense nerves, there was no reason to answer as the phone belonged to the owner of the mansion and had nothing to do with the Task Force.

"Hey," Abby caught her attention. "I'm going for a mug of coffee and a sweet roll. Afterward, I'll pull up the Smith names for you." "You might grab something to eat and drink. Going to be a long day."

Emma hadn't realized she was hungry until she smelled the aroma of toast and coffee in the kitchen. After eating eggs, toast, and drinking a strong cup of coffee, she returned to the den.

She booted her tablet and waited for Abby to give her the file with the Smith names.

"You know the funny thing about my search for the agents?" Abby said as she looked for the needed file. "I find information on many of the Russian men listed," she continued, "including Ivan Popov and his daughter but nothing for Oleg Volkov. You met Ivan, didn't you?"

"Yeah." Her throat tightened with a sob.

Abby appeared to understand it was a touchy subject and changed it. "Here it is." She downloaded the info to a new jump drive and handed it to Emma. "Search the obvious social media sites and any other places you can think of."

"Will do."

The hours disappeared in silence, except for the click of their keyboards. Though Smith was a common name, she hadn't thought there would be so many.

"What if he was employed by a peripheral company linked somehow to the U.S.? Do we have a list of government contractors?"

"Somewhere." Abby stretched and yawned.

"Did you sleep last night?"

"Not long enough," the woman answered and stifled another yawn.

Webb probably didn't get much sleep last night. How was he faring? She hoped no news was in fact good news.

The new list of names included not only individuals but companies, pages of them. She rubbed her eyes, the strain of staring at the screen taking its toll.

"I'm going to grab lunch. How about you?" Abby asked.

"No, I'm good."

A few minutes later Abby returned with a tray piled with several sandwiches, fresh fruit, almonds, and donuts. "Might as well munch while we work." She smiled and downed two cheese sandwiches and a donut.

How did the she stay so thin?

"You sure you don't want a bite of food?"

"Maybe in a little while." Emma returned to the search for Mr. Smith, forcing her thoughts from Webb and his situation.

***

The assignment started in the middle of the night, east coast time. The FBI picked up the Russian infiltrators working on the eastern grid. No problem. This am, if the day went as planned, the western grid would be secured as well.

Tension clawed at Webb's back. Sweat dripped down his neck into his shirt. *Going to be hot as hell today.* He hoped the nine-millimeter pistol, strapped under his left arm, wouldn't be needed.

With his SUV and the team van parked on the road, he nodded to his men and they entered the yard of the single-story home situated on the multiacre property. A good choice for the foreign agents, isolated enough for them to be able to come and go without drawing too much attention from the locals.

The agents had the wherewithal to keep a pit bull patrolling the yard. However, a sleeping dart took care of the animal. The mutt would wake in a couple of hours with a terrible headache.

The dawn would be breaking soon and the team needed to capture the Russians before they woke up. Unfortunately, it might be difficult to be sure everyone they wanted slept in the house last night. If one of them got away... He'd worry later. Right now, he needed to capture this group. By tonight, the assignment should be complete. Afterward, he'd consider his future, assuming he survived the day. *Stop. Nothing's going wrong.*

To keep the noise level down, the team wouldn't use flashbang grenades when entering the home. The best result would be to round up the guys without alerting the neighbors. The fewer people who understood the mission the better. The last thing he needed would be a local reporter or a neighbor with a cellphone taking a video.

"Hold your positions," he whispered to the men near him and used a hand signal to the others to do the same. One member crawled on his stomach dragging plastic tubing and a metal cylinder behind him. Another man did the same in another part of the home. As planned, they placed the tubing into the air vents, and pumped gas into the house.

Webb glanced at his watch, counting the minutes until they could safely enter the house. With a nod, he signaled the team to put on their gas masks and enter, front and back.

The sound of a truck's engine broke the silence as an imported pickup flew out of the opening garage door. Webb jumped out of the vehicle's path and rolled to the side of the driveway. *Shit.*

He waved at the team to continue into the house, ran to start the SUV, to take after the truck. The men would put the other conspirators in the van while he tracked down the person fleeing.

The imported truck appeared big but sleek. In most cases, the type of pickup had no more than six cylinders, but who knew what lay under the hood of this one?

The roads were clear of traffic in the early morning, and they drove without concern for speed limits.

The truck had pulled out first, but Webb lost no time in catching up with the vehicle. To his surprise, the passenger window opened and someone leaned out and fired at him. He swerved to dodge the bullets flying in his direction. He dropped back but stayed close enough to keep them in view. The two-lane road twisted and he lost sight of the vehicle and was forced to speed up again.

The night retreated and dawn's light increased. Commuters would be on the road soon. Better end this chase ASAP. He wanted to capture the men alive but wasn't interested in taking a bullet He punched the gas pedal, flooring it, and rammed the back of the pickup as bullets shattered his windshield. The truck lurched forward but didn't reduce speed.

His grip on the steering wheel tightened as the road curved and the SUV slid close to the shoulder of the road. Easy to lose control on these narrow lanes, but if the truck wouldn't slow down, he had no choice but to speed up. He could try to pass the truck on the inside and pull to a stop in front of them forcing the pickup to stop or run off the road.

A bullet grazed his cheek and he felt warm blood dripping down his face to meet the sweat already there. *Damn.* He swerved again. When the road started downward, he demanded the vehicle give all the power it could muster and took the engine to red line to pull in front and force the truck to a stop or go over the embankment.

He moved forward and blocked their way as a spray of bullets peppered the car. Metal screeched as the truck hit the SUV's back door. Pain seared Webb. He grimaced and held on as the autos, slid toward the embankment.

The passenger in the truck didn't wear a seat belt because when the cars slammed into each other he was thrown through the windshield, his scream piercing the morning air.

***

"Something's wrong," Emma shouted. Quickly turning to face Abby, she knocked a cup of coffee off the desk and it shattered, splashing hot liquid on her. She jumped up and tried to brush the coffee from her pants.

Abby ran to help, grabbing a box of tissues and wiping the floor. "Did you find something?"

"No, not in the files. Webb's in trouble."

Chapter 22

In the den, Abby stood up from the floor after cleaning the spilled coffee, disbelief in her expression.

"Abby, I know it sounds foolish, but I sense he…" Emma let her words dwindle into silence. She wouldn't expect the woman to believe or understand her feelings. Still, fear gripped her and she shivered. Something had gone wrong for Webb.

Abby tossed the coffee laden tissue into the wastepaper basket. "Emma, you're shaking."

"Am I?" She did her best to stop trembling as she picked up the broken cup and dropped it into the basket as well.

"You going to be okay?"

"Uh, yeah." Emma clasped her hands together to stop them from shaking. "I'm sorry. I don't know what came over me. I…"

"No worries." Abby smiled. "This is your first rodeo. We all worry but have learned to suppress our concerns." She hesitated. "It may not be helpful, still, my advice is to keep busy. The time goes faster."

"I'm trying, but my mind is not focusing. I have trouble keeping my concentration on the name I'm searching for. I mean Smith, for pity's sake. How hard can it be?" She took a slow breath hoping to calm her heartbeat and sat at the desk. "I got this. I'm good."

Abby looked skeptical but nodded and returned to her work.

Rubbing her forehead, Emma took another deep breath, then forced her eyes to focus on the monitor.

The hours passed slowly. She nibbled on a sandwich and scrolled down the names in a new file. Smith Plumbing. Smith Electrical, Smith Catering. But none of them H. J. Smith. As she investigated, not a single person was likely to be the one she was hoping to find.

She leaned back and glanced out of the window. The sun was starting to set and still nothing from the Task Force.

In the bathroom, she washed her hands and yanked a comb through her hair. She stared at her face in the mirror, surprised by the grey circles under her eyes, not enough sleep. She swallowed a yawn and blinked. coffee, coke, she needed something with caffeine to stay awake and continue doing her job.

With a cola from the kitchen, she returned to the den. Abby was gone. She had mentioned it was her turn to cook dinner for the team. Emma wanted to help, but Abby thought she would be more valuable searching the documents.

She gulped her drink and turned on a lamp near the computer desk. The answer she needed had to be in the files. The first lady had asked for her help, waited to hear from her, and depended on her ability to do the job. *Damn. No stress.*

It might be easier to find Mr. Smith if she had the first and middle names not only the initials. How many H names were there? Hank, Harry, Harris, Harrison, Harvey, Hakeem, Harland, to name a few. How long would Kate wait before calling to ask if she'd located the person?

She recalled their last conversation. Jen, her secretary, had interrupted them and mentioned Kate might be late for a cocktail party with donors if she didn't hurry. *The donors.* They'd been vetted, hadn't they? She scrolled though the pages of names found on the donor list. For some odd reason they weren't listed alphabetically, but rather by date. Twenty minutes later she found two Smiths, H. J. a Harry James and a Hubert John.

She stretched and searched for Harry first. He might be a donor but a physical threat to the president? Not likely at eighty and recovering from a stroke. Guess he might pay someone to do it, but how would they get close enough? Not probable.

Max Luxury Real Estate Inc. caught her attention. Being a real estate agent, she recognized the name of the famous company and understood they represented and owned the most expensive properties in the country. Rumor and press articles said the CEO of the corporation was a self-made man who worked his way up from a simple real estate agent to one of the richest men in the country. And his name? Hubert John Smith.

Online she read articles going back years, anything she found about the company and the man. He grew up in a working-class family and though he might have gone to a state college, he had little interest in higher education and at eighteen, went to work. Married, no children, his company now constructs luxury properties in California, Florida, Virginia, and Washington D.C. Photos of a well-built middle-aged man at a gala with his young wife on his arm smiled for the cameras. Why would he do anything to harm the administration or the president? It didn't make sense.

With the cell Kate gave her, she dialed the first lady and delivered the information she found. "This is odd. All the donors must have been vetted by your people, but from what I can find, this is the Smith we are hunting for." She prayed the cell she used was in fact secure. "And Kate, the man appears to be linked to the Russian Abby tried to locate. A banker, Oleg Volkov, an oligarch with ties to the Kremlin according to the reports I read.

Silence.

"Kate are you still there?"

"Yeah. Hubert Smith is here at the Sonoma hotel."

"OMG."

"He's a billionaire real estate mogul and was authorized by the Leader of The House, Johnson. The leader is from the other party but… We try to be bipartisan and…" She sounded as if she was digesting the unexpected information. "I met the man. He's pretty nondescript. I'd never mark him as dangerous."

"Maybe that's why he was chosen."

"Damn. Emma you're right. I'm going to take this to the Secret Service."

"What if the man is in debt to the Russians?" Emma asked.

"Possible."

"As a real agent myself, I've heard rumors developers are often in over their heads and on the brink of financial failure if their loans were to come due before they made enough presales to cover the payments. It seems to be their modus operandi."

"Go on."

"Uh, well, right at the moment Hubert Smith owns a couple of apartment towers on Fifth Avenue, New York with views of the park. The units sell from fifty million to one hundred and ten million. I went on line and looked at them. They are beautiful, but it appears only one is sold. Might be important to find out what other building ventures he has and where the funding came from. What if the loans are coming due and he is short? Would he turn to the Russians?"

"Hm, amazing. Living on the edge of financial ruin could change a man's principals," Kate mused. "As an ex-police officer, I've seen men go to the mafia to secure money when they're desperate. Still, if it's true and he is in serious debt to a Russian bank or an oligarch, how would he be a donor to the president's campaign?" A rhetorical question, Emma didn't try to answer.

"All the photos of Mr. Smith are with his young wife," Emma added. "They're the social couple du jour. Why didn't he bring her with him? Meeting you and the president is a social coup. I can't imagine she wouldn't want to be there, unless..."

"Yeah. Something to consider, Emma. If I meant to do something illegal, my spouse would be left at home. Thanks for the info. I'm going to inform my husband."

"I wondered..."

"Nothing from the team yet." Kate appeared to understand her question. "Hang in there. They're good. If there's no word, don't worry."

"I..." Her friend had already disconnected.

***

Webb grimaced and squeezed the steering wheel as the vehicles, still twisted together, spun sideways toward the embankment. He stomped on the brake with all his strength. Even so, they continued their out-of-control rotation toward the perimeter of the road.

Damn!

He turned to look as the driver of the truck struggled to open the door. No luck.

Webb grasped the door handle of his SUV, jumped out and dropped to the blacktop as the two vehicles slipped over the edge. Groaning and holding his right shoulder, he ran to see the pickup heading straight for a vintage oak. It hit it so hard part of the tree fractured and a huge branch landed on the truck, crushing the cab's roof.

Hell. Webb was about to check to find out if the saboteur was alive, when the foreign agent on the ground got to his feet and tried to run, blood dripping from the guy's nose.

Webb grabbed him. "You're not going anywhere."

"Screw you!"

He pulled hand cuffs from his pocket and shackled the man's hands behind him. Ignoring the pain radiating down his arm, he began to drag the foreign agent with him.

The team van pulled up and a Task Force member jumped out.

"Hey, Juan."

"You look like shit, Webb."

"Thanks." He grinned. "Take this piece of crap to the van, then tell me what happened at the house."

Juan took the suspect. "Went as planned. They're all in the back of the van. Where the hell is the SUV?"

"Over the side with the pickup."

"You're shitting me."

"No. I'm going down and see if the guy is still among the living."

"I'll do it. You're bleeding. Take a break. I'll shove this asshole in the van and deal with the other creep."

Webb wanted to disagree, but pain shot down his arm when he moved his right shoulder, hurt when the truck hit the SUV.

"I'll handle this, Webb."

"Yeah. Okay."

His friend had things under control and the other team members would take care of the conspirators from the house. They were sleeping off the gas. They're in the back of the van, assignment complete.

With a deep breath he sat on the side of the road and brushed the bits of shattered windshield glass from his hair, watching it sparkle on the roadside tar. He grimaced realizing he ached all over and that the glass had cut his forehead.

With the back of his hand, he wiped the blood from his face and tried to stand, but a twinge in his shoulder slowed him. He grunted and forced himself to get up and watch as his buddy climbed down the embankment.

"He's dead," Juan shouted. "I'll grab his ID, anything else I find and take the license plates too.

Webb gave him the thumbs up signal. Exhausted, he went to sit in the van.

***

Men's voices woke Emma. She stared into the blackness of the bedroom and tried to decipher their words. Impossible from upstairs, but laughter was clearly apparent.

Relieved, the tension in her neck and back relaxed when she heard Webb's voice. She closed her eyes and said a prayer of thanks.

Later, she saw a light under the bathroom door connected to the bedroom. *Webb*. She hadn't realized he'd entered and gone to take a shower until the sound of the water running woke her. When he finished, would he come to bed? Her heartbeat quickened at the thought and her nipples tightened in anticipation. She sat up against the headboard and waited for him to come to her.

In the open bathroom doorway, a towel around his waist and backlit by the bathroom light, Webb's muscled arms flexed as he dried his wet hair. The aroma of shampoo and shaving cream wafted to her.

"I didn't mean to wake you."

"I wasn't sleeping. I was waiting for you."

He turned and the slice of light from the bathroom touched his face.

"Webb, you're hurt."

"It's nothing."

"You sure?"

"Yeah."

"Did everything go okay?"

"Yep, all good. Bad guys apprehended."

Their eyes met and love for him swelled in her. She sat up and the sheet fell to her waist. "I worried."

"I'm fine," he said, his voice husky.

When he moved closer, she reached up and pulled the bath towel from his waist. His need growing as he stood next to her, she held her arms out to him. "Come to bed, Webb."

***

Webb woke with a start and rolled over. Emma slept, her arm over her eyes to shade the light coming from the bedroom window, her breathing slow and even, her uncovered breasts pink and budded waiting for his touch.

Sweet, kind Emma, he didn't deserve her. *I love you.* If life was different, he'd wake her and... *Enough. Suck it up and do right by her.*

Out of bed, he dressed as quickly as possible, ignoring the pain from the bruising on his right shoulder and sat on a bench to tie his cross-trainers. Plans had to be made to return Emma to her old life. With equilibrium restored, she would forget she'd been entangled with him and his dysfunctional existence.

A new man might enter her life. The thought slammed his heart against his rib cage as he imagined someone else touching her. Anger surged and he wanted to kill the nonexistent male. Better to hold his temper and release her from the vow made under deceptive circumstances. He glanced down at his fisted hands. *You brought all of this on your own head.* If he'd left her in the bookstore years ago, neither of them would be hurting now. Damn his selfishness.

Emma moved. He admired her exquisite face and memorized each detail of her features. After today, he wouldn't see her again, but her image would be etched on his soul.

Let her sleep. He left the bedroom closing the door and his life with Emma behind him.

In the hallway he leaned forward, hands on his knees, and waited for his heartbeat to slow.

The team waited to be debriefed and the first lady wanted a report on the events of yesterday. The FBI had the Russians infiltrators for interrogation, but he had details Kate, as leader of the Rapid Advance Task Force, had earned.

When he entered the kitchen, the men and Abby were eating breakfast. He grabbed a plate of pancakes and bacon and joined them.

After the meal, work started in the den.

***

Emma soaked in the tub, something she'd been unable to do for days. She smiled remembering last night. Her body tingled needing Webb again. She touched her lips still swollen from his passionate kisses. Love for him flooded her. He cared or last night's love making wouldn't have taken place. She hadn't been surprised he'd left the room, letting her sleep, because he was always an early riser.

Out of the tub and digging in her suitcase, she found jeans and a white silk top fitted at the waist. Her hair loose around her shoulders, she applied pink lipstick and mascara, then searched for the new silver earrings bought in Sonoma. With her shirt tucked in, she glanced in the bedroom mirror. For the first time in days, she recognized the person staring back at her.

A smile crossed her face as she let out a sigh of relief. She stepped into navy leather flats before leaving the room. *Everything is going to be okay.*

The team was in a meeting, so she ate alone but not lonely. She turned on the small flat screen TV in the breakfast nook to catch up on the local and national news. If something was wrong with the President Nielsen and the Vice President, the news would be blasting the details on all channels. With no mention of them, she relaxed.

She sipped her coffee. What was happening in Sonoma with H.J. Smith? Would a call to Kate be out of bounds?

Holding a second cup of coffee in hand, she sat on the back patio. Clouds floated in the deep blue sky and she admired the beautiful day. Life had returned to normal. Her worries were over. She grinned and thought of the love she and Webb shared last night.

"I've been looking for you." Webb stood next to her. "We need to pack. I'll see you in the bedroom." He left before she could answer.

***

When she entered the bright and sunny bedroom. A room mirroring her own happy outlook.

With his back to her, Webb stared out of the window.

"Webb, isn't this a beautiful room? Maybe we should think about using these colors in our master…"

"Last night was a mistake." Webb faced her and his eyes narrowed. "I took advantage of you. I should've been stronger. Can't be a future for us, we both understand that—I apologize if you thought otherwise."

"But…"

"Emma, you can go home and start your new life again. Think of this episode as an interruption, a misstep, and move on. It's what I'm going to do. We can because the danger has passed."

She gasped. "I won't believe what you're saying. Last night we…" Tears clogged her tightened throat.

He began to gather his clothes.

"You might have mentioned this last night, Webb. You couldn't speak then?"

"I apologized. What more do you want?" He tossed his clothes into his backpack.

"What if…?" Where was she on the monthly calendar? "Webb, I…"

He stood up and glared at her. "Spit it out, Emma?"

"Nothing. I don't want anything from you because that's all you can give of yourself, nothing. You're pathetic." She wiped tears as they dripped down her face. "Okay, fine, I'm leaving. You'll be alone. You happy now?"

He tensed, his expression becoming grim. "Abby will drive you to our—I mean your home as soon as you're ready."

"I…"

The bedroom door slammed before she finished her sentence. "Damn you, Webb!" she yelled into the empty space. *I wish I could hate you.*

Chapter 23

Emma unlocked the Palmer Company office and entered. Karen, her boss, had surprised her by leaving the company, including the building and all the belongings, to her. Somehow, it was wrong when her connection to Webb caused Karen's death.

A month since Webb left her and there had been no word from him or any member of the team. None expected. Yet, Emma realized the risks he took on assignments and wondered if he had remained safe. Maybe he'd found a new woman to occupy his down time? *Don't.* She wiped a tear. Their relationship was nonexistent. Why wouldn't her heart accept the truth?

Her mother had beamed with joy when she learned Skye was working again. Still, without Webb, the job she had enjoyed, now brought little happiness.

She gazed at the office, the desks gathering dust, the place as empty as her life. However, the Palmer Real Estate Company was Karen's baby. Emma sighed, determined to keep it going.

Her mother often spouted positive phrases. She had one for every occasion. Funny, today Emma couldn't remember any of them. Gone was her pride at being able to find the silver lining in any situation.

The day Karen died had started out as a cheerful one. With loud music blaring, they'd planned a big ad campaign to bring in new clients. Karen had danced to her favorite hit before falling into her desk chair laughing.

Stop. Why drive yourself crazy with memories?

Now no matter how bright the day, to Emma everything appeared a dull gray. If she didn't break out of her funk the business would close and she'd lose what little career she had left.

"Karen, I promise I won't let you down. I'll make Palmer Reality into one of the best in the city."

The first thing to do, network. Karen's favorite word. In spite of her sour mood, Emma smiled.

She spent the rest of the afternoon on the phone arranging to attend meetings and she even offered to speak at one of them. Maybe she could recall one of the positive sayings her mother loved. *When you are given lemons, make lemonade.*

Where did Karen put the ad campaign? Time to use it and move things along.

***

Two weeks later, the phones were starting to ring. She had picked up a few clients and considered bringing in a secretary to help manage the office paperwork and answer the phones.

A man interested in buying her mountain cabin wanted to check out the place. She made an appointment to meet and show him in a week or so. They'd firm up the date when he returned from a business trip.

She glanced out of the store front window and watched a black limo, with U.S. flags flying, pull up and park in front of the real estate office. Black SUVs parked in front and behind the limo.

A man wearing a dark suit and a serious expression entered the office.

"Mrs. Craig?"

"Yes."

"First Lady, Kathryn Nielsen, wishes to visit. Show me your ID."

Suddenly nervous, she dug in her bag and pulled out her driver's license.

He stared at the photo and at her before handing it back. "I'll take a look around." Without waiting for permission, he moved into the room, checking doors, windows, and opening closets, in the storage and bathroom. He walked out of the office without saying another word.

When she went to the window, neighbors across the street also stared out at the men in black suits who stood at attention near the huge limousine.

Appearing to be at ease with the process, Kate entered the office and smiled. "Secret Service." She nodded toward the man standing at attention by the door. "Since recent events, they've tightened my leash." She grinned. "How are you?"

"Happy, flourishing," she lied.

"You don't need to put on a front with me, Emma—we're friends."

"Are we?"

"I hope so. First ladies don't have many, not real friends. There are a lot of folks around me who want something, but not people I can trust."

"Oh, Kate, of course we're friends." As she hugged the first lady, the Secret Service agent tensed and glared at her. Touching the president's wife must be against protocol.

Kate hugged her too and cleared her throat. "Uh, do you have tea?" She changed the subject and smiled. "My Irish grandmother got me drinking the stuff and I can't go without it."

"Yeah. Sure. Sit down. I'll be right back." She ran to the storeroom and searched the food cabinet. "Is Irish Breakfast tea all right?" she shouted.

"Perfect."

She carried two steaming mugs of tea and set them on the desk before taking a seat across from Kate. "Sorry, I don't have milk or sugar."

"No problem." Her friend sipped her tea. "I needed that." She held the mug in her hand and glanced around the room. "It's good to see you again."

"You too."

"The other day I realized you've never been updated on the last assignment. Emma, you deserve to be after all you went through."

"I did wonder what happened to Mr. Hubert John Smith. I checked the news but couldn't find any info."

"The little coward." Kate frowned. "You know he owed millions to Russian oligarchs. His notes were overdue. The Russians blackmailed him when he couldn't pay. They recruited Smith and had given him more advances than he could handle. They wanted his contacts in Washington, hoping he would default, so they could use Smith to reach government officials."

"Wow."

"Yeah. His mission was to poison both the president and the vice President, leaving Leader of the

House Johnson to come to power as president of the United States."

"Oh my God, I thought stuff like that only happened in movies."

"Afraid not. When the Secret Service agents cornered him, he swallowed poison hidden in a capped tooth."

"Damn."

"His obituary lists his death as a heart attack."

"Your husband and the VP are okay?"

"Yes. Thank goodness. Watch for news concerning the Leader of the House of Representatives. He had some involvement too. Representative Johnson will soon retire to spend more time with his family."

"Whoa, Kate, why would he betray the country?"

"Greed, power? He's an old man. Maybe it was his last hurrah. He ran for president three times and lost."

"And no word on the oligarch, Oleg Volkov?"

"Not yet. Might be back in Russia."

"I…" Emma paused, absorbing the news, then said, "More tea?"

"I'm good. You're not going to ask, are you?"

"What?" She looked down at her desk, her cheeks burning.

"Ask about Webb—he's all right. Physically at least." Kate shrugged. "He acts miserable and Juan tells me he's a bear to be around. Still, no one's better at the job than he is."

Emma nodded, but didn't speak for fear of crying.

"Okay, well, the other reason I'm here is to ask you to find a house in San Francisco for us. The president and I love this city. We'll be in D.C. for the next few years but plan on spending vacations here.

When he finishes his term, we want to move and I thought it might be good to secure a place now, rising prices and all."

Stunned, Emma stared. "You're serious, Kate?" *Or being kind to help me keep the office open.*

"Yeah. You found a great place for the team and under terrible circumstances. So, yeah." She finished the tea and set her cup on Emma's desk.

"I'd be happy to find a home for you. Give me an idea of your wants, needs and a budget. I'll look for something wonderful."

"Good. Our staff will need residences too. Can you handle it?"

"Of course."

"I'm so relieved to settle this." The first lady relaxed into her desk chair.

"Kate?"

"Yeah."

"Thanks."

"Not necessary, Emma. I picked the best person for the assignment." She hesitated. "Promise to stay in contact as a friend. I mean it." She stood and the agent came to attention again.

"I will and I'll buy more flavors of tea."

"I'm holding you to that." Kate laughed. "You have the cell I gave you?"

"Yeah."

"Keep the phone and here's my private email."

She took Kate's card and gave her the Karen Palmer Real Estate business card with her private email written on the back.

"Don't be a stranger, Emma." She hugged her and the agent followed the first lady out of the building.

After Kate left, Emma leaned back in her chair and closed her eyes.

Webb was miserable. Good. Why should she be the only one?

Forget him and move on.

Could she?

***

From the back seat of the first lady's limo, Webb stared at Emma standing in the doorway of her office. Her long dark hair touched her shoulders and her blue eyes sparkled as a smile formed on her magnificent face. His hands tingled with the desire to hold her and declare his love.

He sat back fearing she would glance in his direction. She appeared happy. Maybe contentment was out of his reach, but at least Emmy might find peace.

Kate entered the back seat and gave orders to her driver to return to Sonoma.

Snapping her seat belt closed, she said, "Emma's miserable."

"I saw her smile."

"She puts on a good front. Now the danger's over, you sure you don't want to go talk to her?"

"I can't guarantee her safety if she stays married to me."

"Webb, there are no guarantees for anyone, no matter what they do for a living."

"I won't put her at risk again. Not as long as I'm a field agent and I don't know how to do anything else."

Kate cleared her throat. "I wanted to talk to you about that."

"What?"

She pushed a button raising the window between the front and the back seat of the limo. "I thought I could handle leading the Rapid Advance Team and do a good job as first lady too, but the duties of the first wife are occupying more and more of my day. I'm not doing either job to my standards."

"Kate."

She held up her hand. "Let me speak before you contradict me."

"Okay." He sat back and folded his arms across his chest.

"The years leading the Task Force have been some of the best and most important of my life. Don't get me wrong. I'll always be available to help, but being the president's wife is essential too."

"Of course."

She hesitated and he thought about speaking when she added, "I need you. The team does as well. They need a commander. You've done a fine job leading them. Time for you to move up and take the reins from me."

"Kate, you can't be serious. I'd be no good in an office. I'm a field op."

"One of the best. Still, I've seen your computing and social skills, a dynamite combination of abilities not found in most men. How many people can take out an enemy agent, analyze intel, talk tech, then be relaxed at a gala with the heads of state and the president? You're the only one I can think of."

"But…"

"You weren't expecting this. So, give it some clear-headed thought. But remember I want you. The president and I will be returning to D.C. in two days. Give me an answer before we leave."

"Who would take charge of the field?"

"Your choice. You understand the guys' strengths and weaknesses."

Webb rubbed his chin. "I didn't anticipate this." If he took the promotion his life would change in unimagined ways, with more responsibility and men depending on him not to make a mistake. Their lives would depend on him getting it right. Was he ready to take the next step?

"Will you will consider the position?"

"Uh, if you say so."

"Good."

***

Russian banker Oleg Volkov drove from the San Francisco car rental agency in a nondescript, midsize sedan.

Smith had failed to complete his mission. Oleg shouldn't have believed the little weasel had the guts to take out the president and the vice president. Nonetheless, Leader of the House of Representatives, Johnson was still in place and available to be used during the next United States election.

In three days, his flight to Mexico would take off. Forty-eight hours afterward, Oleg would be home in Moscow. His window of opportunity to finish the assignment here was short. His plan to kill Mrs. Ethan Lancaster or Emma Craig, whatever she called herself, would succeed.

Parked across the street from the Palmer Real Estate building later that afternoon, Oleg started the engine of his rental car. The girl still worked in the real estate office, but soon she would leave and head for home. Emma Craig didn't vary her schedule, unwise but expected for a civilian not imagining a threat.

Webb apparently had not bothered to train his wife in the necessity of changing her routine. Or like most good-looking bitches, she didn't follow instructions. Oleg had tracked her for days. She didn't often look at the cars around her and never changed the route she took to her house. Once she'd stared at him but didn't recognize him the next day. He never used the same car more than once and often changed his appearance wearing varied hats and sunglasses. If she noticed him today, she wouldn't next time. He grinned, enjoying the game.

What he would do to her before she died?

Of course, he wouldn't act until he was sure Webb realized her pending danger, but couldn't save her. The American would experience the panic and hurt he'd suffered as a young teen when his papa had been killed by Ethan's father.

Back then, Oleg had been too young to intervene or exact revenge. He'd carried the pain of being without a male role model most of his life. After Emma Craig's death, Oleg would pass the burden of survival to Ethan Lancaster, Webb as he called himself now. Let him grieve while Oleg enjoyed the gratification of retribution.

Chapter 24

No reason to be nervous. Emma glanced at her hair in the bathroom mirror. *Up or down?* She decided on a compromise and pulled the sides back and fastened them with a rhinestone clip. Sophisticated without overdoing the bling.

Why had she agreed to speak at the yearly real estate event in the first place? She shrugged. It seemed to be a good idea when she was asked. Now the time had come, not so much.

And why the stuffy formal attire? Business suits would be all right with her. In her closet, she found the slinky black beaded gown she'd bought at the designer discount store in Sonoma. The black item was a classic and might never go out of style. Letting the dress slither down her body evoked the memory of the night she'd spent with Webb at the Sonoma hotel. How gorgeous he'd been in a tux and how easily he'd traveled in government social circles. The event this evening would've been simple for him. If only he was going with her.

Grow up. Face the facts. You're alone.

The Saint Francis Resort stood on a high bank overlooking the San Francisco Bay with a glorious view of the Golden Gate Bridge and Marin County. A popular choice for events, reservations had to be placed well in advance. She'd attended luncheons in the dining room, but no other affairs.

A doorman took her ticket and opened the entrance. She checked her black satin wrap and set her business card on the glass and metal table nearby. Many real estate agents appeared to have arrived early as well, their cards scattered on the glass top. She read a few of them, hoping to find a friend's name among the bunch.

The ballroom glistened with crystal chandeliers and a chorus of voices filled the warm air. A sea of black and white tuxedos on the men mingled with a multitude of colored gowns on the women.

If she was going to succeed in this business, she'd better excel in networking. Not her forte, so why had she ever considered going it alone without Karen? *You made a promise to her to keep the real estate company going.* She sighed and took a deep breath as if she were about to dive into deep water.

You can do this. With a forced smile on her lips, she stepped into the room.

The good thing about sales people, ask one leading question about their business and they're eager to respond, making conversation trouble-free. So, no worries, all agents were eager to converse with her. She grinned, let them speak, and the evening progressed well.

The wine bar, stocked with fabulous California products, made her choice hard. She chose a glass of chardonnay from a winery she knew.

The evening's speakers sat on a small stage. She joined the others and introduced herself.

Her presentation on using social media to increase business went over well as did another real estate agent's discussion on working with drones to give a bird's eyes view of a property.

After dinner, the music started with a DJ taking the stage.

Awkward without a partner and missing Webb, she wandered out to the backyard, admired the manicured landscape of the garden, and looked to the beach far below.

Music and laughter floated from the ballroom. The sounds of people enjoying the night only increased her loneliness. *I should leave.*

"A beautiful night, no?" a man said.

"What?" She startled and turned to see him, well dressed and handsome enough but…

"A lovely view."

"Yeah." She turned her back on him letting him know the conversation was finished.

"I enjoyed your presentation, by the way."

"Uh, thanks." Why did this guy make her tense? Most women would be flattered by his attention, but they didn't love Webb.

She walked toward the end of the yard, stared down at the steep cliff and the waves crashing on the rocky beach below. Would the man take the hint and go back into the building to choose another woman to bother? No luck—the guy came forward and stood next to her.

"I didn't introduce myself." He smiled and held out his hand. "Oleg Volkov."

***

Webb hadn't seen Emma in days. The time had been spent learning the scope of the job he might accept.

In the Sonoma hotel suite where they had stayed, he frowned and resisted the urge to pace the room. After accepting the first lady's offer to take command of the Rapid Advance Task Force, the realization he'd soon move to the east coast hit like a punch to his jaw. No chance of accidentally running into Emma in the east. If they lived on the same coast, he could keep an eye on her without her noticing.

Now he fought to stop her image from filling his mind. Was she safe? Did she ever think of him? If she understood he would soon move to DC, would she care or be pleased to have him thousands of miles away?

Known for his steely command of his emotions, panic was unfamiliar to him. Still, tonight something akin to it found a home in his gut. *Emmy needs you.*

Wishful thinking? His imagination?

At six o'clock in the evening she might be having dinner. How dangerous could that be? He had followed her routine and understood she'd be giving a presentation at a real estate event in the city. Safe in a large group, right?

He sat down in the club chair facing the television screen and reached for the remote control.

Oh Hell. He grabbed his car keys and ran out of the room.

***

Emma stepped back from the man offering his hand. A gust of air hit her and a chill ran up her spine.

"Mrs. Ethan Lancaster, you know who I am." Oleg's grin hardened into a sneer. "How is your husband?"

"You're confusing me with someone else." She trembled.

"No, Emma. That's your husband's name, but you call him Webb." Oleg's voice rose as the breeze became a cold wind and the fog started to enter the San Francisco Bay.

She glanced back at the building. How long would it take her to sprint to it?

"You'll never make it." He grabbed her arm.

"Let go of me."

She strained get free from his grip and hammered her fists against his chest.

He laughed without humor and pulled her to him. "You fight like a girl. This is going be easier than I thought." He hit her hard in the face.

She screamed, but the sound of her voice blew away in the wind from the bay.

Don't waste your time hitting him in the chest, go for the eyes. Webb's instructions played in her head. She socked the Russian again.

Oleg turned her to him and she jabbed him in the eye. He yelled and loosened his hold on her. She ran, yelling for help.

He grabbed her ankle sending her face down in the grass. She kicked him with her stilettos and crawled away. He jumped on top of her. The air in her lungs swooshed out. Turning her over, he slapped her again. "Bitch. I was sorry to have to kill you, but now you deserve to die. Webb can mourn your death as I lament my father's."

Suddenly, he made sense. She realized her dying would contribute to the retribution for his father's death. She wanted to call him crazy, but laboring to breathe, she couldn't speak.

His eyes narrowed as he came closer, almost as if he were going to kiss her good bye.

"No," she murmured.

His huge hands circled her throat and squeezed.

Fear clawed at her. Breathing impossible, her heart thundered. With her last bit of strength, she slammed her fist into his other eye.

Startled, he released her long enough for her to snatch a breath of air and cough.

Someone punched Oleg. He grunted and rolled off her. She scrambled away from him, clutching her neck and gasping as pain radiated in her chest when she took a deep breath.

A man dressed in black struck Oleg again and again. The men grunted as they exchanged blows. Unable to stand and run, she stared after them in horror. What if the other guy lost the fight?

She squinted in the dark. *Could it be Webb?*

An equal match, the men continued to strike each other. They exchange blows moving closer to the edge of the cliff and the drop off to the sea.

With a blow to the solar plexus, her husband doubled over in pain, but recovered and kicked the Russian, sending the man's head snapping backward. One last punch and Oleg Volkov stumbled, lost his balance, and staggered off the precipice with a deafening shriek. He must have understood he would smash on to the rocks on the beach below, no doubt a fate the man had planned for her.

She managed to crawl to the end of the cliff and peer at the body on the rocks below. Oleg's mouth still open in a silent scream, the breakers surrounded him, the flow of his blood turning the water around him red.

Oh, God. Shaking uncontrollably, she hid her face in her hands.

***

"Emmy, are you hurt?" Webb knelt before her and took her face in his hands. "You okay?"

"I…" She coughed. "I…"

"Never mind. Don't try to talk."

Bruises had already formed on her delicate throat, the mark of the necklace she wore noticeable in purple on her pale skin. He picked her up in his arms and held her to him. "Oleg will never hurt you again."

"Is he dead?"

"Yeah. I'll get the Task Force to take care of him. Do you want a doctor?"

She shook her head. "Please get me out of here."

She clung to him and buried her face in his jacket. Her breathing rapid and uneven, she trembled in his arms. "Don't ever leave me," she whispered, her voice breaking.

"I won't, Emmy. I love you. I'm with you now and forever."

She'd be dead if he'd been a minute later. Her lifeless body would be on the jagged rocks below, cold surf washing over her instead of Oleg. He shivered and held her closer.

On the way out of the building, he grabbed her purse and walked through of the ballroom without stopping to explain what happened.

He set her in the passenger seat of his car, entered the driver's side and fired up the engine.

"Webb, how did you find me?" she asked, her voice hoarse.

"I had your schedule. When I arrived at the ballroom and didn't find you, I was terrified I was too late."

"You understood I needed you, but how?"

"We have an invisible bond, a link, Em. Haven't you experienced it?"

"Yes, but I didn't think you had."

He held her hand, scanned her face, then leaned toward her and gently kissed her cheek. "Emmy, my love, let's go home.

*****

If you enjoyed this book, help the author and other readers by leaving a positive review. And remember to tell your friends about Reggi's books. Thank you.

Learn about Jon Lancaster, Webb's brother.
Dangerous Denial by Reggi Allder.
Reviews: "An enthralling read that takes you in from the first sentence. Read Dangerous Denial!"

"You can run but you can't hide from the truth! 5.0 out of 5 stars will hold you on the edge of your seat as you follow her real-to-life characters."

"If you enjoy California wine, love, and suspense, read the romantic suspense Dangerous Denial!"

Unravel the mystery.
Executive assistant Skye Turner thinks most people are good until her beloved boss is murdered.

The police call his death a suicide. What is the truth? She needs help to uncover the circumstances leading to his death.

United States black ops member Jon Lancaster is restless while he recovers from injuries received during his last assignment. Pretty and diverting, Skye is probably mistaken about the death. Still, he decides to assist her in deciphering the events of the day the man died and also dig though the clues left for her.

Can Skye and Jon control their growing desire for each other? Are they ready for the lurking danger waiting for them?

Books by Reggi Allder
Suspense
Dangerous Web
Dangerous Denial
Dangerous Money
Dangerous Moves
Shattered Rules
Contemporary
Her Country Heart
His Country Heart
Our Country Heart
My Country Heart Her
Her Country Heart Christmas Edition
Historical
With Glowing Hearts
Coming next
Dangerous Sisters
Growing Up in a Small Town

www.ingramcontent.com/pod-product-compliance
Lightning Source LLC
Chambersburg PA
CBHW072128250626
47159CB00007B/2599